# YOUR WISH IS MY COMMAND

He was tall, tanned and wore the gray Armani suit as though it had been made for him. His dancing eyes gazed at her with undisguised humor. He was, in a word, gorgeous.

"I told you, I'm a Djinn."

"I see." If he really was Darcie's replacement, she couldn't have imagined a better looking one. "I appreciate your effort, but I need Darcie. Not you. Call HR and tell them to bring her back." Putting the glass down, she watched the man watching her. A skitter of electricity danced up her spine.

"I'm afraid I can't do that, Meredith." He stepped closer.

"Why not?"

"Because you're my assignment."

"How quaint." She swallowed and looked around her office. It was professional, tidy, just the way she liked things. This man set off "messy" and "complicated" warnings inside her head. "I have just unassigned you. Now, go get Darcie. Please?"

He moved behind her and slid his hands over her upper arms to her shoulders. His touch was immediately calming, soothing in a way that made her forget she didn't know this person, that he could be an escaped ax murderer. Instead of lurching out of her chair and calling security, Meredith purred. Somehow, his almost intimate touch seemed perfectly natural. His long, strong fingers coaxed away stress that had been lurking in her shoulders for weeks.

"Your wish is my command, Meredith." His breath was as light as a sunbeam on her neck.

# MEREDITH'S WISH

# KAREN LEE

LOVE SPELL BOOKS ◆ NEW YORK CITY

A LOVE SPELL BOOK®

October 2000

Published by

Dorchester Publishing Co., Inc.
276 Fifth Avenue
New York, NY 10001

ISBN 0-505-52405-8

The name "Love Spell" and its logo are trademarks of Dorchester Publishing Co., Inc.

Printed in the United States of America.

*For Matt and Ben, who give my life meaning,*
*and for my mother, Dolores Robinson,*
*who gave me my love of books.*

# ACKNOWLEDGMENTS

Writing may be a solitary endeavor, but it takes a bunch of people encouraging and helping along the way to make it work well. Therefore, cheers and thanks to Robyn Amos, Judy Fitzwater, Ann Kline, Barbara Cummings, Vicki Singer, Beth Fedorko, Courtney Henke, Laurin Wittig, Cameron Nyhen, Felicia Ansty, and Denise Timpko—talented writers all—for your patience and for laughing in the right places. To Wendy Schatz and Helen Cook for sharing your worst date stories. And to Catherine Anderson for taking time out of your vacation to read the final manuscript. I will be honored to return the favor. Thank you also to the Smokey Mountain Romance Writers and to Debbie Staley for insisting that I enter their contest.

# MEREDITH'S WISH

# *Chapter One*

## *"Djinn and Tonic"*

*Corporate America, Monday*

"You can't be serious!" Meredith Montgomery, the youngest, and only, female executive at Horton Consulting, shook the file folder in the company president's face. "It's harassment, pure and simple."

"You call it harassment, I call it healthy competition. The first one to bring me a signed contract before the end of the month gets the vice president's office next to mine." Bill Horton sat at the head of the boardroom table and steepled his fingers. "You do want a promotion, right?"

Well, of course she did. "What did Francis say?"

"He's ordering new business cards."

That weasel. Francis Griffin, her primary rival, had been nothing but trouble since Horton hired him. "What account did you give *him?*" At least she should be able to gauge his potential for success.

"East Overshoe, Wyoming, city government."

"Ha! We've been working on them for years without results." Not that her assignment was any juicier. The Duchy of Hertzenstein. She'd never even heard of it.

"Read the brief carefully. You've got three weeks and I suggest you use them wisely." Horton's sly smile should have set off alarms, but Meredith was too busy flipping through the pages in the folder to let "sly" register.

"Oh, my God!" She felt the color drain from her face, and checked her shoes to be sure it hadn't dripped onto her Etienne Aigner pumps. "You really can't do this." She pulled one sheet from the folder. "The Grand Duchess's guards tossed our last rep into the moat!"

"You said you wanted a tough assignment. Go get 'em, Meredith. I want you to succeed." He paused, considering. "I'd hate to share the executive suite with Griffin, but if you're not up to it . . ." She squared her shoulders, narrowed her eyes and glared at her boss. "Never let it be said Meredith Montgomery backed away from a challenge. I'll bring you your contract." There was just one teensy problem. The only deals the Grand Duchess had made in the past ten years were with married women. Married.

Meredith was decidedly single.

"Not to worry," she told herself as she marched back to her office, already working on plans. She tossed the briefing folder on her assistant's desk and said, "Book two first-class tickets to Hertzenstein, schedule a meeting with the Grand Duchess before the end of the month, and find out why she has this quirk about married women." She breezed into her spacious office. A little background information wouldn't hurt. She wasn't about to let a small thing like being single get in the way of her career.

"There isn't an account out there that can resist my presentations. Besides, Devon will be happy to pose as the corporate spouse. After all, he's been trying to get me to talk about weddings for weeks." She hummed happily and dialed her latest beau's number.

"Devon. Hi, sweetknees. It's me, Meredith."

"Meri? Uh, hi." She felt the surprise in his voice.

She explained her problem. "I know how you like to travel, so I figured you'd jump at the chance to . . ."

"I can't, Meri. Not this time."

He'd never said no before. "What's up? Big stock swap? Working on a merger?"

"Of a sort. I'm getting married."

She was only half listening, scribbling ideas for her meeting with the duchess on her pad of paper. Maybe it was tied to a legend, this married-woman thing. "Right. I see. What?" She jerked upright and dropped her pencil. "What do you mean, you're getting married?"

"You were never around, Meri." Devon sounded mildly apologetic. "I'd love it if you could come to the wedding."

"Right. I'll have Darcie schedule it." Dropping the phone receiver into its cradle, she swiveled in her high-backed, custom-designed chair and looked out of her office window. She couldn't decide how she felt—angry or relieved. She knew Devon wasn't the man of her dreams, but jeez, she hadn't even known he was getting married. Earth to Meredith. She shook her head, casting aside any thoughts on *why* she hadn't even been aware of this development in Devon's life, and refocused on the problem at hand.

While she didn't really *need* a man to get the contract and secure her promotion, a stand-in husband would be a clear edge. Devon had taken himself out of the race. Now what?

"Darcie! Come in here, please." How dare he get married when she needed him most? She'd been promoted for her bold, take-no-prisoners style; she didn't understand why it failed to work outside of, well, work.

"Right here, Boss Lady." Darcie Collins, Meredith's executive assistant and advisor on all things relating to men, popped into the office, grinning, a standard-issue cup of tea in hand. Her hairstyle du jour, copper curls piled high, framed her face perfectly, displaying her flawless complexion. "I'll have to contact the duchess tomorrow. It's past dinnertime in Hertzenstein. Did you know it's the smallest independent duchy in northern Europe?" She paused. "Uh-oh. Trouble on the social front?"

"Devon. That creep. He's getting married." Meredith paced around her desk. "Men are so exasperating."

"It's the second definition in my Webster's." Darcie held out a box and a small pamphlet. "Two things. This brochure on Hertzenstein was in the briefing folder. It might help on the whole duchess question. And, your new cell phone arrived."

Meredith set the brochure aside and took the package. It shimmered peacock blue in the late afternoon sun. She rotated the box and it glittered gold, then red. Rather exotic for a simple cell phone. She opened her newest toy. "Thanks." She slid the new battery into place and touched the power button. The slim, red phone came to life with a reassuring "beep" and hummed contentedly in her hand. "Men should be so cooperative." She turned the phone off. "I wish I could find one who would stick around long enough to get to know the real me."

Darcie slid into a chair, crossed her long, shapely legs and sipped her tea. "You're talking love, right? True love. It's the only kind worth looking for."

Darcie was entitled to her opinion. "I'm not convinced there is such a thing. Outside of books, that is." And her parents. They'd found it. Thirty-five years of happily-ever-after marriage were hard to argue with. But fairy tales weren't for serious career women. "Besides, I've got bigger plans. That corner office is as good as mine."

"There isn't anything bigger. Never doubt the existence of true love. There are more important things than financial security, you know."

Darcie thought lots of things were important—herbal tea, fitness tapes, self-help books. But Meredith had seen what happened when money troubles threatened to destroy a family. She brushed a stray strand of hair off her forehead. "Do you smell something? Like aftershave?"

"No. Concentrate on your perfect man. He's out there, Meri. Believe it, visualize it, affirm it. True love can happen."

"Right. Like I could just wish up my perfect mate." She had a sudden picture in her mind of a tall, muscular man with black hair and dancing dark eyes. His tanned body had a definite "come hither" stance. The image disappeared.

"You okay? You look flushed."

"What? I'm fine. Just thinking about that perfect man and wondering how I could convince him to show up to save the day." White horses were optional. "Must be my imagination." True love indeed. If she wanted to wind up like her father, a middle-management victim of a corporate merger, unable to find a new job, all she had to do was sigh and moon about true love. Since she had no intention of being a victim, love would have to wait. She needed a contract.

Mentally, she ran through a list of men she'd trust to help her out of her temporary marriage crisis. No one came to mind. "There was one guy who came close to my idea of the perfect man. Glenn."

Darcie wrinkled her nose. "Why him?" Her assistant had never warmed to Glenn's drive to be the best attorney in Washington, D.C., by the time he was thirty.

"He understood me. He encouraged me, supported me. He didn't mind when I had to break a date because of work."

"Only because he worked all the time, too."

"True, but without his help, you wouldn't have me as a boss. So, don't give me too much grief about Glenn."

"Still, he didn't stick." Darcie shook her head. "You need to change your specifications in men, Boss."

"I suppose." Meredith glanced at the fresh flowers, which she had delivered every Monday. Glenn had started the tradition. He'd sent daisies every week for a month after Meredith had landed the job with Horton. She depended on them to brighten her day, just as she had once depended on him. Today, those smiling daisies and pert, purple irises snuggling up with baby's breath reminded her of all the bridal bouquets she hadn't carried.

Bunk, sentimental bunk.

"At least he wasn't like Terry." Meredith folded her arms across her cream, silk blouse. "Or David. No one was like David." She considered. "Paul was a lot of fun."

"Charles liked the theater. Anthony was too moody. And Pierce, well, he got married. Come to think of it," Darcie said, "all of your ex-boyfriends are married."

"You make it sound like I'm a training ground."

"Hey. Six months is the longest any of them has waited before tying the knot. With someone else."

Darcie's phone rang. "Hold that thought." She sprinted out of the office.

"Six months. Indeed." Meredith pushed aside the problem of ex-boyfriends and went back to the problem of finding a husband, or at least a man she could convince to act as a stand-in. Maybe she should check the personals column in the paper, or try an Internet on-line dating service. Nah, too risky. She wanted to be a vice president, not a headline. CAREER WOMAN DICED BY LUNATIC CORDON-BLEU CHEF. No. Darcie would have an answer. She always did.

Except Meredith should be able to handle this on her own. Most of her college friends were married or engaged. Was she the only woman with a career and no life? Meredith slumped in her chair and stared, unseeing, out of the window.

Something about approaching thirty must have flipped the "contemplate this" switch in her heart. She'd given up, passed by and jumped over so many things for the sake of her career. She hadn't thought much about it until now. Was there some cosmic conspiracy going on here? "I get the opportunity of a lifetime and all I can do is get gooey remembering everything I haven't done."

*Get a grip. You've managed to pull up from the brink of disaster before. You can do it again.* Could she manage the next rung on the corporate ladder? She *had* to get the contract before Griffin did.

She walked to the mirror hanging beside her three Industry Achievement Awards and frowned at her image. A serious, but attractive, woman stared back at her. Short auburn hair, clear complexion, green eyes that tilted up just a little at the outside corner. Makeup professional, not overdone. At twenty-nine, she was a smashing success in business, respected and admired. Why wouldn't the rest of her life work?

# Karen Lee

She touched her cheek, then ran a finger across her lips. Too pale. Everything in her life had been pale lately. She grabbed her handbag and rummaged around for her lipstick, Passion Rose. Deftly, she applied it to her full lips and smiled grimly at the results.

She made a kissing motion. "This is what you're giving up, Devon." She found her blush and dusted her cheeks. She put the cosmetics back in her bag, hoping there was a solution to her problem just around the corner. Swaying her hips with each step, she took the long route back to her desk, walking around the table and past the bookcase and the two wing-back chairs. She paused at the credenza and poured herself a finger of scotch. "It's perfectly acceptable," she told the ornate pendulum clock on the wall. "According to you, it's half past six."

She slumped into her desk chair and turned on her new cell phone. Cradling the receiver between her cheek and her shoulder, she pretended her perfect man had just called to propose a quick weekend wedding in Vegas.

Securing a contract with a duchess who only did business with the very married wasn't the primary thing bothering her. She closed her eyes. What really nagged at her was the stark realization that not only did she not have anyone proposing on bended knee, she didn't even have a guy to *fake* marriage with.

In the small, quiet hours of her life, when her only companions were her computer and her cat, Meredith dreamed of what she wanted more than the corner office, more than the promotion her boss was dangling in front of her. "*I* want to be the one walking down the aisle in the white dress." A single tear dribbled a path across her newly blushed cheek and she rubbed it off with the phone.

18

She wanted true love. Heart-stopping, eternity-lasting, completely mind-blowing true love. The kind Darcie promoted. The kind her sister and her parents had. The "make my life complete and meaningful" kind of love. True. Blue. Purple. She didn't care. Another tear plopped onto the phone. "All I need is a man who wants the same thing—with me."

The image of the darkly handsome man reappeared before her eyes. This time he gave her a broad, erotic smile before vanishing from her mind. Someone like him. She shook her head. "I wish . . ." She felt silly, but the scotch had relaxed at least one inhibition. She closed her eyes and rubbed her temples. Her voice was quiet. "I wish I could find my own true love."

A delicate spicy aroma surrounded her, as the heavy mahogany door to her office swung open.

Meredith opened her eyes, gasped and dropped her new phone on her desk.

The figure in her doorway was male.

Definitely.

He was tall, tanned, and wore the gray Armani suit as though it had been made for him. His dancing eyes watched her with undisguised humor. He was, in a word, gorgeous.

"Who are you?"

"I'm a djinn."

"Jim?"

He shrugged. "If you like. I can be whoever you want me to be." His rich, deep voice flowed like fragrant coffee.

"Where's my assistant?" Meredith demanded.

"She's been reassigned."

"Oh, that's grand," Meredith said sarcastically. She stood and looked past the man. "Darcie, where did you find him? He's lovely." She stepped from behind

19

her desk, unconsciously smoothing her navy, raw-silk suit. She paused in front of him, flicked invisible dust from his lapel and felt a rush of excitement as she caught the mischievous glint in his eyes. "I've got to hand it to you, Darce, you've outdone yourself." She brushed past the interloper. Her assistant was a mind reader. "Darce?"

Darcie had disappeared and—she glanced at her watch—it wasn't even that late. Her assistant had never complained before about calling it quits at eight or nine.

He followed her. "I told you. Miss Collins has been reassigned." His smile revealed gleaming, straight teeth. "Horton put her on a special project."

"Starting when? And why didn't he tell me?" Meredith marched back into her office, stopping at the credenza to think about pouring herself another finger of single-malt scotch. Even a successful woman could handle only so many surprises in one day. "How does he expect me to get this contract without her?"

Yes, she decided, it had definitely been a scotch kind of Monday. A three-"D" day: dumped, as in boyfriend; disaster, as in her new project; and depression, as in her maudlin admission of traditional feminine dreams. And now, Darcie was gone. She poured eighteen-year-old Dalwhinnie into a crystal tumbler. Make that a four-"D" day.

"You shouldn't drink, Meredith. It isn't good for you." The tall man had followed her into the luxurious office and stood in the precise middle of the red antique Turkistan carpet.

"You sound just like Darcie." She set the scotch on the edge of her desk and paced back and forth, then plopped into her desk chair. "I don't have time for this. Horton knows better. He knows she's an integral member of my team and if he really wanted this darned contract he wouldn't pull her off at such a critical juncture."

She snatched up her drink and took a sip. "Who are you, really?" The red stripes in his very conservative tie matched the red in the carpet exactly. She took a bigger sip.

"I told you, I'm a djinn."

"I see." If he really was Darcie's replacement, she couldn't have imagined a better-looking one. "I appreciate your effort, but I need Darcie. Not you. Call HR and tell them to bring her back from whatever remote locale Horton's shuffled her off to, and then, go back where you came from." Putting the glass down, she watched the man watching her. A skitter of electricity danced up her spine.

"I'm afraid I can't do that, Meredith." He stepped closer.

"Why not?"

"Because you're my assignment."

"How quaint." She swallowed and looked around her office. It was professional, tidy, just the way she liked things. This man set off "messy" and "complicated" warnings inside her head. "I have just unassigned you. Now, go get Darcie. Please?" Maybe it was time to find a job somewhere else. The pressure of this one was taking its toll.

He moved behind her and slid his hands over her upper arms to her shoulders. His touch was immediately calming, soothing in a way that made her forget she didn't know this person, that he could be an escaped ax murderer. Instead of lurching out of her chair and calling security, Meredith purred. Somehow, his almost intimate touch seemed perfectly natural. His long, strong fingers coaxed away stress that had been lurking in her shoulders for weeks. Her of-

fice was once more filled with that wonderful, soothing cologne fragrance, overlaid with the slightest
rich coffee aroma.

Maybe a temporary assistant with great hands
who made decent coffee wouldn't be such a burden
after all. Darcie was committed to herbal tea. "I wish
I had some of that coffee you're drinking." She
couldn't help thinking he would also make a wonderful duchess-pleasing husband. What a pity she
couldn't use him, having long ago vowed never to
mix business with pleasure. Nothing would torpedo
a rising career faster than an office romance.

"Your wish is my command, Meredith." His breath
was as light as a sunbeam on her neck.

She jumped up suddenly, spilling the cup of coffee
that appeared from nowhere beside her keyboard.

"Where did that come from?" She backed away.

"You wished it."

"Right. I wished it." Her heart pounded in her
chest. She reached for the tumbler of scotch and
downed it in one gulp. "Who are you?" she sputtered.

"For the third time, I'm a djinn."

"Of course you are. I suppose I wished you, too."

"No, you called me."

She closed her eyes. "Steady, Meredith. You're a
sane, accomplished businesswoman and this conversation isn't really happening." The scent of spice
increased.

"You are indeed sane and accomplished, as well as
quite the most beautiful woman I've encountered in
my long and checkered career. But, I'm here and I'm
real. Closing your eyes won't make me go away."

"What will?"

"You could wish me away, but I wouldn't advise
it."

Meredith opened one eye. "Why not?"

"Because it's tough to call a djinn in this day and age. Too much pollution."

She opened her other eye. "Okay, pal, help me out here. Just what is this gin you keep talking about?"

"Djinn, Meredith, djinn. I'm a genie."

The genie watched the woman's eyes. Frankly, he'd expected a different reaction. He had chosen this form because it matched the woman's dreams. Besides, his genie pals assured him it was the shape of the perfect man.

A cold, prickly itching started in the middle of his broad, Homo sapiens, male back, and quickly spread to the base of his perfectly formed skull.

A Premonition.

This assignment wasn't going to work. He knew it. He'd have to go back to the Djinn Reorganization Board and tell them he'd failed the test. Then he'd be out on the streets of Paradise precisely as quickly as the All-Powerful Chairman of the Board could blink.

The streets of Paradise weren't a pretty sight these days. The Chairman had been reading too many management books. Changes in the djinn hierarchy were happening fast and reorganization wasn't all it was advertised to be. So many genies, afreets, demons and houris were out of jobs, just wandering. Pathetic. Oh, he knew a few genies who didn't mind all that leisure. But he preferred working. What good was a genie on permanent vacation?

Regardless, he was about to join them.

It was really too bad that the Chairman took such a dim view of creativity—this genie's best feature. Although some called it an overactive imagination, he liked to think of it as innovative, creative and entrepreneurial. Not merely keeping up, but leaping

23

ahead. His human heart pounded with the very excitement of it all.

However.

The Chairman and the Reorganization Board revered the traditional, and wallowed in rules so old not even the Elders could say when they had been written. But, written they had been and he was bound to obey. Oh, sure, he'd bent a few rules in his time, but there were two he absolutely couldn't mess with.

*No bringing corpses back to life.* He didn't mind this restriction. As it turned out, a certain carpenter fellow was the only one who had that particular power anyway.

*No making people fall in love.* The Greeks had a minor god who'd experimented with this and all he'd managed to do was get himself in hot water. And this genie certainly didn't need any more of that.

His enthusiasm for his work plummeted faster than a lead balloon with weights. This assignment was his final chance. His one opportunity to save his career. He needed to stick by this Meredith, grant wishes and come back covered in glory—or suffer the consequences.

He couldn't understand why the Chairman, who had created him after all, didn't like him very much. It was never good for one's career to be on the Chairman's hit list.

He planned to maintain a low profile until this latest management craze blew itself out. He was already in enough trouble, and Meredith was his last chance to work in the Reorganized Djinn Hierarchy. He turned his attention back to his project, who had quit staring at him and started to speak.

"You mean to stand there in your Armani suit and Harvard tie and tell me you came out of a bottle or a lamp or something?" She frowned. "I need another drink." She headed for the credenza.

"It's up to you, of course, but it's not advisable to mix alcohol and genies."

"And why not?"

Trouble. He could tell she was going to make trouble for him. Why did the Chairman always give him problem humans? "It's a lot like drinking and driving. Not healthy."

"Well, I'm not driving. I'm celebrating." This time, she didn't bother to measure, just sloshed the aged scotch into the tumbler. "It isn't every day I meet a genie." She saluted him with the scotch, downed the golden liquid and poured another.

"You need to sit." He suggested to one of the wing-back chairs that it move closer to the woman, who was beginning to sway alarmingly. It wouldn't do to have his subject injure herself before he had a chance to explain.

The chair caught Meredith at the knees, and she sat. Solidly. Slopping scotch on her navy skirt. "Great. It goes well with the coffee, don't you think?" She grinned stupidly at him. "Course, if you're a real genie, you ought to be able to make this stain go away completely, right?"

He crossed his arms and rolled his eyes. "Child's play." The stain evaporated.

"A trick of light. When I get home, those stains will be there, waiting for my dry cleaner. Do you cut people in half? Pull rabbits out of your pockets?" She leaned toward the genie. "Do the one with the coins. I like tricks that involve money."

He scooted the other wing-back chair around to face the woman, and sat. "Have you heard a word I've said?"

She nodded. "Most of them. But I've always had a

25

very vivid imagination. I'm hallucinating from too much work and too little scotch."

"You're not imagining me. I'm a one-hundred-percent-real genie, all-powerful, all-knowing, and ready to grant three wishes for my new master." He looked at the woman. The all-knowing part—come to think of it, the all-powerful part as well—wasn't entirely correct, but he figured he'd toss them in for better effect.

He'd just recited the standard Genie/Master verbal contract, but it sounded trite in this technology-worshipping age. One of several reasons the Chairman had his turban in a tangle.

"A genie. Three wishes." She looked around her office. "If I didn't think you up, where did you come from? Out of my coffeepot?" She pointed to the ornate Arabian coffee service. "I had no idea I'd imported a genie when I brought it back from Riyadh." She paused, then frowned. "I thought genies lived in lamps."

"Some of us do."

"But not you."

"No." This was so embarrassing. At least a lamp had a mythic quality about it, an archetypal identification. He felt a distinctly un-genie-like flush suffuse his face. He looked away from her smirk.

"So, Mr. Genie, where *do* you live?"

"You had to ask, didn't you? Not satisfied just to have a genie at your beck and call."

"Well, I don't exactly know genie protocol. Where?"

It was the final condition the Chairman had dictated before he began his assignment, so he'd "fit in" with all the other gadgets. "Your cell phone."

"Excuse me? I have a haunted cell phone?" She reached over and picked it up.

"It isn't haunted. I'm a genie, not a ghost. Take care. You must never let that phone out of your control."

"Interesting." She paused, setting the phone in her lap. "And what is your assignment again?"

"Honestly, Meredith. If you'd just put down the alcohol," he said, "and pay attention, we wouldn't need to repeat ourselves, now, would we?" With a flick of his wrist, the crystal glass floated from her hand back to the credenza and settled, completely empty and sparkling clean, on the tray.

"You don't look anything like that Disney genie. Or Barbara Eden, either, for that matter. Shouldn't you be blue, or green or something? And sit on clouds of smoke?"

Hollywood strikes again.

"Genies can take on any shape they need to."

"Really? So, well-dressed genies are wearing eighteen-hundred-dollar suits these days? And alligator shoes, um, roughly fifteen hundred dollars?"

"It helps me blend in."

Meredith nodded and closed her eyes. "This is exactly how I would have scripted the end to a perfectly horrid day. First, my significant other decides to get married—to someone else. Then, I have to compete for my next promotion. On top of which, Horton takes away my best person. I work late, have a small drink and poof, I hallucinate a genie from Harvard or Yale who doesn't live in a lamp but has set up housekeeping in my cell phone. And, he's here to do my bidding. Three wishes' worth." She opened her eyes wide and hiccuped. "Have I got it all?"

"That about sums it up. Genie, three wishes, no lamp."

"What if I wish for more wishes?"

He shook his head. "Three wishes. Period. If you

wish for more wishes, the whole deal is void."

"Great. Even wishes come with a limited war-ranty."

"I suppose. What's a warranty?"

"It's an agreement that says the dealer will replace defective products, free of charge, unless the pur-chaser voids the warranty by messing up the prod-uct. You know, like trying to repair the vacuum cleaner yourself, only there's leftover parts when you put it back together?"

"Innovative concept." He wondered if the Chair-man had ever considered anything like this. "Except, wishes generally don't break. And they aren't defec-tive unless the person making the wish botches the job."

"Hmmmm." Meredith leaned back in the chair. "My very own genie." She squinted at him. "Still, a genie in a suit? It doesn't quite work."

"Okay, okay. Fine." He stood, whirled, and sud-denly, the gray suit and Harvard tie were gone. In their place was a blue apparition in the general shape of a man with muscular blue arms folded across a muscular blue chest and wide, gold bands at his wrists.

No legs. Just a wisp of bluish smoke that danced and swirled around the office. His face was recog-nizable, still handsome, but blue. His eyebrows had developed mischievous peaks, and his ears had gone all pointy. His head was bald, except for a topknot, caught in a gold clip of some sort, from which flowed a long, shining black ponytail.

"The beard is a nice touch."

"Hey, you want stereotypical genie, you get the goatee." He stroked the neatly trimmed black hair on his blue chin.

She watched him, thinking she hadn't had dreams like this since her sorority raided the fraternity house and drank all their beer. "I wonder. How do genies reproduce? I mean, what else have you got under your belt besides smoke?" She would regret the scotch in the morning, but it was fun, watching her hallucination wriggle.

"You're being rather personal."

"Sorry. I'm a management consultant. I don't spend time with genies. I didn't know you had feelings."

"I *do*." He whirled once more and the tall, tanned and impossibly handsome man was back. He loosened his tie.

"That was a great trick, Jim." She sighed. "Still, I would like an answer."

"Harrumph." The ad-agency–gorgeous genie paced in front of her desk. "Genies don't reproduce. They are brought into being fully formed by the Big Man, the Chief Executive, the Head Honcho, the Big Cheese." He stopped pacing and sat in her desk chair.

"I get the picture. No sex."

"I didn't say that."

"No. I did. Why am I talking to an imaginary something? Admittedly a very handsome something, but imaginary nonetheless. I should be working on my twin problems: no man, no promotion." She rolled her eyes. "Unreal."

The vision in the suit walked toward her, placed a strong, tanned hand on each arm of the wing-back chair and leaned close. "Do I look unreal to you?"

"Hard to tell. You're all out of focus." She blinked up at the blurry image just inches from her nose and took a deep breath. "But, you smell wonderful. What kind of cologne is that?" Spicy. Exotic. Erotic. She hiccuped.

The genie rolled his eyes and sat on the edge of her desk. "It's not cologne. It's my natural fragrance."

"I wonder if it could be reproduced. I could get rich selling it to young execs on the prowl." In the barely conscious back of her mind, she was hatching a marketing scheme to sell genie cologne in twisty, blue bottles.

"First, she wants a man. Now, she wants money." He scratched his cheek with a perfectly manicured, long, slender finger and looked at the ceiling. "I really hoped she'd be different."

Meredith hiccuped again. Maybe she wasn't inventing both sides of this conversation. She was sure she wouldn't actually ask herself these kinds of questions. She shook her head. *Don't even go there, Meredith*.

"Look, Jim. You've been a perfectly polite and quite entertaining invention of my work-weary brain, but I do have a project to complete, so, please, go away."

"My name isn't really Jim." Her figment, getting more attractive by the minute, folded his incredibly strong arms across his expansive, muscular chest and stood solidly enough in the middle of her office.

"Really?" Were mind-fictions supposed to argue with their sources? "What is your name, then?"

"Aha! Thought you could trap me, did you? Well, I'll have you know that, while I didn't graduate at the top of my class at DU, I did pay attention the day they covered rules on how to bind a djinn." Her poster boy for the incredibly good-looking actually smirked.

"Uh, okay, I'll bite. How do you bind a djinn?"

"You must know the djinn's name."

# Meredith's Wish

"Like Rumplestiltskin?"

"He wasn't a djinn, of course, but it's the same idea."

"Well, then, Genie, creature of my imagination, how shall I summon you to do my bidding if I don't know your name?" There. That should stop her impertinent hallucination.

"You've got your phone. You can call me." He smiled, and her heart flip-flopped like a fish on a hot tin roof. Pity he wasn't real.

"Good. That's good. Any particular number? Say, 911?" She chuckled.

"I suppose we could agree on that, but really, you just need to speak into the cell phone and I'll come to you."

"Every woman's fantasy." She picked up the phone.

"I beg your pardon?"

"To have a man come when you call. It's every woman's fantasy." She turned the phone on. *Especially when they look like you, pal.*

"I can be your fantasy."

This was getting out of hand. "Fine. Be a fantasy, be a figment. Heck, be a fig leaf. Just leave me alone. I really need to find a solution to my latest work crisis."

"You could wish for a solution, you know."

Meredith paused, considering. "Wishes. I have three of them, right?"

"You have been listening."

"So, I could use up a wish to fix my problem?" Her personal genie nodded. "Good, I need to find a man."

The genie cocked his head and raised one eyebrow. "I'm pretty good at finding things. Who have you misplaced?" He stood, feet balanced and slightly apart, arms folded across his chest. "I'm ready. Wish

31

away. Anything you want. Be as outrageous as possible. But be sure you state your desire in the proper form, as in 'I wish for fill-in-the-blank.' "

Meredith toyed with the cell phone. This *was* simply a dream, this enticing specimen of the male gender, she told herself. "Okay. Assuming for the moment that you *are* a genie and you *can* grant wishes, I wish . . ." Her thoughts wandered back to what she had been doing right before her life turned into a sequel to *Aladdin*. "I wish, not just for any man, but for my true love." She sat back and relaxed. It sounded almost reasonable.

The genie closed his eyes, took a deep breath and blinked. "What did you say?"

"I wish for my true love. And, if it wouldn't be too much trouble, I'd like him before Saturday."

# *Chapter Two*

## *"Slow Djinn Fizz"*

"I can't do that." The genie leaned over her.

"Why not?"

"*You* weren't listening when I explained the rules."

"*You* didn't mention any. Except not wishing for more wishes. What kind of genies have rules?"

"All kinds." He frowned and walked across the red carpet to the window and back again. "You'll simply have to wish for something else," he whispered. "I can't have you making wishes I can't grant. My boss will have my head on a pike and *then* he'll fire me. Sure as spit."

"You mean you'll lose your job?"

"She can listen. Yes. Make another wish. Quick."

Meredith couldn't believe her hallucination had the audacity to argue with her. It seemed everyone was against her today.

"No. That is my wish. Take it or leave it."

"I can't take it. It violates ancient laws older than

33

the invention of time." He paced around the office. "I can't leave it, either. You're my mistress and I must do as you command. Only, I can't do this."

Meredith sat quietly. She had learned that one sure way to win a negotiation was to be silent. The first one to speak lost. She stared out the window. Besides, it was her fantasy. She *should* be in control.

The seconds ticked into minutes. She sat comfortably, enjoying the silence. Her imaginary man wandered nervously around the room, a sheen of sweat on his handsome brow.

"I give up," he said. "I don't have a choice. My number is up anyway. It was pure hubris, thinking this assignment would save me." The genie stopped midstride, as if he'd had a revelation of major proportions. "Look, Meredith, you've got problems, right?" She nodded. "I've got problems, too. Why don't we work together to solve them? I'll rub your shoulders if you rub mine. What do you say?" He held out a tanned hand.

What an intriguing twist on normal hallucinations, if one could consider hallucinations normal, that is. Make a deal with your imagination. She shrugged.

"Why not? I'll have my people call your people with the contract sometime next week." She grabbed her illusion's hand to seal the agreement. No doubt when she woke she'd find herself shaking hands with her umbrella. "The deal's struck, Fantasy Man. Now go somewhere and wait while I figure out how to, one, convince the duchess to let Horton Consulting help increase their tourist trade. And, two"—she sighed—"find a date."

"Dates is it? Now, I'm a genie who knows his dates. There's chopped dates, stuffed dates, whole dates.

Dates from California, dates from Greece. What kind did you have in mind?"

Meredith sighed deeply. No more scotch. Not on an empty stomach, no matter how bad a day she'd had. "Not that kind of date. A take-me-out-to-dinner kind of date. I just need time to think about my situation." She narrowed her eyes.

"You're certain? You couldn't make just one tiny wish right now? Could you?" He glanced at his gold wristwatch. "I'm in kind of a hurry."

"I wished a wish. True love. Go grant it."

He started to protest, rolled his eyes and said, "Okay, fine." Her imaginary man faded faster than an East Coast sunset until only his voice remained. Low, sexy. "You know where to find me."

Meredith stood unsteadily and walked to her desk, her Hertzenstein briefing documents still open and demanding answers. The smell of cinnamon faded. Slowly, she scanned the office.

No drop-off-the-edge-of-the-universe gorgeous man. No man at all.

It had been a great dream while it lasted. Love always seemed to work that way for her. She took a deep breath and turned her attention back to the Duchy of Hertzenstein. She leafed through the folder Horton had given her. It included bios on the duchess and her duke, stats on population and exports, descriptions of the castle, coupons for ten-percent savings at certain hotels. But not one word on why married women succeeded where the single did not.

There was an answer here somewhere. She just had to find it. Maybe the Duchy had a Web site. She reached for her mouse.

The screen saver on her PC monitor swirled fantastic, dizzying shapes. Why had she chosen Frenetic

# Karen Lee

Fractals anyway? She bumped the mouse and the figures disappeared, replaced by Horton's earlier e-mail summoning her to his office.

She leaned her head onto the keyboard, momentarily overcome by exhaustion, scotch and her obviously overdeveloped imagination. She jerked upright again when the phone rang, interrupting her brief catnap.

"Hello?" She sounded fuzzy.

"Meredith?"

"Oh, Darcie. It's so good to hear your voice. Where are you?" Meredith sat back, reveling in the relief that rushed through her. "Are you all right? Did Horton really reassign you or did I dream it? Why didn't you tell me?"

"Whoa, slow down. I'm fine. I'm actually just two floors below your office. I'm sorry I didn't have time to call you, but Francis insisted that I begin work immediately. He said he'd call and explain everything."

"Francis Griffin?"

"Don't go ballistic on me, Boss. This is temporary."

"Horton reassigned you to Griffin?" He *was* trying to torpedo her career.

"Yes. Griffin didn't give you the details?"

"Griffin wouldn't give me the correct time unless there was something in it for him. He certainly hasn't provided any details." Meredith held her head with her free hand.

"Really? He said he'd either call you or stop by."

The only visitation she'd had was an imaginary man too sexy to be real. "What's this about, Darcie? I need you for this project and Horton knows it." So did Griffin, for that matter.

There was a pause on the other end of the line. "I really thought you knew or I wouldn't have left with-

36

out talking to you. Horton explained that it wouldn't be a permanent move, just a couple of weeks."

"Horton explained?"

"Yes, I met with him and Francis just after lunch. Griffin needs my graphics expertise, Boss, and it's good exposure for me." She paused. "You can have my evenings and weekends if you need them."

She'd need them, three times over. "No, Darcie. I understand." A lie, but Darcie was her friend. "And I wouldn't dare steal time away from you and Ben now that things look like they're headed for the altar." Another opportunity not to be the bride. "I do need one small favor."

"Already done. In fact"—Meredith heard the clicking of a keyboard hard at work—"I just e-mailed it to you."

"What?"

"The background you wanted on the duchess. About married women. It's all there."

Now she was getting somewhere. "Thanks, Darce." She retrieved the e-mail and glanced at it. "This will be very helpful."

"Good. Well, I've got to get back to Francis's presentation."

"Wait, please. One more favor?"

"Sure."

"Find me a date?"

"What? Not again."

"Please? If I don't take a husband, or at least a stand-in, with me to see the duchess, well . . ."

Darcie was quiet. "That's why you needed to know about the married bit. You can't close the deal without a ring on your finger and the I-do's to go with it."

"I could get the contract on my own," Meredith said indignantly. "It's just that every advantage helps.

Trust me, you do not want Griffin to be vice president."

"The last time I fixed you up with a guy, I never heard the end of it."

"This is different."

"Different as in he simply needs to be breathing, or different as in he should eat with utensils?"

Meredith sighed. She hated the desperation that crawled in her stomach. "Different enough to be able to pass as a husband. So, I need someone reasonably intelligent, who wouldn't mind tagging along on an all-expenses-paid business trip."

"A tall order. I'll have to think about it."

"Think quick. You'd hate working for Francis full time."

"I've got an idea. Let me put you on hold and see if I can arrange this." She paused and Meredith could hear the chuckle beginning. "There's an extra charge for rush orders, you realize."

"No problem. This is a certified emergency. I'll buy lunch next time." Meredith listened impatiently to three verses of "I Got You, Babe," wondering who Darcie could find at this time of night. Another workaholic, no doubt. The music segued into a syrupy version of "Unchained Melody" as she doodled on the Hertzenstein folder. Who picked this stuff? She made a mental note to check into it.

Darcie clicked back in. "Meredith, you're in luck. My dentist, the very unattached Dr. Alan Rademacher, has agreed to go out with you."

"There's too much enthusiasm in your voice. What's wrong with this guy?" The doodle was shaping up to look just like Mr. Imaginary.

"Nothing. Nothing at all. He's charming and articulate."

Meredith had been burned so many times recently, she wanted to carry a fire extinguisher. She added a quirked eyebrow to her doodle man. "Don't tell me he has a great personality." Her head hurt. "I think we should have a trial run before I try to pass him off as something as important as a husband."

For a nanosecond, she considered the possibility that the man she had imagined was this Dr. Rademacher. She shook her head. No one in the real world was that attractive. She looked around her office, but the handsome man hadn't returned. And he'd been such a nice figment. She x-ed out her doodle. "What do you think he'd agree to?"

"Don't be so caustic. Alan is a really nice man when he doesn't have his hands in someone's mouth." Darcie chuckled. "Perhaps dinner. He frequents the Tivoli."

"Well, at least he has decent taste in restaurants, which supports your claim that he uses utensils. But he'd better keep his fingers away from my molars." Meredith had relaxed. "Thanks Darce, you're a real friend. I'll bring all my future needs to Collins Imaginative Dating Service."

"If you'd quit trying to manage men the way you manage work, you wouldn't need my services. Let me set up dinner for Wednesday night."

"I'll meet him there, say, around seven?"

"You won't have trouble recognizing him. He's tallish and blondish and has perfect teeth. Enjoy." Darcie hung up.

Maybe it wouldn't be all that bad. How many times did a gal get a chance at a guy with perfect anything, much less perfect teeth?

Saying a final good-bye to her doodled Adonis, she dropped the folder into her briefcase and turned her attention to Darcie's e-mail. Her friend had done an equally good job on research.

"While William the Conqueror was busy making plans to invade England, several of his captains decided to have a go at the small country of Hertzenstein," she read. "Sir Guy d'Boncey and Armond du Chat, Duke of Plantain, gathered their knights outside the walls of Hertzenstein. They issued demands to speak with the duke." Meredith yawned.

"Inside the walls, Hertzensteinians prepared for siege. Unfortunately, the duke, Adelard the Plump, was mortally wounded by his own archers during a practice session. That left the duchess, Hermione the Bold and Beautiful, to deal with the invaders. Her faithful lady-in-waiting, Alice Bourneville, suggested the duchess negotiate a treaty. So, she did." Meredith was suddenly interested. She hadn't done well in history, but the idea of an eleventh-century woman taking control of a desperate situation made her feel somehow comfortable with Duchess Hermione. Even if her nickname was a soap opera.

"In 1062, Hermione and Alice signed a treaty so favorable that the Duchy of Hertzenstein survived. Because of the bravery and creativity of these two married women, to this day, married women negotiate all business deals with the Duchy."

Kind feelings toward Hermione or not, history had always made Meredith's head hurt. Especially the kind that interfered with her career. It looked like she definitely needed a significant other.

She logged off and shut down her computer. Tomorrow. She'd worry about it then. She could barely see, much less think; home in bed was where she belonged.

Thanks to Darcie, at least she had a prospective candidate culled from the general herd.

\*   \*   \*

The fourth time Meredith rolled over and glared at her alarm clock it read five-thirty-five. In the AM. Her assignment with the duchess kept marching through her dreams, with columns of numbers dancing the limbo, getting lower and lower until they disappeared altogether and were replaced by a tall, handsome and all too exotic man who smiled at her and said, "Your wish is my command," and then disappeared. Most annoying.

She sat up and looked around. Her head hurt.

She reached out and scratched her cat's ears. Here was another fine example of what men weren't. Stanley was faithful, quiet, and slept with her even when she was in a rotten mood. Admittedly, he shed. But the constant battle to keep black and white cat hairs off her suits was worth the unquestioned loyalty.

She ran her tongue around her dry mouth. Water. This situation definitely called for water. She slid out of bed, jammed her feet into her slippers and shuffled to the bathroom. She turned on the light, reached for the faucet and about jumped out of her flannel nightgown.

The man who had declared himself her personal genie leaned against the clear, glass blocks that formed her shower. The bottom half of very expensive silk pajamas hung low on his lean hips, and his excellent physique shouted "I work out." He smiled. "I didn't mean to startle you, Meredith, but you called."

Meredith sat on the edge of her Jacuzzi tub, shaking. "Startle me? You've frightened me out of a year's growth." Her heart was doing a quality imitation of a kettle drum. All the other times she'd had a man in her bathroom, semidressed, she'd invited him. She considered sprinting for the phone and dialing 911.

"Actually, a person can't really be that frightened."

She rolled her eyes. "Try looking at things from my point of view."

Without discernible movement, suddenly he was sitting beside her, his nearness aphrodisiac-strong. "Nope. Looks the same." Instantly, he was leaning against the shower again.

"Don't do that! You make my head hurt worse." She rose and filled a glass with water, drank and sat down again. "I figured you for a one-hallucination appearance. It must be the stress of this competition with Griffin."

"You know, Meredith, for a bright woman, you can be exceptionally dense sometimes."

She looked up at him and shook her head. "So I've been told." One more sip of water. "Refresh my memory."

He walked toward her, his long legs quickly eating up the distance between them. "May I?" He motioned to the edge of the tub. She shrugged. He sat down. The exotic scent that seemed to follow him permeated the room. "I know it's not high-tech, but I am a genie and you are my assignment."

She wondered if he'd disappear into smoke if she touched him. "I remember that much." The idea of touching him, all over, was very appealing. She felt drowsy, but warm, like she'd just finished making love. She swallowed.

"You know," he said, "if you're really interested in catching a man, you should consider alternative nighttime fashion. Flannel is so very déclassé. And the bunny slippers? Well, I wouldn't like to speculate about those."

Erotic thoughts vanished, no smoke. Men, even imaginary ones, would never appreciate the need for flannel.

"If you had a man in your life, he'd keep you warm," said the genie.

"Maybe. If he'd stay around long enough."

"That's just the problem I've agreed to help you solve."

"What? Keeping me warm at night?"

"An interesting prospect, I'm sure, but no. Don't you remember our deal? I'm crushed, deflated, demoralized."

Somewhere in the middle of the conversation, Meredith began to believe in the existence of this genie-man in her bathroom; she started to embrace the thought that he might just be real. "I remember wishing for true love. But I was imagining you, wasn't I?"

"Do I look like a figment of your imagination?"

"You're better than my best dreams, that's the truth." She traced his square jawline with a slender finger. Electric chills danced up her arm. She jerked back her hand. "You're real."

"Of course I'm real. That's what I've been telling you since our meeting. And we have a pact. I'm going to help you. You're going to help me. Remember?"

"Something about being on a tight schedule."

He clapped. "By Djorge, I think she's got it."

"So I didn't hallucinate you this evening at my office? Wandering around in your very expensive suit?"

Jim shook his head.

"And the bit about the cell phone?"

"Unfortunately true."

"But I didn't dial you up just now. I was only dreaming about you."

"Strong thoughts from the subject person work just as well for advanced genies."

"So any time I simply think about you, you'll appear?" Scary. Especially since her personal genie was such an attractive specimen. Clouds of sleep swept away as layer upon layer of possibility unfolded. There could be some real advantages to having her own genie.

"Generally speaking, yes. Although I do have enough manners to know not to pop in when it would reflect badly on you. Like in the middle of a shower, or a meeting with the president. Things like that." His eyes sparkled mischievously. He raised one dark, enigmatic eyebrow. "Unless I think I'm needed."

"Uh-huh. Right now what I need is sleep." It wasn't what she wanted. Not with Mister Tall, Dark and Magical within jumping distance. But, she had her career to consider. Not to mention her mental health. "So, be a good genie and slip back into my phone. We'll talk about this in the morning." She yawned and padded back to bed. Sleep was definitely required.

She'd consider psychiatric help later.

Jim was sitting on the edge of her bed, long silk-clad legs crossed, and a "take-me-I'm-yours" look on his face. "It's almost time to get up anyway. Why not pop into the shower? I'll fix breakfast." He smiled and disappeared.

Meredith squinted at her clock. Five-fifty-three. Just her luck. She'd found a genie who liked mornings.

She wandered back into the bathroom and turned on the shower. The jets of hot water convinced her she was awake. Lathering her hair, she realized she felt wonderfully refreshed, almost like she'd spent a restful eight hours in bed rather than a fitful few.

"Stanley. Do you smell something? Like bacon?" She snagged an Egyptian cotton towel, wrapped it around her slim figure and wrestled with the decision of what to wear. In the end, a navy print dress with a white, geometrical pattern won out over a gray skirted suit. She tied a bright red scarf loosely around her neck and critiqued the effect in her mirror. She added gold earrings, a small but elegant pin, and she was once more the dedicated, single career woman her mother had warned her about.

Emphasis on single.

"I'm working on it, Mom. I'm working on it," she murmured.

The aroma of bacon grew stronger as she slipped into her pumps. Stanley, hungry himself, twisted furry figure-eights around her legs.

She positively bounced into her kitchen, the worries of the previous day banished.

He was there, her genie, decked out in a chef's hat and long, white apron.

"Would Mademoiselle care for coffee?" He waved a hand and a cup of steaming liquid materialized. "Cream?" Out of nothing, a slender stream of white poured into the cup. He made stirring motions with his finger and gave it to Meredith.

"Thanks." She cradled the cup in her palms. "You're pretty handy in a kitchen."

"One of my many talents. How do you like your eggs?"

"I don't usually eat in the morning."

"You should never ignore breakfast. It's the most important meal of the day." Bacon, eggs and toast danced through the air to land decorously on a plate. "*Mange.*"

"I don't have time." She remembered with a jolt of adrenaline what she'd been working on when the genie popped into her office. Her weekly team planning session. She had to bring them up to speed on the

new developments in Hertzenstein. "I need to prepare for a meeting at eight"—she glanced at her
watch—"which I might make, depending on traffic,
and I'm not even quasi-ready." She squeezed her eyes
shut and gulped the coffee. She opened her eyes,
shoved the empty mug in the general direction of the
counter and tried to remember where she'd left her
briefcase.

"Meredith, take a deep breath. There's nothing to
worry about." He pushed her gently into a chair.
"You have a genie on your team." The briefcase appeared beside her.

The food did look tempting. "What, no orange
juice?" Meredith laughed when a glass filled before
her eyes. "Wait. Does all this count as wishes? I remember a three-wish limit."

Dishes clattered to the floor: eggs, bacon, juice and
coffee an all too real mess.

"You can't tell anyone. It could mean my job. And,
they aren't really wishes, after all, just small tokens
of assistance to help you achieve your penultimate
wish: true love. Think of them as product demonstrations."

Meredith could see real panic on the genie's face.
Being out of work was tough. She'd watched her father grapple for almost two years before he found
employment. "They're not going to fire you for product demonstrations, so calm down."

"You'll be willing to explain that to the Chairman,
won't you?" With a wave of his slender, long fingers,
he cleared the mess off the kitchen tiles and whipped
up another breakfast. "He prefers entries in triplicate, using the appropriate Wish Deviation Form,
number zero-eight-five-two-dee-dash-dee-jay."

"Whatever you need. We're partners, remember?"
She checked her watch again. The hands hadn't

moved. So, genies could stop time. Helpful. "Tell me about this famous Chairman of yours."

The genie shivered in midstride. "He is all-powerful." He tiptoed across the kitchen and sat next to Meredith. "We must be very quiet," he whispered.

"Why? Does he have supersonic hearing?" She matched his hushed tones.

He nodded. "Sees all, knows all." He glanced nervously around the pristine white kitchen as if waiting for a plague of dust balls. "He's prone to surprise inspections, like a demented drill sergeant."

"Hmmm. I had an art professor like that once. Really broke my concentration."

"Exactly! How can he expect me to perform flawlessly if he keeps watching?" He scooted his chair closer. "You got an A in that class, right?"

Meredith smiled. "I barely passed." Of course her C− was mostly her fault. The primary reason Professor Lomax rattled her so badly was her all-consuming crush on the handsome young artist. "Ancient history."

"I'm good at history."

"I bet you are." She considered the breakfast waiting in front of her. "I don't feel like eggs, and bacon is just fat in strips." She sipped the fragrant coffee, which had appeared in the empty mug. "Partner."

"Partner." He pondered the word, nodded, apparently liking the concept. "Partner. Something healthier, then? After all, you can't find true love if your body chemistry is always in an uproar." Eggs, bacon and toast turned into yogurt and fresh peaches, topped with a small sprinkling of wheat bran. "Happy now?"

"Much better, thank you." She picked up her spoon and then glanced at the clock on the wall. Seven-fifteen. Her wristwatch may have stopped, but

# Karen Lee

time was marching forward. "Yikes! I'm so late. I'll never make it and then what will Horton do?" And how would Francis take advantage of it? She jumped up, grabbed her briefcase and coat and raced to the door.

April morning sun illuminated her driveway. The same driveway where she remembered parking her Mercedes the night before.

The drive was empty. Just like her career was going to be if she didn't get to the office, pronto. Only one explanation came to mind.

"Jim! Where's my car?"

"You were in such bad shape last night, I couldn't let you drive home. It wouldn't do to lose my assignment to an accident or an extended jail sentence." He put his arm around her shoulder. His touch was warm, comforting. "Come, finish breakfast. You'll make the meeting. Trust me. I have a way with clocks."

"That car is my pride and joy. I worked very hard to get to the place where I could afford a Mercedes and . . ."

"And what has it gotten you? A lot of time stuck in traffic, or driving home late. Alone. Sit down, Meredith. Relax. Enjoy the morning."

"Right." She allowed him to lead her to the chair.

"Tell me what this meeting is about and why it's so important." Her genie sat in the air, his legs crossed, a stenographer's pad and pencil at the ready. "I'll create an agenda that will blow their socks off."

"How do you do that? Float, I mean."

"Very well, thank you. Now, if you'd just give me the basics, I'll improvise."

Meredith was more than a little suspicious of what he might improvise, but she outlined the meeting.

"Of course, Darcie would have arranged coffee, bagels, that sort of thing, as well as had copies of all the relevant information already set out in the conference room next to my office."

"Consider it done." Jim snapped his fingers. "Ready?"

"What do you have planned, Jim? Is this another product demonstration that won't count as a wish?"

"Consider it a sample." He stood behind Meredith, held her shoulders, and as her designer kitchen faded to black, her equally well-appointed conference room appeared. "Here we are. I do hope that whole-wheat bagels with herbed cream cheese are a good choice. I worked so hard on this meeting."

Meredith looked around her. Everything was perfect. Briefing papers arranged in tidy piles at each chair around the table. Overhead projector warmed-up and focused. He'd even added fresh flowers next to the coffeepots.

"Close your mouth. It isn't becoming for an executive vice president." Jim stood next to her, grinning broadly.

"Hey, Meredith." Jack Williams from Finance walked into the conference room. "I was here not five minutes ago and the room was empty. How'd you manage this? Magic?"

"Could be, Jack." Meredith walked to the head of the table and motioned Jack to his seat. "Coffee?"

The rest of the team arrived more or less on time. Meredith smiled at Jim as she opened the meeting. "I'd like to introduce my new, temporary assistant. Folks, this is Jim. Darcie is on special assignment."

Jim the Djinn, horn-rimmed glasses perched on his perfect nose, and looking the proper assistant in gray slacks, a button-down red striped shirt and sleeveless V-neck sweater, passed out copies of the agenda. His appearance had changed subtly. Gone was the throbbing animal passion, replaced by a calm efficiency Meredith usually associated with librarians or high school English teachers.

She glanced up to see Francis Griffin checking out her meeting as he passed the conference room slowly. "Still unmarried, I see," he called as he stuck his head into the room.

Meredith gave him a tight smile. She would never understand what his wife saw in this short, flabby man whose piggy eyes glinted malevolently. "Don't you have your own challenges, Francis?"

He pulled his ever-present monogrammed handkerchief from his pocket and dabbed at the sweat that had suddenly appeared on his forehead.

"A little nervous, are we?" Meredith cocked an eyebrow.

"I'm not the one who has reason to be nervous, Montgomery." He straightened his collar and jammed the handkerchief back in his pants pocket. "I'm thinking of demoting you to file clerk after Horton promotes me." He stalked away.

"What's he talking about?" Eileen from Systems looked worried.

"Let's get started, people." Meredith consulted the agenda. "First item: Requirements for the New Assignment."

As an assistant, Jim was efficient and quick to learn. As a genie, he was difficult to control.

"It's part of the genie mystique," he assured her, gazing out at her from her computer screen, his dark eyes alluring between columns of a projected income statement.

"Please get out of my computer. I can't concentrate

with you staring at me." Why couldn't he have been an old, ugly, wart-covered genie?

"Technology has ruined humans." Jim appeared in front of her desk, just as handsome and unwart-covered as ever. "You have no appreciation for the mythic."

"Quite possibly." She adjusted her scarf. "I assume you'd like to pin down the details of our arrangement. That's why you're hovering."

Jim glanced from side to side, then looked at his polished brown loafers. "My feet are solidly on the floor. I'm not hovering. And yes, we do need to confer." He slid onto the edge of her desk. "I've got a real crisis brewing."

The phone rang. "Hold that crisis." She answered with her standard "Meredith Montgomery."

"Good news." Darcie sounded very tired. "I've talked with my dentist. He's excited about dinner tomorrow evening, but he's got a late extraction and wondered if eight would work instead of seven. I already checked your calendar. You're fine."

"Thanks, Darcie. I owe you." She hung up the phone and smiled at Jim. "Your first opportunity to assist."

"Really?" He slid closer. "Give me details."

"My *real* assistant has arranged a blind date for me."

"And you need me to act as his guide dog. Demeaning, but if it helps you find true love and saves my job, okay."

"Why are you so very literal?"

"I'm not just literal, I'm legendary." He chuckled. "Blind date simply means I've never met him before."

"And he's your true love?"

51

"Anything is possible. We're having dinner at the Tivoli restaurant. I'd like you to . . ."

"Make the evening perfect in every way. Almost too easy. Rest assured, I'll have him begging on bended knee." He stood. "Say no more. I have arrangements to make." He leaned close and whispered in her ear, "One order of True Love, coming up." He disappeared in a breath of blue, trailing cinnamon across her cell phone.

"You having trouble with the electrical system, Meredith? All your lights just blinked." Francis Griffin leaned into her office, his brown suit more rumpled than usual. "Can I talk to you for a sec?"

"Sure, Francis. As long as you're not here to abscond with my new assistant, too."

"Hey"—he held up pudgy hands—"don't blame me. Horton suggested it." He entered the spacious room and reached for her cell phone. "Is this new?"

She snatched it from his grasp. She wasn't entirely comfortable with this genie in her life, but the thought that Francis could take advantage of him was not a pretty one. "Yes. And not for sharing." She tucked it carefully into her briefcase. "What was it you needed?"

"Who were you talking to when I came in?"

"No one. As you can see, we're the only two here."

Griffin narrowed his eyes and glanced around. "I was sure I saw someone, heard something. No matter. I wanted to apologize about Darcie." He shifted from one foot to the other, then pulled out his handkerchief and dabbed at the sheen of sweat on his face. "I'm not clever with graphics like you are and I really wanted to give my presentation to the folks in Wyoming some zing. I figure you have to capture their imagination to bring in the big-bucks contract."

"You think slick graphics will get you the promotion?"

"I deserve it. I've given my life to this company for the past few years. I started in a mail room, you know. I educated myself."

"And I've always admired your tenacity, Francis, but this company needs new ideas."

He blinked his porcine eyes. "And you're the one to have them, is that it?"

"Look, Horton clearly needs me in that corner office. Why would he have given me the tougher assignment if he didn't think I could handle it better than you? If I had your project, I'd have the deal closed by noon tomorrow. It'll take more than stealing my assistant for you to beat me."

He gave her a martyred look. "For your information, there's nothing easy about East Overshoe, Wyoming. Besides, I know the grand duchess prefers doing business with women. Obviously, I don't qualify and that's why Horton gave her to you. It has absolutely nothing to do with skill. If that old bat would join the rest of us in the twenty-first century, I'd have had her signature by noon yesterday." He walked to the door. "The company also needs seasoned experience."

"Some experience is too heavily seasoned." She smiled at him.

"Don't cross me, Montgomery. You won't like the results. This is *my* promotion and I'll do whatever it takes to make sure Horton gives it to me." He spun on his heel and stomped out of her office.

# *Chapter Three*

## *"Djinn Game"*

"Watch where you're going!" Heading into his office as fast as his chubby legs would take him, Francis Griffin almost walked over Jim. "Why are you here? What do you want?"

"Excuse me, sir," Jim apologized. "I'm here to talk with Miss Collins." Griffin's office area certainly didn't compare to Meredith's. It was smaller and darker, somehow more appropriate to its occupant.

"Something she can help you with?" Meredith's rival wrinkled his brow, an evil glint in his eye.

"Miss Montgomery sent me over to be briefed."

"Fine. But don't take too much time." He snagged a pile of file folders and stalked away. "She's mine now."

Jim didn't like the sound of that, but then, he didn't like much of what Meredith's rival said or did. He indicated the retreating Griffin with a slight nod. "What's up with him?" He sat in a straight-backed chair in front of Darcie's temporary desk. It was covered with computer disks, file folders, papers and scribbled notes.

"Ah, my new and very challenged boss. He's tired of watching the garbage trucks outside his window." Darcie nodded sagely. "Until he joined the marketing department alongside Meredith, our Mr. Griffin was on the fast track up the corporate escalator."

"Something tells me Miss Montgomery has gummed up the works." Jim liked Meredith's assistant. She reminded him of one of his favorite houris—sharp, sassy, and pixielike.

Darcie picked up her cup of tea and took a sip. "You might say that. Meredith brings her own style to business negotiations, bends all the rules and succeeds beyond even his wildest dreams." She wrinkled her nose. "Consequently the nervous Mr. G will try just about anything to stop her from occupying the office real estate next to Horton's."

Jim recognized himself in Darcie's description of Meredith. He, too, pursued his assignments with panache, making waves where he had to, bending and sometimes breaking rules. They should be a perfect match, so why did he have the feeling he was headed for disaster whenever he thought about her? He turned his attention back to Darcie. "Pardon? I didn't catch that last comment."

Darcie ran her tongue across her upper lip. "I was just saying that she won't be wanting me back with you taking dictation and pouring coffee."

Jim cocked his head and smiled. Modeling himself after an ad for men's cologne had been a stroke of brilliance, if he did say so himself. Every woman he'd met at Horton's had practically swooned. Darcie had just joined his growing group of admirers. Only Meredith hadn't succumbed to his Adonis-like appearance. Her reaction to his obvious charms was difficult to judge. She should have simply fallen at his feet. Instead, she remained aloof, businesslike. He adjusted his glasses. He'd have to see what he could do to change that.

"She's always had an eye for the extremely good-looking." Darcie smiled broadly, her charcoal eyes twinkling.

"I've found her to be completely professional." More or less. He chalked up her lukewarm reaction to his physical assets to an excess of distilled spirits.

"What did you want to know about Meredith?" Darcie set down her tea and began straightening the file folders. "She usually comes in around nine, likes her coffee with a touch of cream, no sugar. Hates tea, especially herbal. She stays late almost every night. Works out at her gym several mornings a week." Darcie added one more file folder to the growing stack. "She's a demanding boss, but a fair one."

Jim cleared his throat. "I wanted information of a more personal nature. To get to know her, you understand."

"Of course."

"What kind of things does she do for fun?"

"Fun isn't in her standard vocabulary. She's more of a work-every-waking-hour kind of gal."

"Surely she must have some outside interests. Like golf, or theater or art?" He suspected the answer was a solid, unwavering "no." He'd seen her intense focus.

"She plays golf. She claims it's an insipid game invented by some Scotsman who'd been cut off from his supply of haggis." Darcie laughed. "But she keeps it up, because it's good for business relations. She plays with clients, and as far as I know, she and Horton play together fairly regularly." Darcie rested her chin on her hands. "She used to be artistic. Did some kind of painting, or drawing, I think. Then the demands of the job overtook her spare time and the paintbrushes and pencils went into mothball status."

Art. That explained the half-sketches and doodles on every exposed piece of paper on her desk. "I know she's single. Is there someone in her life at present, someone whose calls I should anticipate?" He opened his steno pad, poised to take notes.

"Hmmmm. Ticklish subject actually. Her latest beau just entered the swelling ranks of ex."

"Hard to believe a woman that attractive, that bright would have trouble with men." He paused. "What kind of men does she like?"

"Well"—Darcie pursed her lips—"I guess she wouldn't mind my telling you. She generally goes for tough-minded career guys. The ones with wing tips and a matching MBA. That way, they can compare balance sheets over their crème brûlée and double cappuccino."

"If they're both career-minded, why is there a problem?"

"You tell me. I can't figure it out. I guess she's too committed to her job to pay enough attention to her relationships." She removed a dangling, gold hoop from one ear and played with it. "Consulting is a tough, competitive business, and Meredith is the best of the best. She's convinced nobody in the industry takes her seriously because she's a woman. I've tried to tell her she's wrong, but she doesn't listen. She drives herself so hard, sometimes I worry about her." Darcie put the earring back on. "If you ask me—which she would never 'cause she knows she wouldn't like the answer—she needs balance, time to relax, a project or some interest outside of this office."

# Karen Lee

"Maybe she should go back to her art." He'd had experience with artists. In general they were a lot of fun. At a minimum, they were colorful.

"Maybe. From what I hear, she was good. When she was younger she had aspirations to go professional. She gave it up, though. No money in art."

"Why did she need money?"

"It wasn't Meredith so much as her folks. They had some hard times several years back. Her dad got squeezed out in one of those mega-mergers and tried his hand at a landscaping business. It didn't do well. She quit her art to help them and wound up with a business career. From what I understand, if it hadn't been for her efforts, her parents would have gone bankrupt. It would have ruined their lives."

So, his subject was dedicated to family. And artistic. And minus any possible male intrusions. Strike that, complications. Strike that, candidates. Yes, candidates was the word. He had to keep his priorities straight. He needed to assist, not intrude. Or so the Chairman would be quick to remind him. "You've been very helpful, Miss Collins. Thank you."

"Not at all, Jim. You come by anytime and we can chat again. Take care of my Boss Lady, you hear?"

"Thank you so much, Dr. Rademacher. The corsage is, ahem, lovely." Meredith turned her face away from the enormous greenish orchid her "date" had pinned to her coral, raw-silk suit jacket and tried not to sneeze. "You really shouldn't have." It took her back to her high school prom.

The prom had been a disaster.

"Come, come, Meredith. Call me Alan. And, you're right, I probably could have skipped the flower, but I thought, why not? It's our first date and I wanted

58

it to be a night to remember. Darcie said you liked flowers."

"What a romantic thought." Meredith normally enjoyed the quiet elegance of this restaurant, with its low lighting and attention to every detail.

"Darcie speaks quite highly of you, you know. How long have you worked for her?"

Meredith coughed quietly. "I don't actually work *for* Darcie, Alan."

"I understand." His voice took on a conspiratorial tone. "Part of the secretarial pool. Your secret's safe."

Why had she agreed to go out with this person? She'd made a wish. Two days ago. Federal Express, heck, even the U.S. post office, delivered faster than that.

She thought of an appropriately stinging retort to the doctor's comment, and then took a deep breath. Perhaps the fair-haired dentist would grow on her.

"Zeese way, Mademoiselle. M'sieur." A tuxedoed maitre d' materialized at Meredith's elbow. "A private table for zee 'appy couple, no?"

"My regular, please," said the dentist.

"Oui, M'sieur."

Meredith followed the broad shoulders of the maitre d' to a table in a quiet corner. There was something familiar in his walk, the way he carried himself.

"Voila!" He pulled out the damask-covered chair and swept Meredith into it, snapping open the elegantly folded linen napkin and draping it across her lap. From nowhere, it seemed, he produced a menu.

She looked inquiringly across the table at the orthodontist. He smiled. Darcie was right about the teeth. Perfect. She decided to let the slight about her job go unanswered. For now. She glanced at the menu, then looked at Alan once more. Was it her

59

imagination, or did the candlelight glint off his incisors?

"Mademoiselle, M'sieur. May I offer you a cocktail?"

She smiled up at the matire d' and choked.

"Are you all right?" Alan cocked his head, worried.

Meredith grabbed the glass of water and gulped a mouthful. The maitre d' was Jim. She coughed, sputtering water all down her blouse and on the tablecloth. "I'm—I'll be fine. Just swallowed wrong. That's all."

" 'Ere, Mademoiselle, let me assist you." The "maitre d' " proffered a handkerchief, bowing slightly. "I am so sorree." As he leaned forward, he whispered in her ear. "Is this the man who's going to understand and love you anyway?"

"Maybe. It's possible. What are you doing here?" She tried to speak quietly.

Sotto voce to Meredith, Jim said, "Holding up my end of the bargain by helping you get your wish." Out loud, so that the good doctor could hear, he applied his newly minted French accent. "I believe Mademoiselle eez fine now. I'll get your waiter." Jim bowed, pivoted and disappeared.

"Are you quite certain you're okay?" the dentist asked.

"I'm fine, really. It's nothing. Happens sometimes."

The Toothman opened his menu. "Would you mind terribly if I chose a wine for us? I'm rather particular about the label and the vintage."

"No, please. I'm sure you'll choose well." She gazed out the window, watching the lights of Washington, D.C.

"Do tell me you prefer white over red. Red wine has such a deleterious effect on the teeth. Stains, you know." He stuck his nose in the wine list.

Actually, she preferred a good, full-bodied red wine, but, what the heck, she could be a discriminating termite and enjoy a dry, white pine. She chuckled at the old joke. As long as he didn't choose something sweet.

The sommelier hovered a few feet away. Alan signaled with a lifted finger. "Sugar Loaf Vineyard, '92 Chardonnay Reserve, if you please, garçon."

"Very good, sir." The wine steward bowed and backed away.

"I think you'll like this. It's a humorous little wine, not too pretentious. Fruity, sweet."

Meredith coughed into her napkin. "I'm sure it's lovely, Alan. What do you recommend as an entrée?"

"Don't rush things. The night is young." He signaled their waiter. "Fried calamari for two."

The night was aging rapidly.

"But of course, M'sieur." The waiter smiled as Meredith looked up at him. Jim, again.

"Uh, waiter?"

"Yes, Mademoiselle?"

"I'd prefer the vegetable platter, no dip, please." She narrowed her eyes at the dentist.

"As Mademoiselle wishes."

"Don't you care for squid, Marguerite?"

"My name is Meredith. It's not the squid so much as the fried part. I don't do fried anything. Sorry." She raised her water glass and took a small sip, watching Alan over its rim. She set the glass back down. "You go right ahead with the squid. I don't mind, really."

"Fried calamari for one, then."

"Very good, sir." Jim cocked an eyebrow at Meredith as he left their table.

The sommelier brought the wine, opened it and handed Alan the cork. At Alan's nod, he poured a small amount into the wineglass. Alan swirled the liquid around and then held the glass up to the candlelight. "Legs, Melinda. This wine's got great legs. Just like you." He sipped, sloshed the wine around in his mouth, held it for a moment and swallowed.

"Meredith. My name's Meredith."

"Right. Sorry." He looked at the sommelier. "Excellent. You may pour." The sommelier did so, filling Meredith's glass first.

"To our evening." Alan raised his glass.

"Indeed." She touched his glass with hers and drank. Sweet. Entirely too sweet. Let's see, the good dentist had flunked the name test, the food test and the wine test. She wasn't seeing any true love here.

Their appetizers arrived. Alan waxed ecstatic over the calamari—fried just right, not too oily, tender, not rubbery. "It takes a delicate hand not to ruin good squid, you know."

"Really?" Meredith pushed celery sticks and strips of red and yellow pepper around her plate with a carrot, arranging them in tidy rows. Her mind wandered to the Grand Duchess, securing the contract and her own move to the corner office.

"I'm sorry. What were you saying?" She dragged her attention back to the dentist and his squid.

"Your teeth. The bottom incisors are crooked. Misaligned teeth can cause serious problems if they're not attended to. A little straightening, eighteen months to two years in your case, and, bingo, no more trouble with dental occlusion."

"I've never had any trouble with my bite, Alan."

"Ah, that's where most people go wrong. They think things don't change. Misaligned teeth throw off not only your bite, Meredith, but put undue pressures on your jaw."

The Toothman nattered on about basic principles

of orthodontia while Meredith smiled, nodded and pretended she was actually listening to what he said. "Could you excuse me for a moment? I need to visit the ladies' room." Without waiting for a response, she fled the table for the sanctuary of the women's lounge.

Once inside, she sank into an overstuffed chair and stared at the gold embossed wallpaper. She was quite certain she couldn't stomach another moment of this excruciatingly boring evening. She'd even settle for a conversation with Jim. She pulled out her cell phone.

"I enjoy our conversations, too. I find them quite enlightening, as a matter of fact." Jim materialized in the chair beside her.

"What if someone comes in? It is the ladies' room."

"It's okay. I put an 'out of order' sign on the doorknob. Now, tell the genie what's wrong. I sense that your evening isn't running smoothly."

"To put it mildly." Meredith unpinned the large offending orchid and looked at it. "What grown man brings a corsage on a date? It looks like something you'd give the mother of the bride at a wedding. And the color clashes with my Chanel suit." She pushed the wilting, green flower aside.

"I'm sorry things aren't working out. Maybe if you engage him in conversation about his work. Men like that sort of thing, you know." Jim reached across and put his hand on Meredith's knee. Heat blazed up her leg. Shocked, she pushed his hand aside.

"That's what I've been doing." Meredith sighed. "I suppose I could try again. He's not The One, but you never know. Even dentists might need Horton Consulting's management services." She stood and walked to the door.

"Don't forget Mother's orchid." Jim held out the

drooping bloom. "The doctor would be certain to miss it."

"Hrummmph." Meredith snatched the now-purple flower and jabbed the pin through her lapel. "I doubt he can see past my pearly whites."

Meredith approached the table. Dr. Rademacher had stopped the young woman refilling water glasses and was mumbling something about jaw kinetics and the dynamics of temporomandibular joint dysfunctions. Meredith rolled her eyes and sat.

"Ah, Marilyn. I'm glad you're back. I took the liberty of ordering for us both." He held up a hand. "Nothing fried."

"Thank you. And it's *Meredith*, not Marilyn."

"Of course. Meredith. Ha, ha, ha." He laughed a short, punchy sound, as though he were a plastic bottle squeezing out blobs of ketchup. Splop, splop, splop.

Meredith squared her shoulders and told herself she could get through this evening, really she could. And, he might turn out to be a fine conversationalist. "Tell me, Alan, why did you decide to be a dentist?"

"Not just a dentist, an orthodontist. It's a demanding specialty area, you know." He took a swallow of his Chardonnay. "Smiles, Meredith. Smiles."

Shades of *Fantasy Island*. "You decided to become an orthodontist because someone smiled at you?"

"Exactly. My third-grade teacher, Miss Plumly, had a terrible overbite. That woman could have eaten apples through a picket fence. I always thought it ruined her as a teacher. Kids called her Horse Face."

The Caesar salad was prepared table-side and served on chilled plates. Meredith had picked her way around the anchovies before the good doctor got through the third grade and started in on the rest of his education.

It seemed he had tagged likely future patients at every grade level. Students, teachers, acquaintances, they were all described according to their teeth. "Lisa in the fifth grade, now she could have benefited from a headgear. Mrs. Johnson, the seventh-grade teacher, good bite, but horribly stained teeth, too much coffee, you know." Meredith took a sip of wine, wishing it were a little stronger. The entrées arrived and she zoned out as the Toothman droned on.

"And then, just last year, I perfected a marriage of technologies, you might say, combining the power of the computer and virtual reality with the challenges of orthodontic dentistry."

"Really?" Meredith poked at the veal piccata congealing on her plate, boredom eclipsing even her acute ability to think about more than one thing at a time. Listening to the good doctor was affecting her brain. How did the Toothman manage to eat and talk at the same time and not dribble on his impeccable white shirt or get steamed asparagus stuck between his teeth?

"Absolutely. I've developed a method, using virtual-reality software, to calibrate optimal dental occlusions without the use of standard radiographic films. Fascinating, actually. You would benefit from it, Marlene. You really should have those lower incisors seen to." He motioned for the waiter. "We'd like to order dessert."

"Meredith. None for me, thanks. Decaf coffee."

"You shouldn't drink coffee. Stains the teeth." He leaned closer. "Actually, I could get you a reduction in fees, cover both the straightening and whitening."

"I beg your pardon?"

# Karen Lee

"Well, I don't normally mention such things, but your teeth could use brightening."

"My teeth are fine, thank you very much. And, furthermore, *Albert*, they are no longer a topic of conversation. In fact"—she tossed her napkin on the table and shoved her chair back—"I just realized I have a brief to prepare for the company president." She smiled at his shocked look. "Yes, *Altoid*, I'm an executive and I've never worked in the secretarial pool. In fact, we don't have a secretarial pool. That went out with spats." She gathered her bag. "I can truthfully say I've never had a date like this before. Thank God." She turned on her heel and stalked out.

"I'll call you tomorrow, Maureen." The Toothman's parting words drifted across the restaurant.

This wasn't a good beginning in her search for true love. In fact, it was horrid. If she had to be saddled with a genie, why did it have to be one who couldn't grant wishes?

# Chapter Four

## "Djinn Up"

Outside the restaurant, Meredith took a deep breath and hailed a cab. "What a jerk." She removed the offending orchid after she'd slid into the backseat of a White Top taxi. "Here, give this to your wife." She handed the flower to the cabby.

"Ah, but djinni don't have wives." Jim smiled back at her and pulled out into the late-night traffic.

She had ceased to be surprised by anything a being in male form did. Especially her genie. "I shouldn't wonder," she said, "given the fact that you can't seem to grant a simple wish. Men are so infuriating, I don't know why we put up with them. I swear I'd be better off with my cat. At least Stanley listens when I talk." She slumped into the seat and noticed Jim watching her in the rearview mirror. "What are you up to, now?"

"You're obviously unsatisfied with my service thus far. This doesn't bode well for my continued em-

# Karen Lee

ployment, you realize. Satisfied customers are what the Chairman wants, not whiny, disgruntled ones." At a red light, he swiveled around and pinned her with his lovely, magical eyes. "Try being gruntled for a change."

"Frankly, I've had enough grunting for one evening. Take me home, please." Looking too long into her genie's eyes was having a deleterious effect on her libido. Home alone was the answer.

Jim turned his attention back to the road. "Tell me about the other men in your life. Maybe I can give you some pointers."

Meredith sighed wearily. It wasn't like she really *needed* a man to close this deal. It would just ease the way with the duchess, and Meredith always liked to approach a prospective client with every advantage. In this case, a husband was that edge she needed. Plus, and Meredith realized with a start this meant far more to her, there was an outside chance Jim might actually succeed in granting her wish for true love, even though he'd started out a little rough.

"You were going to give me a list of suspects," Jim reminded her. "For your wish? Hello?"

"I'm sorry. I was just thinking about tonight." She paused, the edges of a plan coming into focus. "Part of what went wrong with Dr. Rademacher was my fault."

"Really? This is new, not blaming the genie."

"I've just got to get this promotion. To do that, I've got to get the contract." She took a deep breath. "To do *that*, I've got to find a husband, an impossible task given my track record, so I'll need a stand-in."

"A place-holder until we find your True Love?"

"Right. And, since I can't seem to concentrate on both of those at once—the substitute and the real thing—I was wondering if you could help."

In the rearview mirror, she saw a bit of doubt slip across his forehead. "That's what I'm for—helping."

"Good, then you can come with me to see the duchess, posing as my new husband, and I can concentrate on other things. Like love."

"What!"

"It's perfectly logical. If I don't have to worry about meeting the duchess sans spouse, I'll be more open to amour." She sighed. It was all so simple. Break a problem into its sub-parts and the solution fairly jumped out.

"Can't."

"Why not?" She hated it when people didn't immediately see the brilliance in her ideas.

Jim coughed, choked, and she recognized the ugly sound of panic bubbling up in his throat. "Djinni rules forbid it." He didn't sound convincing.

"No wonder you guys are having image problems. Too many rules."

"I see the logic in your suggestion. I'm not stupid. But, it won't work."

"Fine. Just take me home, then." She'd find a better time to propose the most obvious solution to her problem.

Silently, Jim faced the windshield and drove. Past tree-lined streets of old, established homes. Along winding Virginia roads arched with foliage so thick Meredith swore she was going through a green tunnel. Slowly, she began to relax and settle back in the seat. Barely three days into this new project and she was already counting the injuries.

"I was just thinking about a suitable man I know. You might enjoy meeting him." Jim smiled in the mirror, all panic erased for now.

She was instantly wary. "I didn't think genies had friends. How do you know him?"

"Hey, I don't live in the cell phone permanently, you know. I get around. I've had other assignments. Successful ones, I might add. Ones where people actually wished for something I could deliver."

"What good is a genie if you can't wish for what you want?" He was attractive, her genie, but she was beginning to believe he wasn't a top performer in geniedom, or wherever it was genies lived when they weren't granting wishes.

She could feel him bristle. "What if I call my friend and have him meet us at your house? It's not that late. And it would show you that I'm working on this wish."

"Not tonight. I'm beat and I really need to outline alternative strategies for the duchess."

"Did I mention that my assignment—you—has an expiration date? And it's approaching fast." Jim pulled onto the parkway.

She reconsidered. Her evening was already ruined and she was certain nothing and no one could top the dentist in the annals of dates from hell. "What would we talk about? I have enough trouble making sane conversation with one genie. How would I ever handle another?" She shuddered.

"No need to get nasty. Besides, he's not a genie. Trust me. You'll like him."

Right. "As long as he's not Freddie Krueger or a closet comedian, I suppose it'll be fine. But I really can't do it tonight, Jim. Set something up for Friday. Unless I can talk Darcie into helping out again"— and *that* would never happen—"you're my only hope, Obi-wan."

"If you're trying to guess my djinni name, you aren't even close." He smirked. "Besides, you're obviously not happy with my performance."

"It isn't an auspicious beginning, no." She touched

her purse, strangely comforted by the feel of the cell phone. "I'll be able to call you if things with your friend get out of hand, right?"

"Absolutely. Seven days a week, twenty-four hours a day, I'm at your disposal, provided you haven't lost your trusty phone."

"I'll let you know whether or not your taste in men corresponds with mine."

"Very good. He'll be waiting for you Friday evening when you get home from work." Jim whistled as the cab sped toward Meredith's house.

They rounded the corner into her neighborhood and passed the guard at the front gate. She lived in one of the many new developments that dotted the northern Virginia landscape. Jim stopped in front of her house, one of the smaller dwellings in this exclusive neighborhood. While it wasn't quite the starter castle her sister accused it of being, Meredith's brick, three-bedroom house was more than she needed. She'd been enchanted by the hardwood floors and the windows that gave her sanctuary a light, airy feel. But she'd really bought it as an investment.

The fact that her teddy bear collection lay artfully arranged in what would make a wonderful child's bedroom was irrelevant. And never mind that the smallest bedroom housed an art studio, just waiting for the day she had some spare time. She could dream, couldn't she?

"Awfully big house for one person." Jim opened the cab door and offered his hand to help Meredith out.

"If my ever-ready genie would get on the stick and grant my wish, maybe I'd have someone to share it with."

"And I was just beginning to like you." He took her hand.

71

Once more, streaks of heat sizzled up her arm. She pulled away. "Would you kindly stop doing that?"

"What?"

"You know what I mean." He followed her up the steps. "Where do you think you're going?" she demanded. After an evening that had sunk faster than the *Titanic*, she was in no mood to entertain her all-too-appealing genie with small talk. Maybe he was right. Having him pose as her husband wouldn't work.

He crossed his arms. "The cell phone? It's in your purse, right?"

"Right."

"Well, I live there, if you'll remember. Whither thou goest and all that."

She blew stray wisps of hair off her forehead. "Fine." She unlocked the door and disabled the alarm system. Jim brushed past her and Meredith's spine tingled, all too aware of his closeness. She shivered. Good thing she was tired. Her libido had taken such a beating tonight that even a magical being was starting to look good. She reset the alarm and then turned to the hall table to riffle through day-old mail, absentmindedly clucking for Stanley who usually came to greet her.

The djinn sat on the bottom step of the broad, curved stairway that led to Meredith's bedroom. If he was any judge of women, and he'd known a few thousand, Meredith was a woman who desperately needed loving. While he was just the djinn for the job, rules were rules. He couldn't get involved. That was why her scheme to take him with her to Hertzenstein wouldn't work, not now, not ever. He was fine being her assistant in an office filled with people. He was fine locating gentlemen callers for her. He wouldn't be fine trying to convince the duchess he was her husband, not because he couldn't beguile an old woman, but because he couldn't trust himself. Being a man around Meredith was a dangerous proposition.

When he finished his assignment, and he hoped he would finish it, it was back to the old routine. Occupy the odd lamp or bottle—maybe a laptop computer if his current living situation was any indication of future prospects—until someone bumped into it and released his spirit. Then, three wishes, poof, back in the vessel. He frowned. When you looked at it like that, his djinni life wasn't all that exciting.

"You want to discuss the evening? Debrief, so to speak?"

"No." Meredith picked up her cat, Stanley. "We're going to bed." She tossed Jim the cell phone. "Go to sleep. We'll talk in the morning."

"Meredith?"

"Jim?"

"I really need to talk. Now would be best."

"I don't have the energy tonight."

"That's part of what I need to talk about. *Tempus fugit*."

"*Fugit* along with it won't you. Please?" She turned off the master light switch for the main floor of the house and left Jim holding the phone.

"But . . ."

"Tomorrow, Scarlet. Worry about it in the morning."

"Who is this Scarlet?"

"Stop it, right now!"

He held his retort, watching her mount the stairs, her long, slender legs going higher and higher. "I could come tuck you in," he suggested hopefully.

73

"Not part of the job description." She yawned. "Find me that elusive true love thing."

He heard the door to her room close and lock, as if that futile effort would keep him away. He paced the hall. No need to panic yet. He was only three days on the job, after all. He had oodles of time. Oceans. He was drowning in time.

What a shame that it would be the last time he'd have if he couldn't figure a way around Djinni Rule Number Two. The probability that he could actually find true love for Meredith approached zero. And so did his continued employment at Djinn Central.

The Chairman had made it painfully clear that this was Jim's last and final chance. Ol' Blue Eyes wasn't the type to forgive. And he never forgot.

"Boss, I'm really sorry about Dr. Rademacher. He seems so nice in his office." On the phone the next day, Darcie sounded truly contrite.

"That's because he can do all the talking and you only get to grunt. Insufferable boor. Couldn't even get my name right half the time." It was the middle of the afternoon, Meredith had two dozen things to do and she still hadn't gotten over her anger from That Date.

"Come to think of it, he has that problem with his patients, too. He calls me Denise half the time."

Meredith could hear Darcie chewing on a pencil. "You've got something else on your mind."

"Well, with Alan out of the picture, what are you planning for the Grand Duchess? Today's Thursday, I remind you. The end of the month waits for no woman."

"I know." Meredith sighed and an image popped into her head of Jim in a tuxedo, playing waiter, trailing a heady, sexy fragrance. "Perhaps it's time to approach Jim again."

"Jim? Your new assistant? What a great idea!"

She coughed. "You know about Jim?"

"He's wonderful, Boss Lady. He introduced himself yesterday. He wanted a little insider info on what kind of boss you were." She lowered her voice. "Wherever did you find him? The temp agency never has people like that when I call to fill a position."

What could she say? She'd rubbed her cell phone and now had a genie in waiting? Even Darcie would have trouble with that one. "I guess I was lucky." Let her think he came from the agency. "I may keep him." She chuckled.

"I know I've botched a few blind dates for you, but do you really think you need him?"

Meredith detected the hurt tone in her friend's voice. "Oh, Darce, you're the perfect friend and the perfect assistant. It's just that desperation increases my stupidity. You've got an opportunity with Griffin and I can't keep coming to you to patch up my dreadful personal life. Besides, a fresh set of eyes"—and what lovely eyes they were—"might see something you've missed."

Darcie laughed. "When you put it that way . . ." She trailed off. "Why *not* ask Jim? He's so charming and warm. I'm sure he'd be glad to help out."

"Jim has, um, extraordinary credentials, that's true. He's spontaneous and creative. But he's opposed to it." She shook her head, remembering the warmth of his touch.

"You can talk him into it. Oops! Can I call you back, Boss? Mr. Griffin just walked in."

Meredith pictured Darcie covering the mouthpiece of the phone. Through the muffling, she heard Griffin ask about reservations to Wyoming. That snake! He was ready to go only four days into this contest and what was she doing? Mooning over a man who wasn't even a man. She'd better get hopping or she'd lose out.

"Darce? I've got to go anyway. We can talk later."

"Thank you for calling. I look forward to hearing about future developments." Darcie adopted a business tone, clearly not anxious for Griffin to know she was speaking to Meredith.

Meredith hung up and scowled. Then she grabbed her electronic address book and looked up the Grand Duchess's number. Without thinking further she stabbed in the digits, and paced her office while the overseas connections clicked through. There was no way she was going to let that sleaze Francis Griffin beat her to the corner office. None.

Suddenly, she realized it was late in Hertzenstein, too late to call. Why did she have to deal with six time zones when Griffin only had two? She slammed the phone down, breaking the connection. Just what she needed to start off a relationship. She was sure the Grand Duchess would be delighted to leave some state dinner to talk to her. Although, realistically, she'd probably wind up talking with a very grumpy secretary.

There was medium-to-heavy panic brewing in her stomach. She had two first-class tickets to Hertzenstein, had reserved a suite at the *Auberge des Cygnes*, the best the Duchy had to offer. And—she pushed the calendar button on her electronic address book— she had just ten days until that flight left Dulles Airport, bound for a minuscule nothing of a country nestled between the Petrusse River and the Ardennes. The whole place wasn't as large as Rhode Island and it held the key to her future.

She let out her breath. It *was* time to reintroduce

the subject of corporate travel with her genie. After all, if she took her cell phone with her, he'd have no choice.

She picked up said phone and dialed YO GENIE. Jim shimmered into being, dressed in tennis whites, carrying a racket and two green tennis balls.

"You rang?"

"Are you sure you're working on my wish?"

"Absolutely."

Skeptical, she said, "Sit down, Jim. I've got a proposition for you."

He slipped into the wing-back chair opposite the desk. "This sounds promising. It's been a hundred years, at least, since I've been propositioned."

"It's not that kind of proposition, exactly. Besides, you've been after me for days to talk. I thought it was important that we take some time." Meredith felt uncharacteristically flushed at the sight of Jim's well-formed, tan legs crossed almost within her touch. "I didn't realize genies played tennis."

"We invented it. Silly game, actually. We fiddled around with the scoring just to make it more interesting. One-love, match point. All that keeps a fellow's interest up. Much better than one, two, three."

Meredith rested her chin on her hand. "Really. What else occupies a genie's time?" If she eased into the subject of husbands, instead of her usual bulldozer approach, maybe she'd meet with less resistance.

"Lately? A lot of worrying."

"I shouldn't think a genie would have anything at all to worry him. Other than housekeeping in a cell phone."

"Ah, but that's where you're wrong. I, of all my genie brethren, have much to be concerned about." He paused, raised an elegant eyebrow and set down

# Karen Lee

the tennis racket and balls. "You could offer advice. As part of our deal."

"Maybe. What's wrong?"

"Well, it started a century ago, maybe more. People, real people like you, gradually quit believing in magical beings. You know, sprites, leprechauns, fairies and, of course, djinni."

"And gnomes and dwarfs and goblins."

He snorted, disgusted. "Troglodytes. All of them. A completely different order. Gnomes and their ilk are of the earth. Djinni are fire and air. Significant differences."

Meredith nodded. "But you're all in some kind of trouble, right? What happened?"

"People got all involved in technology. First steam engines, then lightbulbs, then airplanes. Next thing you know, boom, we've been replaced by gadgets." He snickered. "Like that phone of yours. Darned cramped in there. Electrons whizzing around. Can't get a decent night's sleep."

"Do you have to stay in the cell phone?"

He gave her a dumb smile and rolled his eyes. "Unfortunately. Part of my, shall we say, reeducation."

This was getting interesting. "Please, go on."

"Where was I? Oh, yes. Technology. Then, some goofball invented motion pictures and, quicker than you can say pita bread, everybody thinks a djinn is something created by Industrial Light and Magic." He leaned back in the chair, looking at the ceiling. "What were we to do, I ask you?"

"We?"

"We. All the mythical folk who populate the world of the djinn." He gave her a doubtful look. "You probably wouldn't understand what it's like to be brushed off as a mere special effect." Jim flexed his exceptional biceps. Meredith's heart certainly didn't

78

consider his actions a special effect. It pounded away as if Jim were real. "Never noticed for what you really are, what you can really offer. No one understands."

Ah, but she could understand. "I've been there."

He squinted at her, disbelief easy to read on his face.

"Really. I'm a woman in a man's world. I know how it feels to be a second-class citizen who only gets attention when she's done something wrong. Trust me. I know."

"Then you can understand how I felt when the All-Powerful Chairman of the Board called me into his exalted presence to announce that I'd been selected."

"For what?" She knew about Chairmen of Boards.

Jim sighed, long and sad. "About ten years ago, the All-Powerful Chairman met with the leaders of the other sects of magical beings. When he returned, he set up a Reorganization Board and began to implement his strategic plan to downsize the djinn who had worked for him—faithfully, I might add—for centuries."

Downsized? Fairies and genies reorganizing? Meredith managed to stifle a chuckle. "And then what?"

Jim looked grim. "They were all my friends, the djinni and the afreets. And especially the houris. All of them gone. Outplaced. Rightsized. Reengineered out of jobs." He stood. "It wasn't one of the Chairman's better ideas. Picture this." He swept an arc through the air with a graceful hand. "Dozens of djinni with retirement packages, bored in Paradise, getting fat and flabby. Causing trouble." He cocked an eyebrow. "That much mischief concentrated in one place, I mean, what would you expect?" He leaned against the window, gazing at the Potomac.

"You have to channel mischief or you get, well, trouble with a very large T."

He drew in a deep breath. "So, the Chairman simply stopped offering outplacement packages and eliminated excess djinni. Now it's my turn."

He'd spoken so quietly that Meredith barely heard him. "Your turn? You mean the Chairman . . . ?"

"The All-Powerful Chairman of the Board."

"Right. Him. He's going to fire you?"

Jim nodded morosely. "The old pink slipperoo. Out the door without so much as a 'Thank you very much' and no chance for the traditional silver retirement salver. And to think, I placed second in a class of two hundred in magic carpet navigation." He sighed again.

"You have a magic carpet?" She waved away his retort. "Never mind. This is more than just breaking djinni rules, isn't it? That first night you mentioned that I was your project. What did you mean?"

"Pretty simple, actually. I have one chance to prove myself to the All-Powerful Chairman. To show the Reorganization Board that I can bring added value to the Order of the Djinn." He wandered away from the window and slipped into the chair once more.

"And if you don't succeed?"

"I'm history, so to speak."

"Why is it that you're in so much trouble? Why has the Reorganization Board targeted you?"

He closed his eyes, as if the light suddenly hurt. "I only wish I knew."

"You must have some idea. Have you insulted someone important? Spilled coffee on someone's lap? Screwed up someone else's wish?"

Ah, that hit home. He winced and opened his eyes. "I followed all the rules, exactly. For a change."

Meredith's Wish

There was more to this.

"It wasn't my fault. I'd been out partying, dancing. The war was over and people hadn't stopped celebrating. I must have picked up a bug of some sort because my normally perfect hearing wasn't perfect." He looked at her, sadness etched on his face. "I thought he said he didn't want to resist her, talking of his assistant. What he really said was, 'I want to invent the transistor.' So, I granted his wish and, bingo, the techno revolution started." He leaned forward and held his head in his hands. "Last year, when the Chairman realized that I'd started this whole technology thing by not clarifying one simple wish? My days were numbered, sand running out of the hourglass and onto the beach. If I don't improve my performance, add value, I'm done."

"So the Chairman thinks you started people not believing?" He nodded slowly. "What, exactly, do you have to do to add value?"

"I must succeed in making your wishes come true."

"Your track record thus far isn't promising."

"I do just fine on reasonable wishes. Even yours wouldn't be so difficult except it violates an ancient taboo of the Order of the Djinn." He looked at her, his dark eyes sad. "I can't make anyone fall in love. It just isn't done."

"What if I wished for something simpler? Like becoming CEO of this company? Could you do that?"

"Easy as falling off a minaret." He stood and paced a nervous trail across her red carpet. "But that isn't what you wished for."

Meredith hesitated. Her career was very important, certainly. But lately she'd noticed signs that her life was out of balance. Her college and graduate school friends were all married and had families.

Most of her old flames were comfortably settled with someone else. Only she was alone, with just a cat to welcome her at night. It wasn't at all what she had planned.

Even the company president recognized what she had only recently acknowledged. "You're an attractive woman, Meredith. And smart. Why, any number of men would be happy to capture your heart." Bill Horton told her that a dozen times a week. Minimum.

She supposed he was right. Throughout college she'd had suites of fraternity men drooling after her. They'd swooned at her auburn hair, gazed gaga into her sea-green eyes. Stood in line to put their arms around her slim figure. They'd proposed in four-part harmony. And she'd rejected them all because she had goals that didn't include an MRS. degree. Was it her fault she was good at what she did? That she'd stumbled into this career because she loved her family?

She watched Jim watching her. "Honestly?"

"That's best when dealing with a djinn."

"I've always known I had the talent, the energy, to run a company of my own. But lately, I've been wondering if it would be enough to make me completely happy. I really need a partner in life." She felt tears threaten. She hated getting emotional. She gave a small smile and tried to lighten the moment. "If you ever tell my mother I admitted that, you won't have to worry about the Chairman, I'll have your head." Her smile disappeared. "I can't believe I'm going to say this, but my heart's desire is to be happily paired with someone who loves me."

There was that love thing again. It was much easier to maintain her hard-edged-businesswoman role if she didn't actually admit she was a hopeless romantic. What would happen now that the proverbial cat was out of the starting gate and racing after sunbeams? "I guess I wasn't kidding when I wished for true love."

"See, that's our problem. About all I can do is maneuver men into your path and see that the circumstances are as ideal as possible. Hopefully, we'll have better results than last night." He grimaced. "Unfortunately, you and he will have to do the falling without my help."

"I see."

"It gets worse. I have until the end of the month to accomplish this Herculean task."

"What?"

"I've been trying to tell you that all week, but you've been too busy to listen."

She glanced at her watch. "I've been busy? What have you been doing for five days?" She saw a mixture of sadness and fear flit across his face. "What will really happen if you don't grant my wishes?"

Jim reached out, picked up one of Meredith's crystal tumblers and turned it to catch the light. "If I don't succeed, the Committee will mark me to be downsized."

"Downsized isn't all that bad. It happens in business all the time. Think of what else you could be doing. Making commercials, working in some theme park." Meredith hoped her tone sounded cheerful.

"It doesn't work like that since the Chairman changed the rules." He held the glass up and watched it fill with ruby liquid, then handed it to Meredith. "Pour the wine onto your desk." He smiled at her horrified expression. "Really, it will be fine. Pour."

"If you say so." She turned the tumbler and, as the liquid spilled out, it disappeared in a fine carmine mist.

"That's what happens to a downsized djinn."

She set the glass down and shivered. "Oh."

After a moment Meredith stood, silent. Thinking. She looked up at Jim, standing in front of her, shoulders slumped in a posture of defeat she hadn't seen before. "If I could concentrate, really concentrate on love, would that help?"

"It couldn't hurt," he sniffed.

She walked slowly toward him and placed her hand on his cheek. It was surprisingly warm. She decided the tingly feeling in her palm was just energy emissions. "If you would reconsider your decision not to go with me to see the duchess, I'd feel so much better. I'd be able to give true love my undivided attention." She blinked, just a little.

Jim took her hand between his, dwarfing it. His dark eyes deepened as he kissed her fingertips. "Yes, I will accompany you." He turned her hand palm up and kissed the center of it. He shivered out of focus for an instant, the edges of his perfect form momentarily transparent. Then, he let go. Had she imagined it? He cleared his throat. "It will have to be as a last-ditch effort, though. If we find Mr. I-Love-You-Truly in time, I'm off the hook."

Meredith stood for a moment, dazed at her physical reaction to this man. "Oh. Absolutely." She sat on the edge of her desk. "It'll work out for the best. After all, when I bring back the signed contract, I won't need my substitute husband anymore, assuming you take on that task. And then there'd be just that one last little item. And, the staff has already met you and knows you're on the job. It'll be perfect." She nodded absently and moved to her chair.

"This is only a meeting with the duchess, right? What aren't you telling me?"

"It's a simple extension of the Hertzenstein assignment. Besides, if I bring you along, Griffin will be pea-green with envy." She chuckled. "And wouldn't that be a wonderful sight?" She smiled. "You'll go, won't you?"

"Your wish is my command, my lady. I'd follow you through Hell and back again. But, I'd like a little information about which Hell we're going to and who the devil is going to be there. What is it you business types say? Poor planning produces putrid performance?"

"Something like that. You, James Goodman, Ph.D., will accompany moi, the next vice president, to the annual Company Gala where Horton will announce my well-deserved promotion." She leaned back, a satisfied smirk on her face. "After we secure the deal with our friendly, neighborhood duchess, that is."

"Goodman. Ph.D. Does that mean Potent Happy Djinn? Never mind. Sounds nice. Useful. Full of added value. What will the All-Powerful Chairman of the Board think?"

"How can he do anything but approve? Having the worry of how to approach the duchess removed is merely part of your wish-granting assignment, isn't it?"

Jim shrugged. "I guess you could describe it that way."

"Besides, if I happen to stumble across true love along the way, you're home free." Meredith opened her desk drawer and dug around. "I know I've got it here somewhere." She pushed papers around and pounced on a dog-eared business card. "Here it is. Murray can fix you up with a tux as soon as we get back." She reached for her cell phone, and had begun to dial when Jim walked into her line of sight. "Oh, my." She put down the phone. "I keep forgetting you can do this without help."

# *Chapter Five*

## *"Djinn Down"*

Jim leaned elegantly against the desk, his arms crossed over a crisp white tuxedo shirt, black tie perfect, lapels satin smooth. "Is this what you had in mind?" He executed a runway-model strut across her office, glancing seductively over his shoulder.

Actually, he was better than what she had in mind. *Calm down, heart.* "Perfect."

"And what are you wearing?"

"Oh, I've got a few old things."

She suddenly felt herself propelled gently out of her chair, turned around in the air and bathed in bright light. "What in the world?"

"Something old won't do at all. If you're going to attract someone suitable for falling in love with, you're going to have to dress to attract, Meredith. And, since you have no taste in clothes, I thought I could lend a hand. I certainly ought to know what will turn a man's head and make his heart leap into his throat. I've had a couple of centuries to study the species." He waved his hand.

She settled back to earth, only slightly shaken, and took a few experimental steps on finely crafted black pumps with three-inch heels. Slowly, she turned around, admiring the way the black crepe of the dress flowed exactly and perfectly over her slender figure. "This is wonderful. Better than wonderful. How do I look?" She walked toward the mirror and watched, no longer amazed, as the reflective surface grew into a floor-length, three-way version better than the ones at Saks.

She watched her reflection and caught her breath. "Oh, Jim. This is perfect." The dress was simple, yet superbly elegant. A high collar, accented by a smattering of diamonds, gathered the soft crepe at her throat, leaving her shoulders completely bare. The fabric skimmed her hips and stopped just short of the tops of her shoes. She stepped forward. The side slit in the skirt moved to reveal a long, shapely leg.

"Take a look at the back." Jim put his hands on her shoulders and moved her so she could see.

"Oh." The high collar that held fabric in the front held none in the back of the dress. Instead, the crepe draped gracefully low. "This ought to turn a few heads."

"Indeed."

She smiled up at her genie, stood on tiptoe and kissed his cheek. "Thank you." She stood beside him and looked at their reflection in the glass. "We make a pretty nice couple. I'm sure the duchess will approve."

*Yes, we do make a fine couple. Very fine.* "I don't know about the duchess, but I expect we'll blend in well at this Gala."

# Karen Lee

"Oh, I think we'll do more than blend. Look at how well we're matched."

He had already noticed. His dark, good looks. Her mahogany-red hair and porcelain skin. How many men would be able to watch the two of them and not feel a rise of envy, of wanting? He cocked an eyebrow. *If I were a man, instead of a djinn, I'd snatch you up in a heartbeat.* "You're a beautiful woman, Meredith. All those men who've left you for someone else must have been blind as well as stupid."

She dimpled, and he felt a corresponding heat jet through his human body. The sensation spelled trouble. He was too old to react like this. Usually, he felt scorn for poor, limited humans. And, sometimes, he even took advantage of their lack of imagination. For some reason, Meredith, out of all of them . . . no, he couldn't contemplate or even shape the thought. The Chairman would not understand.

"Well. I think this takes care of *my* promotion, Jim. Now, what are we going to do about your quandary?"

"Huh?" He'd been so absorbed watching her in his creation, he'd not been listening.

"You know, add value or, pfffft, downsized."

"Oh, that quandary. I thought you were speaking of Dean. He's the last real quandary I knew. Dean was quite a guy. He had such a way with the ladies."

"Are you trying to tell me there's a magical being called a quandary?" He nodded, and she punched him in the arm. "Stop kidding around, Jim. If you're going to solve a problem, you need to get serious."

"Maybe. Maybe what I need is to be more ludicrous. Serious has always gotten me into trouble."

"Serious works for me, and you've asked for my advice." She led him to a chair and gently pushed him into it. "So listen."

Her phone rang. Saved by the proverbial bell.

"Hello?" Meredith rolled her eyes and grimaced at him. "Yes, Mother, it's good to hear your voice, too." She walked to her desk and slumped into her chair. "Really? I'm so glad. Janice always wanted more children." She played with her diamond earrings and mouthed the words "my sister." "Me? I've asked you a zillion times to forget about my love life. It'll happen when it's supposed to happen." She paused. "Of course I'm seeing someone." She glanced at Jim. "You've not met him yet. Don't start planning receptions. We just began dating, Mother, so, no, it's not serious."

Jim whispered, "You just told me to be serious."

She covered the mouthpiece and whispered back, "Not about this, silly."

"No, Mother, it's just that you've interrupted a rather important business meeting." She whirled around in her chair. "What? Dinner next Friday? Not possible. I mean, I don't think . . . I . . . I suppose I could ask him." She looked at Jim, her face a mask of panic.

"Just tell her yes."

She sighed. Her mother meddled too much. "Yes, Mother. We'll be there. Seven? Fine. Love you, too." She hung up and swung around to face her genie. "You don't know what you're getting into, Jim. I'll call her on Thursday and beg off. I'm sure I can figure out some reason why you won't be coming to dinner at the Montgomery household."

"Hey, I'm there if you need me. I've had experience with mothers. Trust me, you pick up a lot of skills negotiating family meetings for emirs with harems." He whistled. "You wouldn't believe the arguments."

She had cocked her head, looking at him curiously. "And just what kind of arguments might you have been negotiating?" She didn't really have arguments with her mother, since her mother wouldn't argue. She just stood her ground, insisting that Meredith would only be completely happy if she were married.

"Standard things. Which wife would share the emir's favors, whose costume was more elegant. How to educate the children. That sort of thing."

"Why would the emir allow you to handle these disputes?"

"Because the emir's second wife, Esmee, discovered the secret of my lamp and released me." He polished his immaculate, manicured nails on his shirt.

"No cell phones, I take it?"

"Great Djinn, no. This was, let me see, early in the eighteenth century. Technology hadn't infested the world and people still believed."

He watched Meredith, deliberately putting a sparkle in his dark, almond-shaped eyes. "You have nothing to worry about in regards to your family. Mothers love me." He paused. "You were about to offer advice."

"Right. It is obvious that the primary goal of your Reorganization Board is to increase awareness and appreciation of the ephemeral world in general and of genies in particular. I believe your Chairman fellow . . ."

"The All-Powerful Chairman of the Board," Jim corrected her, proper reverence to his tone.

"That's the one. He's taking absolutely the wrong approach to solve his problem. Why, without djinni, what does he have? Nothing. Nada. Nyet. Zip. Zero."

"I get the picture. I'll be nothing, nada, nyet, zip."

"No. I mean, you can hardly have magical beings without the beings. What the All-Powerful Chairman needs is a different approach to this market." She stood and began to pace around her office, ticking off items on her fingers. "First, he doesn't grasp the basic principles of a solid marketing strategy. Clearly he's missed an opportunity to deliver his message to the people of the world, techno-bound though they may be." She stopped pacing.

"What are you saying? That I should"— he paused, and quirked a doubtful eyebrow at Meredith—"question the motivations of the All-Powerful Chairman of the Board? It isn't the done thing, Meredith."

"Nonsense. Give me a month, no, two, and I could have a top-notch plan in place that would accomplish everything he wants." She strode purposefully to her computer and turned the machine on.

He reached out and stopped her. "We don't have two months." He liked the way her hand felt. Warm. Solid. Real. "Besides, I don't think there's an exact parallel between your company and Djinn Central. The All-Powerful Chairman of the Board doesn't run a free-market democracy."

He let her take her hand back. She stroked her chin and smiled. "Then, we'll just have to give you alternate ways to add value, won't we?"

"I guess. In the meantime, we're clear that the coffee, the breakfast, the new dress—none of those were official. You've got two more wishes. Perhaps we could start on those. Sort of get my wish-granting warmed up." He strolled around her office. His future might be secure. Maybe she could come up with a plan that would wow the Chairman. After all, this was a modern woman. A technologically sophisticated creature unlike other women he'd known. He watched her very feminine curves. Well, maybe not entirely unlike.

"I've thought about that, Jim. But, I don't want to waste my wishes, so I think I'll take my time and do it right." She busied herself at the computer, opening files and calling up spreadsheets. "You might want to take a nap, or finish your tennis game. I want to capture these marketing ideas before I lose them. Then, of course, there's the duchess."

Jim nodded and faded, but didn't really go away. He wanted to watch her, his project, and see if he could determine why she affected him so. In his experience, women were not to be trusted. Every time in his colorful past that he'd gotten involved, in any way, with a subject of the female persuasion, his career had suffered. No, women weren't good things to mess with.

But if he were to take that plunge once more, Meredith would certainly be his first choice.

He was hovering, invisible, above her computer when her arch-rival entered the office.

"Interesting choice in office attire. You got a designer stashed away in a file cabinet?" The man's eyes were definitely hungry, looking at her in the formal dress. Jim bristled, correctly identifying the protective rush of jealousy flooding his brain.

"Glad I've caught you," the man said. "Got a minute?"

Meredith looked up and her smile faded faster than Jim had. She put her hand over the cell phone. "Francis Griffin. What a surprise." She wisely ignored Griffin's comment on her dress.

"Don't start in on me, Meredith. What's so special about that phone? You're always protecting it."

"I've got all my favorite pizza delivery numbers stored in it. Couldn't let those get into enemy hands." She slid the phone into a desk drawer.

"Is that how you think of me? As the enemy?"

"You're taking prisoners—specifically Darcie. Actually, I hope she works out for you. She needs exposure to the underside of this corporation. Give her some balance." Meredith smiled sweetly, but Jim heard the ice in her voice. "What do you want?"

"Two things, really. First, here are the results from the marketing survey on customer service. Thought you might be able to use the stats to shore up your presentation to the Grand Duchess."

"My presentation doesn't need shoring up, as you put it, now that I've decided on a strategy. But, thanks all the same. I'll look it over." She took the spiral-bound pages from the man and tossed them into her in-box, on top of a pile of unread industry reports and newspaper clippings. "You said two things."

Jim noted that Griffin's complexion had paled when Meredith mentioned her strategy. Perhaps there was skullduggery afoot. At a minimum it was wearing tasseled loafers.

"I can't seem to find those charts showing increased tourist revenues from the Alaska project. I wondered if you had a copy handy?"

"Really, Francis, you must think I'm a complete fool. You're the one who flung the gauntlet at me. Why should I cooperate with you?"

"Because you're going to wind up working for me and you can never establish a close relationship with your superiors too early." He'd placed a little too much emphasis on "superiors," and began mopping his forehead with his handkerchief.

"You must be kidding," she said. "You're just as likely to work for me. More, in fact." Jim watched her spine stiffen, and knew she could hold her own with this clown.

Griffin tried to smile. "Look, I'm sorry about all this. The whole competition thing was Horton's idea. You think I like the prospect of wandering around Wyoming? The wind never stops blowing. And, there's all that space." He stuck out his hand. "Truce?"

She hesitated. *Just say "no."* Jim wanted to shout. "Okay. The charts are in the top drawer of Darcie's old desk." She shook hands quickly.

"By the way, what is your strategy, precisely?"

"Truce doesn't imply giving up professional secrets."

"So, you don't really have one, then."

"Don't make rash assumptions, Francis. When have you ever seen me without a plan and a damned good one at that?"

"Whatever you say. Just wanted to let you know I'm available to lend a hand if you need me." Griffin smiled an evil smirk if Jim had ever seen one, and he'd seen thousands. Hundreds of thousands. If Meredith weren't warned . . . He waited until Francis skulked into the hall, and then Jim shivered back into existence.

"You've got to watch out for him, Meredith. He doesn't have your best interests at heart."

"Tell me something I don't know." Meredith glanced up at him. "Be careful." Her eyebrow raised in panic. He had perched on top of her cherry-wood bookcase.

"Don't worry about me, I have perfect balance." He put his hands on the heads of Meredith's lion bookends and executed a djinni handstand off the top of her bookcase. "See?" He felt the left lion quiver and begin to slide. "Yeeeee! Aaaahhhhh!" He landed with a thud on the carpet. "Dumb cat, did that on purpose." He was sure the granite lion was grinning at him.

"Great balance. I see you've abandoned the tux for the casual, English country look."

"Is that what this is?" He smoothed the front pleats

in his brown wool slacks as he stood, adjusted the tan, V-neck wool sweater, the elegant silk cravat, and put one strong hand into the pocket of the tweed jacket. He waved his other hand and a pipe appeared, curling fragrant smoke.

"Funny, Jim. Smoking's not allowed in the building."

The pipe disappeared. "That's not the point. The point is that the man who . . ."

"By the way, Meredith. Horton's called a senior staff meeting for tomorrow morning. Seven-thirty. Sharp."

Francis Griffin poked his head into the office, then stepped all the way in. Again. "Who's he?"

"Another Saturday meeting? I'll be there. As to Jim, I was going to send you a memo, but since you've interrupted my work a second time, I'll simply introduce you. Francis, you remember Jim from when you interrupted my team meeting? Since you've snatched Darcie, I've asked Jim to be my assistant."

"Really? I suppose it's only fair, and you'll need all the help you can find." Griffin strode toward Jim. "Jim?" He stuck out his hand.

Jim gripped it in a bone-crushing handshake. "Pleased to meet you, formally. It's an interesting competition, isn't it?"

Francis extracted his hand, grimacing. "Very interesting. Where did you say you came from?"

Meredith intervened, a flicker of concern on her face. "Did you find your charts?"

Griffin ignored her. "Weren't you here a minute ago? When all the lights flickered?"

Jim shook his head. He knew Griffin suspected something was afoot, and Jim wasn't interested in giving Francis any information.

"Well, welcome aboard." As Francis turned to leave, he stage-whispered to Meredith, "It'll take more than a pretty boy to help this project, Meredith." He held his hand gingerly as he left.

Jim waved his pipe into existence again, sans smoke. "How'd I do?"

"Splendid. Simply splendid." Shoving papers into her briefcase, she nodded at the clock. "Time to head home." She looked down at the elegant, black gown Jim had whipped up. "Could you change me back into my suit?"

"Is that an official wish?"

"No. It just seems polite to give me back my original clothes when you're the one who's been messing around with my wardrobe. I'm hardly dressed for driving in D.C. traffic."

"Okay, okay. Point taken." He waved his hand and she was once again dressed in her slim navy skirt with the bright yellow jacket. He shivered. Yellow. Gaak. Good for flowers. Bad for business attire. Especially with dark red hair. And green eyes. And clear, smooth skin, long legs, elegant hands, generous lips. He watched her reach the door.

She turned to smile at him. "And don't forget you promised you'd have your friend waiting for me when I arrive."

He'd forgotten. There really was too much pollution. Or else it was sleeping with the electronics in that damned phone. He could think of better places to sleep, but he didn't mention it. No need to incite the ire of the Chairman. "And he'll be there. With bells on." Well, maybe he'd forgo the bells.

As she pulled into her driveway, Meredith strained to see just what kind of surprise her djinn had left her. All she was able to discern was a figure relaxed in her doorway. It looked like the mailman bent under his weary load had stopped for a brief nap.

She got out of the Mercedes and bounced up the steps. The figure in her doorway stretched and unfolded into a slim man with a shock of black hair. Dressed in black runner's tights, a white T-shirt, and a black and white windbreaker, Jim's friend flowed toward her and held out his hand.

"Jim sent me." His voice was a rich tenor that purred with pleasure at seeing her. His eyes were large and had a luminous, almost golden color.

"Well, he's outdone himself this time." She watched the man move with catlike grace. She extended her hand. "I'm Meredith Montgomery."

"I know. I'm Stan DeLeo." He kissed her hand.

This was certainly a better beginning than icky green orchids. Looking around for Jim, she nodded in approval. "Pleased to meet you." She felt certain her genie would have wanted to see how his friend managed.

"Jim tried to explain your predicament. I think I can help." He blinked at her.

She raised her eyebrows. Great. She'd just been introduced to what appeared to be a very interesting guy and her genie had already given him a transcript of all her failures. She shook her head. She felt like her life had turned into the subject of an afternoon talk show: one woman's search for true love, aided by her very own genie. Even Montel wouldn't believe this. She smiled at Mr. DeLeo. "Why don't you come in and we'll talk, get to know each other." She fished a key from her purse and unlocked the door, unarming and resetting the alarm. "Can I get you something to drink? Beer? Soda?"

"Milk, if you have it, please."

He followed her into her gourmet kitchen. Copper

pots and pans to make a chef jealous hung from a wrought-iron rack suspended over the island cooktop. "You must be a runner. You're certainly built like one, and the only men I know who prefer milk are athletes."

"I've been know to run a bit. Jump. I like to stay trim. Milk's a treat, though. I usually just drink water."

Meredith moved to the fridge and took out the milk. She poured a large glass and handed it to Stan.

"Thank you." He sipped the creamy liquid, tasting it with much the same enjoyment that the dentist had demonstrated with his dreadfully sweet wine. He smiled broadly and slowly closed his eyes and drank.

Meredith motioned to the round oak table in the breakfast nook, just off the kitchen. "Make yourself comfortable. I'll be down in a minute." Meredith danced up the stairs and across the thick oatmeal-colored carpet in her bedroom.

Perhaps she'd been hasty in her condemnation of Jim. She couldn't fathom where he'd found Stan, but she felt immediately comfortable with him. He was graceful, calm. It was like she'd known him forever.

Not a bad start, she guessed. She took off her suit, pulled on a worn pair of jeans and a pale yellow cotton sweater and ran a brush through her hair. Slipping into a pair of comfortable shoes, she went back downstairs. She really wanted to know about the Stan-Jim connection.

Her guest had moved from the kitchen to the formal living room and was sitting in her cat's favorite chair, his long legs folded under him, staring out the window. Speaking of cats, where was her four-legged pal? DeLeo looked up as she approached.

"You have a lovely yard. Your trees must attract a lot of birds."

"Are you a bird watcher?"

"I like birds. And small animals. Furry and feathered creatures are fascinating, don't you think? I could watch them all day."

"Would you like another glass of milk?"

"No, thank you. If I drink too much, I'll fall asleep."

Spectacular beginning, but declining rapidly. This was one of the stranger conversations she'd had. But, all things considered, not any stranger than talking with Dr. Rademacher about occlusions. "How do you know Jim? Are you a djinn, too?"

"No, I don't have that kind of magic in me." Stan unfolded gracefully, stretched, arching his back, and sat back down. His tongue flicked out and caught the edge of his top lip in a quick swipe. He closed his golden eyes slowly, then opened them and watched Meredith.

Hmmm. This was odd. "Where did you meet Jim?" She came farther into the room and stood beside her baby grand piano. She adjusted the bouquet of flowers on its shiny, black top.

"Here, at your house."

Curiouser and curiouser. "I see. Have we met before?"

Stan stood and walked toward Meredith, his movements fluid and elegant. "You don't recognize me, do you?" He took her hand, a soft, gentle gesture, and led her to the sofa. He sat next to her and draped his arm across the back cushions. He licked the palm of his hand and smoothed his black hair out of his eyes.

She felt her stomach sink and scooted back into the corner of the sofa. "Stanley?" That particular

99

movement was entirely too familiar and not at all human.

Stan ducked his head and smiled. He tucked his legs under him and put his head on his arm. He watched her through half-open golden eyes, then closed them and slept.

"What have you done with my cat, Jim? Front and center, Mr. I-Grant-Wishes. Now."

"At your beck and call, my dear." The djinn emerged from the shadows in the corner of the room. He bowed gracefully, a dangerous grin on his face.

"You, you . . ." Meredith sputtered to a stop.

"I, I what? I did just what you asked for. You said you'd be better off with your cat." He walked toward the sleeping man and leaned low, turning his ear toward the figure's head. "You can hear him purring." He straightened and put his hands up in protest. "Hey, you asked for it."

What a wonderful week this had turned into. Genies on Monday, threats from Griffin on Tuesday. Then, for entertainment, a dreadful dentist dinner on Wednesday and propositions from Edgar in accounting on Thursday afternoon. To round things out, she had just had a "date" with her cat. Could she fire her genie, she wondered, for insubordination? Meredith shook her head. She looked at Stanley, reached out and touched the man's hair. He shifted his weight, opened one golden eye and kissed her hand, then went back to his nap. "Amazing."

"I am, aren't I?" Jim stood tall, puffed out his magnificent chest and preened. "Better than the average djinn. Of course, you wouldn't know that, would you, never having met any other djinns." He moved toward her, put his hand on her shoulder. "Trust me."

She'd already tried that. "Can you make him less

catlike and more like a real man?" Meredith looked deep into Jim's eyes.

"If I did that, I'm afraid I'd destroy the qualities you love about Stanley. He'd become just another boorish male with irritating habits who'd leave his socks in the middle of the floor and expect hot meals in the evening." He snapped his fingers and Stanley the man shrank back into Stanley the cat. "He's much happier this way." He picked up the silky cat, stroked his head and nuzzled him. Then he handed Stanley to Meredith. The cat was purring like crazy.

"You're right, of course." Meredith settled the black and white pet on her lap, where he curled into a ball and continued sleeping, oblivious to his brief adventure.

Jim breathed a little easier. She could have taken his head off after this stunt. The Chairman certainly would have, and might still. He watched Meredith stroke the cat, who responded by stretching full across her lap and turning over. She rubbed his tummy.

Jim shifted uncomfortably. The stupid cat didn't know what a deal he had. Djinni loved to have their tummies rubbed. Along with other things.

"This whole week was a net loss, love-wise. At least I've got my proposal for the duchess outlined." She continued stroking the cat. "And, of course, a most intriguing magic marketing plan."

Jim shivered. He could feel her fingers tangled in his hair, imagine her caresses raising the hairs on his arms and chest. He coughed. If she didn't leave that cat alone, he was going to have to take matters into his own hands.

Stanley would have to fend for himself.

Meredith was back at the cat, gently stroking his ears and smoothing his whiskers.

Jim closed his eyes, shutting out the tempting thought of trading places with the cat.

"You were right about Stanley. He's much better as a cat. I don't react well to men who fall asleep in the middle of a conversation." She smiled at Jim when he opened one eye to peer out at her.

"You really love that cat."

"I suppose you could call it that. It isn't like loving another person, though."

"I wouldn't know. Most djinni aren't infected with silly human emotions." Passion. Lust. Those infected him at the moment. They were growing. And tough to ignore.

"Most?"

"Oh, genies can experience lust, passion—the mischievous, minor emotions, but none of the more serious emotions, the Big Ones, so to speak, like love. But I've heard stories, and that's all they are, mind you, that every so often a djinn is created with near-human characteristics. Theoretically, it's supposed to make him more effective in dealing with people."

"What happens to these special genies?"

"It's only a legend." He leaned back against the plush sofa cushions, imagining her touch. "Of course, if I wanted to adopt an emotion, I wouldn't pick love. Waste of energy, that." He sat up. "Not that it isn't a noble pursuit, you understand. I mean, it's your wish."

"Indeed it is." She set Stanley beside her. "Now, how are you going to make it come true?" The cat stretched, yawned and ambled to Jim's lap.

The unanswerable question. How? After watching her all week, first with the dentist and then with Stan, he had three main observations: She was always thinking about her work; she never really re-laxed; and she was entirely too alluring for her own good. Or rather, too alluring for his own good. It was going to be challenging to be around her for the rest of the month and keep his feelings aloof. The ones he wouldn't, couldn't admit having.

"First, you need to relax. Look at you." He set the cat on the sofa beside her. Standing, he reached for her hands and pulled her to her feet. Great Djinn, her hands were delicate and set up such a throb of wanting in him he wasn't sure he could proceed. "There's enough tension in your arms to launch a rocket."

She laughed. A sound so appealing, so endearing his heart did a triple flip before it settled back to its normal rhythm. "You are such a contradiction, Jim. Half the time you'd be at home in a comedy impro-visation team. The other half of you is pure, unadul-terated romantic."

Was he that transparent? He held up a hand and tried to look through it. "Think what you will, Mer-edith. I'm neither a comedian nor a romantic. I'm a genie. And, for the moment, the genie knows best." He tucked her hand in the crook of his arm and took her on a slow tour of the house. "Look at these." He pointed to a collection of framed pencil drawings on the wall in the formal dining room. "They're quite good."

"Thank you. I did them a long time ago."

He traced the outline of an old woman playing a piano. "You've captured her spirit, her essence." He smiled down at Meredith. "You should draw more."

She snorted. "Who has time for silly things like that? I have a career to manage. Responsibilities. Commitments."

"When you drew this, you didn't consider it silly."

"No, I didn't. But there's a reason for the phrase 'starving artist.' The only time art makes enough money for a lifestyle beyond bare subsistence is after the artist is dead. I'd rather enjoy a lifestyle while I still have a life."

"The whole point, Meredith my dear, is you don't enjoy the life you have. You have a lovely house, a beautiful garden in the back. A hot tub. All the accoutrements of success. But you never take the time to appreciate them. This room is a great example of what I am talking about," he said shortly. Jim had led them upstairs to Meredith's third bedroom—the one set up as a drawing studio. "You have created the perfect space to work on your art." He motioned to the picture window that ran along one wall. It overlooked Meredith's backyard and let in the last rays of the day's sun. A drawing table and stool stood before it, collecting dust. An unopened box of charcoals sat on the corner of the surface. "You must have some desire to sketch and paint again, or why did you even bother with this room?"

"Well, I always thought when I got some free time, I would go back to my art."

"Exactly my point, Meredith. If you don't create the time it will never happen. Work can—and does in your case—eat up all of your time if you let it. "Now . . ." He waved his hand and a pencil appeared. "Here. Draw something."

"You can't just turn the inspiration to draw on and off. I need to be in the mood." She blushed prettily. "What I mean is, I need a proper subject, something to inspire me."

"Well, we can fix that. Lights, maestro." Carefully positioned lamps illuminated the work surface. "Sit, Meredith." He pulled out the stool and eased her into it.

"But, what shall I sketch?"

"Well, you could attempt some of the other decorations in the room." He motioned to a large dust bunny resting comfortably in the corner of the almost empty room.

"Very funny. The cleaning lady rarely bothers with this room, because I so rarely use it."

Jim raised his eyebrows pointedly at her.

"Okay, okay, I already admitted it, I never use this room. I get the point. I should make time to draw again."

"You could try your hand at a djinn."

"What? Oh, draw you, you mean." Meredith's face was flushed again. Jim wanted to reach out and stroke her cheek. To feel her soft lips under his. To see if her blush extended the whole length of her body.

"I haven't picked up a pencil for such a long time, I'm not sure I remember where to start." Meredith stared at the blank paper. "I'd hate to botch such a fine subject." She stood. "Still, it would be fun to get back into my art. Perhaps tomorrow."

Jim took her hand between his. "Tomorrow, then." He kissed her fingertips. "For inspiration." He grinned and disappeared in a fine blue mist.

Meredith sat staring at the blank sheet of white paper, twiddling the pencil Jim had created for her. She missed the escape of drawing, the pure right-brain experience. Shaking her head, she began to doodle. She remembered her classes in life drawing, and felt a slow blush heat her neck and face. Nary a model had looked like Jim. She closed her eyes, trying to imagine him posing nude, leaning against one of the props from the theater department. He'd look nice against the Roman column. She picked up the pad

# Karen Lee

of paper and fanned a breeze adequate to cool the heat that image generated.

She wondered, briefly, if there were rules about how close the genie/client relationship could be, and then discarded the thought as the crazy residue of a life filled with more responsibility than laughter. Well, until this last week, anyway. She'd laughed a lot more since Jim showed up. And felt better for it.

If you were going to wish up a man, Jim sure met all her qualifications. Turning to a clean page in the sketch pad, she realized she'd gotten used to his insane comments, that she really enjoyed his cockeyed approach to life. Of all the men she'd cared about, Jim was the only one to recognize how important the creative side of her was. He didn't think her drawings were silly. Perhaps there was more to him than mischief. Slowly, she began to sketch her perfect man. Dark hair, dark eyes, broad shoulders, an arched eyebrow . . . how to capture that playful smile . . . ?

# *Chapter Six*

## *"Djinn Mill"*

Monday rolled around too quickly. Following an uneventful Saturday morning meeting with Horton, Meredith had played eighteen holes of golf with him. And won, thanks to a little help from her djinn. But after watching Meredith work on her presentation instead of taking a walk in the sun, or riding her bike down the canal bank, or doing a dozen more interesting things, Jim had decided he needed to take matters into his own hands.

He paced across the carpet in Meredith's office, wondering briefly what her reaction would be to his latest plan. He was in deep trouble as it was. What was one more transgression?

"There you are," she said. "I've been wanting to talk with you about these product brochures." She handed him a sheaf of glossy, multicolored pages. "Are they too forward? Too direct? I don't want to offend the duchess."

Karen Lee

He tossed them onto the table, unread, unconsidered. "You have a phone call."

"No, I don't."

"Yes, you do." Jim handed Meredith the phone. "Have fun." He swirled away in a cloud of blue.

Rats deserting a sinking ship didn't move that fast. The phone rang on cue and Meredith answered. Then gasped. "Oh, hello, Your Grace. Thank you so much for taking time out of your busy schedule to talk with me. I appreciate it." She tried to catch her breath, surprised the duchess herself had returned her call.

Her Grace, the Grand Duchess Edwinna of Hertzenstein, chuckled. "It's no trouble at all, I assure you. Our little Duchy is lucky to be able to attract a prestigious firm like yours."

"Thank you again, Your Grace." Meredith was struck by the friendliness in the woman's voice. Nothing in the briefing papers on Hertzenstein would have led her to suspect anything warm about the duchess. "I assume you recieved my packet of information about Horton?"

"Yes, yes, it arrived yesterday. Isn't it amazing how quickly information travels these days? It's a small world, and getting smaller." Meredith heard the movement of papers. "This is a quite an impressive list of clients you've had, Miss Montgomery."

"Horton has been fortunate to have many opportunities to shine." How should she handle the "Miss" question? Correct the duchess? Tell her the proper honorific these days was "Ms." or launch the fiction that she was married? Nothing ventured, no promotion. "Actually, Your Grace, I've just recently exchanged the Miss for Mrs." Well, Jim *had* agreed to accompany her. "If Your Grace doesn't mind, I'd like to bring my new husband, Jim, with me to Hertzen-stein."

"Mind? Of course not. And, congratulations, my dear. It is such a wonderful day when two hearts find each other and pledge their love for eternity. I couldn't think of a better way to begin our business relationship than with a visit by you and your husband. Jim, you said his name was?"

"Yes, Jim Goodman." Meredith had relaxed a little when the duchess mentioned beginning a business relationship. A good sign. Heck, a wonderful sign. She could feel the contract in her hand. "Thank you so much. It would have been so difficult, leaving him here."

"Of course, I understand, you being newlyweds. Such a delightful time." The duchess paused. "Would you prefer postponing our meeting? I could easily make time, say, at the end of May or early June if you'd prefer to spend your honeymoon unsullied by dreary business."

Great. She should have just kept her big mouth occupied with coffee. "Oh, no, Your Grace. We don't have to move our meeting. Jim doesn't mind accommodating my business plans. He's quite used to it, as a matter of fact. No problem at all. Actually," she continued, not wanting to give the duchess a chance to change her mind and clinch the corner office for Griffin, "we agreed that there couldn't be a better place to spend part of our honeymoon than Hertzenstein. It'll give me an up-close-and-personal experience with the charms of your country, and that'll help me even more when I am designing the plan to increase tourist traffic."

There was a long pause before the duchess spoke. "Yes, I can see certain advantages for Hertzenstein in your coming with your Jim, but I wouldn't want to interfere with the start of your lives together. No. We'll simply have to move the meeting. After all," she went on before Meredith could protest, "our discussions about your proposal shouldn't be hurried, and I've seen enough newlyweds to know you'll need all your time to, well, explore each other."

Meredith felt her face flush. Exploring her gorgeous genie was an unspoken fantasy she'd had since he showed up in her office. "Thank you, Your Grace, for your understanding. I can't tell you how I appreciate your consideration. I wonder, however"—she paused, gathering her thoughts—"you did say you wanted to implement the plan to increase tourism this year, right?"

"Correct."

"If we postpone our meeting, Your Grace, you run the risk of missing your targets for summer and fall tourism. I've talked this over with Jim and he understands completely. We're partners, he and I, a team, in everything we do." It was true. "Actually, he suggested that we work together on this project. He'd be terribly disappointed if we didn't make the trip." *Oh, please, please, don't cancel this meeting.* She'd never live it down, and Jim wouldn't be around much longer.

"Well, you certainly make a persuasive argument. I understand now how you've managed to succeed in your career, my dear." The duchess cleared her throat. "Very well, then. Come visit Hertzenstein and bring your groom. But, you must join my husband and me for a simple dinner during your visit."

Yes! "That would be lovely, Your Grace. I know Jim will be excited to meet you and the duke. Thank you again and, if you have any questions, please don't hesitate to call." *Whew, disaster averted.* She concluded the conversation with more niceties and small talk.

When she hung up, Jim was there, looking delicious at the edge of her desk. "You have another call." He smiled.

Meredith's stomach flip-flopped. He was so handsome and charming when he wanted to be. Yes, the duchess would be most pleased with Meredith's new husband. "How do you know these things?" she asked.

"I live there, remember?"

The phone rang. She frowned and answered it. He watched her expression soften and her smile broaden. Then, she blushed. She grinned stupidly, said, "I'll be right there," and hung up.

"Well?"

"That was my former boyfriend, Glenn. Something about problems at home. He wants to talk and he sounds serious."

Just her kind of guy. "Great. Have fun." Jim watched her exit, looked at himself in her mirror and gritted his teeth. "Just not too much."

He was about to disappear when the air in the office got heavier and a pair of dark blue eyes, accompanied by frowning eyebrows, swam into his field of vision. The Chairman of the Board himself. This could mean only one thing.

He was in trouble again.

Jim stood tall and, turning slowly, addressed the glowering visage. "Yes, Your Immenseness?"

"What kind of mischief have you cooked up here?"

"The best kind, the kind that brought me to the pinnacle of my powers. The kind that Meredith will appreciate." Even though he knew he needed to be respectful, he couldn't stop his cocky tone.

The blue eyes gazed around the office. "You're

pushing what little luck you have left. You know that, don't you?"

Jim nudged the edge of the carpet with his toe. How could he forget, with reminders like the one staring at him? "I'm mortified, of course, sir. You'll have to admit this is an unusual assignment."

"Don't screw this up!" The Chairman's temper, barely under control at the best of times, was definitely about to blow. "There *is* a correct way to handle this woman and her wish. You just need to figure it out." He winked out.

"Oh, sure. Tell me there's a solution but don't give me any hints. What kind of Chairman are you, anyway?" He knew the answer to that question, but it didn't help.

Deep down he realized the reason he was having trouble with Meredith had nothing to do with breaking, or not breaking, any sacred djinni rules. He wanted her for himself. And he'd just sent her off to meet her self-described almost-perfect man.

Now would be the appropriate time to let things be. Instead, he decided he wanted coffee.

Meredith sat in the corner of The Capital Grind Coffee Cafe, tapping her fingernail nervously against her Tall Skinny Latte. She glanced at her watch for the dozenth time. Where was he? Glenn was the most punctual person she knew.

She took a sip of her coffee and looked up to recognize Glenn's broad shoulders filling the doorway. He came to her immediately and leaned down to kiss her cheek.

"Sorry I'm late. I forget how wretched traffic can be in this town." He took her hands. "I've missed you."

Meredith watched his eyes. The normal clear blue

was ringed with red. "Me, too. You look tired."

"Right on the money, as always." He gave her a half smile.

"Sounds serious." She noticed the dent of an absent wedding ring. "Looks serious."

"Serious enough, I guess." He pulled his hands back. "Debbie and I are separated."

Meredith gulped. Here was her wish come true, walking right back into her life. Why wasn't she doing back flips across the room?

Glenn twisted in his chair, looked at his lap and then at Meredith. "I need caffeine." He walked to the counter, got in line behind a long-haired young man wearing a George Washington University sweatshirt and grinned back at her over his shoulder.

A rush of memories of hot nights and feverish passion flooded her brain. That part of their relationship had always worked. She drank in Glenn's boyish good looks, the tall, lanky frame, straight brown hair that never would stay in place. Certainly preferable to the shabby appearance of the dreadlocked student in front of him.

But as Glenn returned and slid into his chair opposite her, she noticed his casual grace had been replaced by a foreign tension that creased his face with worry.

What was she supposed to do? She'd loved him, had mourned the end of their relationship, and, a couple of days ago, would have given almost anything to have him back in her life. And yet . . .

"Tell me what happened." She clutched her cup of coffee.

He leaned back and bumped into the passing GW student, who looked strangely familiar. "Yo, dude," the student mumbled, and sat at the next table. Meredith glanced at the book the kid had opened. *Studies in Persian Mythology*.

"You never were good at small talk." Glenn smiled thinly. "That's what I like about you, Meri, direct and to the point. You cut through all the bull. Unlike my lovely wife, who can't seem to articulate at all."

"Hmmmm." Meredith watched the student from the corner of her eye. He was hunched over his coffee and his book, his black dreadlocks an odd contrast to his long, elegant fingers. His coffee gave off a familiar cinnamon smell.

"Has Horton promoted you yet?" Glenn sipped his coffee.

"Hmmmm? Oh. Not yet, but he will. How about you? Is the newest partner at Johnson, Webster and Morse busy?"

"Nights and weekends lately. I've got some incredible cases. Groundbreaking." His face glowed with excitement. "I might actually argue a case before the Supreme Court, Meri. Can you believe it?"

Meredith was having trouble focusing on Glenn's eagerness. The student sitting next to her kept flipping pages in his book and mumbling. It couldn't be Jim. He'd promised her that he wouldn't show up at awkward moments. Like this. With effort, she dragged her attention back to Glenn. "Easily. You're a talented lawyer. I've never doubted it. I imagine Debbie is proud of you."

"If she is, she hasn't told me lately. Sometimes I wish I'd stayed with you. We were a team."

A sudden strong scent of spice drifted past Meredith's nose and she sneezed. "Be careful what you wish for, Glenn. You just might get it." Jim didn't look bad in dreadlocks.

"Look, Meri. Have dinner with me tonight. We can talk and decide what we want to do."

"Do?"

"About us." He reached out and stroked her cheek. "Come on, Miss Successful Corporate Career, take out your calendar and make time for me."

The fragrance of cinnamon grew stronger. Meredith glanced at the student genie and caught his smile. "Okay." She slid out of her chair. "I've got a few things to clear up first. Pick me up at my office at, say, eight." She kissed his cheek and walked out.

Jim was waiting for her when she returned to her office.

"What was that all about?" she asked. "I thought you only appeared when I called, or thought about you." She plopped her bag on the credenza and sat on the corner of her desk.

Jim looked sheepish. "I've got a lot riding on your wish. I figure I've got a right to protect my interests."

"Your interests? Look, while it's kinda fun trying to figure out who you're going to be next"—she cocked her head—"sometimes it's not the best idea. Guess who's not coming to dinner." She patted his knee. "One genie."

He caught her hand before she could withdraw it. For a moment she enjoyed the tingle of sensual warmth that spread from her hand to the center of her body.

"Are you sure about Glenn? I sensed hesitation at the coffee shop, and it didn't have anything to do with their dreadful excuse for coffee. Honestly. Coffee is a beverage of epic, almost holy, proportions. It should only be served by Those Who Know. And never, never in paper cups." He let go of her hand.

Meredith realized with a start that she missed it. "You mean you're not an instant Capital Grind fan? I doubt it'll impact their stock prices. As to Glenn, you're very perceptive, for a genie. He's moving pretty fast. But, I'm a big girl and, if he really split up with Debbie, then I think I can handle this. If not . . . well, you'll have to shift into wish overdrive." Jim's presence became dangerously tempting. She turned her computer on. "Right now, I need a magical briefing for Horton's next meeting."

Jim walked around the desk and stood behind her, leaning low and breathing on her neck. "Let me guess. You don't have a strategy for the duchess identified yet?"

She shivered. "Two perceptions in one evening? Jim, you surprise me. No, I don't." She opened a spreadsheet. "Look at that. I'm sure I changed the sales-to-expense ratio this morning." She highlighted a series of numbers.

"You've been under a lot of pressure. It's possible you imagined changing it." Jim whispered in her ear. "You're awfully tense, Meredith. Why not let me relax you before you jump into this mess?" He trailed a long, slender finger from her earlobe down her neck to the top of her raw-silk T-shirt. "I'm rather good at it, you know."

She could only imagine. "I wish you were good at . . ." She looked up at him. "Oh, no, you don't. No use trying to trick me into using up my other wishes on silly things. I can solve this problem myself." She tried to ignore the excitement his touch set stirring in her. If only her genie weren't so good-looking, so charming and so right about the need to relax. Her shoulders felt like they had steel rods through them.

"Fine. Play Reject-A-Genie. After today, I'm used to it. Even though you haven't begun to plumb the depths of my various and sundry talents." Jim slogged back to the chair and slumped.

"One of those talents is maintaining a fine pout."

She chuckled. "For a magical being, you are so obvious." She looked at the computer screen. "Of course. And so is the problem. Check this out." She nodded at the column of numbers. "Hidden in plain sight."

"If you say so." Jim yawned. "Does this mean your problems with the duchess are over? And we can get down to some serious wishing and save my crumbling career?"

Work ethic and career drive pushed physical attraction aside. Meredith ignored him. She opened documents, checked databases and accessed files. She fussed and fiddled, moved information, recalculated. Her frown of concentration gradually changed to a small smile of satisfaction as she worked. Her excitement built and her satisfaction grew as her ideas started to come together. That promotion was soooo close.

An hour and a half later she stopped and looked at her genie. "As my new assistant, it would be appropriate for you to be at the review in the morning. Which part of this would you like to handle?"

Jim wandered back and looked at the presentation in neat slides on the screen. "None of it, actually. I'm not much on formal speaking. I'm more of a seat-of-your-pants kind of guy. You know, think fast on my feet, maximum creativity."

Meredith shrugged. "So don't come. Now that Glenn's back in the picture, your career is looking pretty secure anyway. The rest of my wishes will probably be a piece of cake for a genie with your experience."

"You're wishing for a piece of cake? Seems a trifle silly, but, if that's what you want, so be it." Jim assumed the proper Djinn Wish Granting Pose—shoulders backing a tall stance, arms folded formally

# Karen Lee

across his chest and weight distributed evenly over his slightly separated feet.

"Hold it, pal. I didn't say, 'Simon Says.' No wish, no magic. Right?"

Jim let his muscular arms drop to his sides. "Who's Simon? Is he in the running for The Man Who Will Understand? How many ex-boyfriends do you have, anyway?"

"None of your business." Meredith stiffened. "Simon isn't anyone. It's a children's game, 'Simon Says.' You can't do anything unless Simon says you can."

"Hmmmphhh. Games are silly. Young djinni don't play games. They train. They practice."

"Hmmmphhh yourself. I think you need a rest, Genie-Jim." Meredith held up her cell phone. "Bye-bye."

"You're absolutely right, Project-Meredith. Hanging around humans too much isn't healthy for djinni." Jim swirled in a cloud of blue smoke and disappeared into the cell phone. "You've got my number."

"Men. They're all the same, magical or not," Meredith mumbled under her breath.

"I heard that."

"Go to sleep, won't you?"

The phone rang. She snatched it from her desk and flipped it open. "I mean it, Jim. Go away."

"Excuse me, Miss Montgomery. This is Horace in the lobby. A gentleman to see you. Shall I send him up?"

"Oh, Horace, I'm sorry. Of course, thank you."

Moments later, Glenn entered her office and swept her into an embrace. "I wasn't sure I could wait until eight."

She relaxed into the familiar feeling of his arms. "You feel great. I've missed your hugs."

"Indeed. This one's powered by the full weight of the law. I've got a subpoena requiring you to have dinner with me. Now." Glenn's face broke into a cautious smile. "I've arranged all your favorites: a solid Merlot, steamed shrimp, stir-fried veggies and me." He looped her jacket over his arm. "Ready?"

There was an insistent knock at the door, followed by a muffled "Cleaning Service."

"I'll get that"—Glenn moved quickly across the room—"while you finish up."

Meredith tidied her desk as Glenn let the cleaning lady into her office. "Could you come back later, please? I'm in a meeting," Meredith said, looking up briefly as she stacked a number of folders into an organized pile on the corner of her desk.

The cleaning woman, a rounded lumpish person with gray streaks in her untidy hair, chuckled. "Right, miss. A meeting. Like the ones that fellow Francis, down the hall, has after hours." She shuffled around the desk. "Just let me get this trash and I'll leave you to your . . . business." She emptied the wastebasket into her garbage bag and waddled out the door, trailing essence of cinnamon. "Closed or open?" Jim's dancing eyes sparkled from the woman's face.

"Closed. And, quit spying on me." Meredith shut down the computer. "It's so hard to find quality cleaning contractors." She hesitated, then stuck the cell phone in her purse. If Francis was staying late, she didn't want the phone anywhere close to him. Jim might be a screw-up, but he was the only genie she had.

A brief ride later, she and Glenn pulled into the Four Seasons Hotel and a uniformed attendant helped her out of Glenn's Jaguar. "I didn't realize the Four Seasons had added steamed shrimp to their restaurant menu." Meredith slipped her hand into Glenn's arm and walked beside him across the plush lobby toward the elevators. "Where are we going?"

"I've rented a suite for the evening. I figured it would be more romantic than my office conference room."

She'd been in his office and he was right, but a suite? "What exactly did you have in mind?" Nagging doubt crept into her buoyant mood. How could something that sounded so much like a wish come true feel so wrong?

"Besides dinner? Reminisce about all the good times we had, about how we finally solved your father's problems with his pension. Talk, get caught up, you know."

She entered the elevator and he punched the button to the top floor. In for a penny, in for a 401K.

Glenn opened the suite's door and engulfed Meredith in his arms. He kissed her quickly, an almost brotherly peck. Frowning, as if that wasn't the outcome he had planned, he led her into the rooms and kicked the door closed. A bottle of Merlot was uncorked on the table, and two crystal glasses gleamed in the light.

"A toast to us." Glenn poured the deep red liquid and handed her a glass.

Involuntarily, she shuddered, remembering the glass of wine Jim had used to illustrate his probable fate should her wish go unfulfilled. *If I can manage things, that shouldn't be a problem after tonight*, she thought, and smiling at Glenn, took the glass and kissed him lightly. Somehow she had to reignite their old feelings for one another, even if it had been five years ago. "To wishes coming true."

Meredith's cell phone rang. "I thought I turned that darned thing off." She crossed the room, took the slim phone from her bag and flipped it open. "This is Meredith Montgomery."

"Meredith?" The voice was a raspy whisper. "We need to talk. I have bad vibes about Glenn."

"I told you to take a hike." Meredith's voice matched Jim's whisper, but didn't cover her irritation. "I'm busy helping you make my wish come true."

"He's not right for you."

"Who is it, Meri? Someone from work?" Glenn offered her more wine. "Tell them you're in a meeting."

"I can't talk right now. I'm busy." Meredith pushed "end" and tossed the phone on the sofa as she turned into Glenn's embrace.

"You always tasted better than the wine." Glenn took the glass from Meredith and set it on the table. He guided her to the sofa and pulled her down onto it. His action set up odd sensations in the pit of her stomach, but they felt more like a stomachache than impending true love.

Maybe you couldn't go back.

There was an insistent knock at the door, followed by a muffled "Room service, sir."

"Dinner is served." Glenn stood. "Don't go anywhere."

Meredith stretched, trying to ease the tension in her shoulders, and wondered how to relieve the tension in the room. This should have felt good, being back with Glenn. They'd been so close during her family's financial crisis. Instead, she felt confused. She leaned back, sipping her wine as the white-jacketed waiter set up their dinner on the table in the alcove.

"That smells wonderful." She walked toward

# Karen Lee

Glenn, slipped her hand into his and smiled. Another doubt settled in her stomach, joining its cousins. This had all the earmarks of djinn interference.

The waiter piled the dish covers onto the cart and asked, "Will there be anything else, sir?"

As Glenn reached into his pocket for a tip, a cloud of cinnamon fragrance drifted around Meredith. "No. No tips." She stomped toward the amused waiter, who was backing away quickly, his dark, almond-shaped eyes sparkling. "Get out! I told you not to bother me this evening." She slammed the suite door, and could hear Jim chuckling over the squeak of the cart wheels.

"What was that about? You're not usually that hard on waiters."

"Ooohh! That man! He's not even a man. Why can't he understand that I'm fine, that everything will turn out fine. If he'd just go back into the phone and be a nice genie."

"You're babbling. What do you mean he's not even a man? And how can he go into the phone? I don't understand."

The cell phone rang. "What now?" she shouted into the mouthpiece.

"I knew it. Glenn isn't the right one, Meredith. He just admitted he didn't understand and that *was* one of your conditions. Dump him and let's spend the evening . . ."

Meredith stabbed at the "end" button and then removed the battery from the phone. "There, that should do it."

"I'm worried about you. Couldn't you just turn the silly thing off? You don't have to disassemble it."

Meredith slumped on the sofa. "I'm so sorry, Glenn. I don't know what came over me." A lie. She knew exactly what the problem was. A colossal case of excess djinn. "Sometimes this job demands too much."

"I know. As I recall, however, you chose the career." Glenn sat in the chair opposite Meredith and loosened his tie. "You never were able to leave the job at the office. Even when we were together."

"Maybe I just need some food. It's been a long time since lunch." She moved quickly to the table and began serving herself shrimp and vegetables. She hurriedly speared a shrimp and shoved it into her mouth. "Ish grade!" she mumbled around the food. "Dry shom."

Glenn cocked his eyebrow and sat next to Meredith. "Slow down, Meri. These babies aren't going to wriggle away." He pulled off his tie. "Do I want to know what that display of intense emotion was all about?"

Meredith shook her head.

"Didn't think so. Pass the vegetables."

After the meal, Meredith excused herself. She walked to the bathroom and shut the door. She opened her purse, looking for her dental floss, and glanced in the mirror. She wasn't the least surprised to see Jim's face gazing out at her. "Thanks for staying away till we finished eating."

"Don't mention it. I did promise I'd be sensitive."

"Right. Sensitive. That's you, in a nutshell. What in the world are you trying to do?"

"I'm simply protecting my interests."

"Your interests are doing just fine." If polite suggestions wouldn't keep Jim away, perhaps something direct would work. "I intend to enjoy myself to the fullest extent possible. Have you had a look around this suite on your frequent passes through it? There's a bedroom through that door. With a bed."

## Karen Lee

Jim raised an eyebrow and gave her a half smile. "It's lumpy. And the pillows are hard."

"I don't even want to think about how you might know that particular tidbit of information."

Jim shrugged. "This whole thing isn't right."

"And what would you know about it?"

"As a djinn, I don't have many scruples. None, actually. Not part of our makeup. Mostly, we are renowned for mischief."

"You're doing a bang-up job tonight. I'll be sure to tell your Chairman of the Board what a fine mischief-maker you've turned out to be."

"Don't even mention his name." Jim's image shivered. "Where was I? Scruples. I don't have any. But you do, and I know you've had second, third and fourth thoughts about this guy who's plumping pillows and pouring wine in there, hoping that you're changing into that dainty little number he's left hanging conveniently on the door." Jim pointed to an elegant black negligee that was mostly lace and totally sinful.

Meredith put her hand over her mouth. "I didn't notice that when I came in." She fingered the gossamer garment. "Goodness."

"Goodness isn't what he has in mind."

"Don't treat me like a child, Jim. I know Glenn. We used to be an item, remember?"

Jim's image squinted one eye and managed to look unconvinced. "Turn around. Please."

"Fine." Meredith faced the sunken tub, and jumped as Jim leaned out of the mirror and began rubbing the tension away from her shoulders. "How did you do that?"

"It's a matter of supreme concentration of molecular density and finely calculated comparison of—"

"Sorry I asked." She began to relax. "You've got two hours to stop that."

She could feel Jim smile. "If you stay in here that long, ol' Glenn will be worried," he said.

Meredith nodded, stretched her shoulders under Jim's ministrations and sighed. "Right on that one, genie." She shrugged out from under his strong fingers and faced him. "I appreciate your concern, and fully understand why you're worried about me. You're worried about yourself."

"What, me worry? Not this djinn."

"Don't kid me, pal. I've spent my career carefully honing the ability to identify worry in the people I'm working with." She drew her finger along the creases in Jim's forehead. "Worry. Definitely."

"Bah! You think too much. That's your problem, Meredith. Too much brain time on things you know nothing about, like djinni."

"If you say so. Now, I'd like to freshen up so we can get about granting my wish and saving your sorry blue hide."

She grinned. Then frowned. "Does it look blue, or is it just this light?"

Jim stepped out of the mirror and stood behind Meredith. He squinted at their paired reflection. "Nah, just your imagination. See?" He held out his hand in front of her face. "No blue."

Meredith grasped his hand, admiring once more Jim's elegant digits. "Be a good genie, won't you, and go home. I've got my cell phone if I get into trouble."

Jim stepped back into the mirror, flickered and disappeared, leaving behind his dangerous eyes, sensuous lips and straight white teeth. A modern rendition of the Cheshire cat. "You be careful," the lips whispered. And faded.

"I always am." Meredith fished in her bag for her

125

lipstick and blush. This was a nice conundrum she'd gotten herself into.

Consider the facts. If her wish came true with Glenn, she'd be helping to end a marriage. If she abandoned Glenn and her wish failed, Jim would be permanently erased.

She sat on the side of the tub. Wishing shouldn't be this difficult, she reflected. She'd wished a hundred things in her life and none had ever caused her this much trouble. Of course, none had come with a genie attached, either.

*Nonsense, Meredith. Get a grip. Glenn called you, not the other way round. If there's something wrong with his marriage, that's his problem. Isn't it?*

She stood, applied lipstick and blush and squared her shoulders. Could she help it if Glenn still found her attractive?

She remembered something Darcie had told her, weeks ago. Glenn had called, asking for the phone number of a mutual friend. She hadn't been in the office, so Darcie'd talked with him. *He and Debbie are expecting their second baby. He sounded happy, as if he had good sense.*

Glenn had wanted children, almost more than his law career. At the end of their relationship, she'd been adamant that her career was as important as his was and children, if there were to be any, would have to wait. By then, she'd helped her parents through the worst times and had discovered she had a gift for marketing. Her career had become very important to her. She certainly didn't want to wind up in the same boiling cauldron her folks had.

However, no man who talked about kids the way Glenn did would easily agree to a separation from his wife and then come running to an old girlfriend unless something else was afoot. She needed to ask a few questions.

Glenn had not, as Jim suggested, moved to the bedroom. And, while he'd removed his jacket and tie before dinner, his very expensive pinstriped shirt remained firmly on his person, only a single button undone.

"I heard you talking." Glenn looked puzzled.

Ignoring his questioning glance, she sat at the table and took a sip of water. A clear head was required. "Glenn, we have to talk."

"Okay, you first."

She shook her head. "No, I mean about you and Debbie. About why we're here tonight." She paused. "What's wrong?"

Glenn sighed, stood and ambled to the sofa. He plopped into the generous pillows and held his head. "I have no idea. Last week, everything seemed to be just fine. Debbie's so excited about the new baby. She's picked out wallpaper for the baby's room and gone shopping with Alex for his own big-boy bed. Sure, she's had a bit of morning sickness, and she's had trouble sleeping, but that's normal.

"Then suddenly, bam. I came home Friday and Debbie was ranting about my never being there, about Alex and the new baby growing up without a father, half orphans. She gave me a bag packed with some of my things, handed me formal separation papers and told me to leave." Glenn looked stricken. "Meri, I don't have a clue what happened. I miss Debbie. I miss Alex. He's only two. I don't know what to do."

Meredith sat beside him, her arm around his shoulders. "Sometimes women are irrational when they're pregnant."

"This goes way beyond that."

"Have you talked with Debbie since this happened?"

"I call several times a day. She doesn't answer. Sometimes I get a wrong number." He shook his head. "I can't figure it out."

"Friday, huh?"

"I figure she started packing sometime before lunch. I got home just after six."

Before lunch. About the time Meredith had asked Jim how he was doing, finding her the perfect man. "Ah, Glenn, could you excuse me a moment? I just remembered an important phone call I need to make. It won't take a minute." Meredith rose and dug her cell phone out of her bag, reattached the battery and dialed. She cocked her head and smiled at Glenn before exiting to the bedroom and shutting the door.

"Come out, come out, wherever you are."

Jim popped into existence, reclining seductively on the bed, dressed in the same silk pajama bottoms he'd sported that first night. "I must have been mistaken about the lumps."

"Why am I not surprised." She sat on the bed beside him, forcing herself not to stare at his chest. "I'm going to ask you a question and I need a straight answer. No genie high jinks, no djinn dodges."

Jim propped his head on his hand. "Ask away."

"How did you arrange for Glenn to be here tonight?"

"Why, Meredith, I'm shocked, shocked, I say, at your lack of faith in my talents, my discretion. I—"

"No tricks, Jim. Answer my question."

Jim twisted a strand of his shiny black hair around his finger. "There once was a churl with a little curl right in the middle of his forehead. When he was good, he was very, very good." Jim raised an eyebrow and gave Meredith a heart-melting smile. "And when he was bad, he was popular."

"An answer."

"Oh, all right. Spoilsport. I have your future at heart, you know. I kind of, sort of, carefully hinted to Glenn's wife that he'd been seeing someone else and was thinking of filing for divorce."

Meredith felt a slow burn begin. "And when did this happen?"

"Just after you made me change your cat back into a cat. But I only did it because of your discussion with Darcie. You did say he was your perfect match, didn't you?"

"Irrelevant in the extreme." She stood and paced the room. "You broke it, you fix it. Now. Put things back."

"Is that a wish?"

"It's a demand. If there *were* such a thing as a warranty on genies, you've voided yours and you owe me."

"Hey, you made the wish. A defective wish, I might add. Maybe you owe me. Warranties, indeed." Jim mumbled and shuddered. "This could be hazardous to my health, you know. The All-Powerful Chairman of the Board doesn't like reject wishes." He levitated a foot above the bed, his arms crossed over his enticingly naked chest. Slowly he returned to the mattress, a slight bluish aura surrounding him. "I hope you're happy." He blinked and disappeared.

Meredith smiled grimly and went back to Glenn. "Sorry about that—an important phone call I forgot I had to make. Listen, I was thinking about it, and you should call your wife." She handed him her cell phone. "I'm sure she's waiting by the phone, hoping you'll call. She's pregnant; maybe it was her hormones in overdrive. Regardless, I'm sure you're clever enough to make her forget she's the one who kicked you out."

Glenn took the phone. "Do you think so?"

"Absolutely."

He dialed, and Meredith wandered into the alcove, tidying the dinner dishes, trying not to listen in on the conversation. Tears welled up in her eyes when she heard Glenn tell Debbie he loved her. And the concern in his voice when he asked after his small son was almost too much for her to bear.

He could have been hers. She sniffed. But, no. She had a career. And a defective djinn. She sighed.

"Meredith, you're a wonder. I don't know how you knew, but Debbie was waiting by the phone. She actually apologized. I guess you were right about these hormones." Glenn hugged her. "Where did I put my tie?" He snagged it from the chair and tied a sloppy knot.

"I'm glad you're back in the good graces of your family." She reached out and straightened his tie.

He glanced at his watch. "And I'm late. Two days late." He kissed her cheek. "Thanks a lot, Meredith. You're a good friend." As he reached the door to the suite he turned. "The place is paid for if you'd like to stay the night. You've earned it." He grinned and ran out the door.

Meredith sat at the table, thinking. Monday evening, day eight of this game, and she'd practically sealed Jim's fate. She shook her head, stood and paced the elegant suite. It wasn't fair. Not that fairness had ever played a part in her life. Just once, though, it would be nice to catch a break. She sighed.

Her cat had plenty of food and she could always leave really early in the morning to go home and change. Or, she could wear the same clothes tomorrow. Who would notice? Maybe she'd take Glenn's suggestion and stay here tonight. It would be a pity to waste a perfectly good suite.

More the pity she didn't have someone to share it with.

The thought of Jim, lying on the king-sized bed dressed in a come-to-me smile, flitted across her mind.

Right. Spend the night with her genie.

On second consideration, the idea wasn't all that bad. They'd really not had time to talk about how to implement the marketing plan she had half prepared in her head. The one that was going to knock the socks off that old Chairman of the Board. If Djinni wore socks, that is.

She continued to pace, running marketing ideas around in her mind. Advertising might be a challenge, but the ad copy would be fun to create. She wondered if there was any market research on things like beliefs in magical beings. She'd have to ask Darcie.

Darcie.

She hadn't talked to her in days, it seemed. Maybe she'd have some useful ideas. At minimum she'd provide a sounding board, and Meredith badly needed to talk to someone.

She dialed Darcie's number and paced as the phone rang, then rang again. And a third time. She and Ben must be out doing something this evening. Meredith hung up. It was silly to think anyone would believe a tale about a djinn who lived in a cell phone. Even someone with an imagination as active as Darcie's.

Still. She dialed her sister's number.

Meredith was about to hang up when a very relaxed voice answered, "Hullo?"

"Janice? I'm not interrupting anything, am I?" She knew the answer was "Yes."

"Meredith? What time is it?"

Oh, no. It was past midnight. "I'm so sorry. I didn't know it was this late. I'll talk to you tomorrow."

"No, don't hang up. If you've lost track of time, you're in trouble. Tell your little sister all."

"I don't even know where to begin."

"The beginning is usually best. What's up?"

In halting phrases, punctuated by sighs and expressions of frustration, Meredith laid out the tale of the djinn in the cell phone and his thus far unsuccessful attempts to grant her wish.

"If he doesn't succeed, he's going to be downsized out of existence and I don't think I could live with myself if that happened."

There was a long pause on the other end of the phone. "You're not making this up?"

"No."

"You haven't been drinking?"

"Just wine with dinner. Trust me, I'm completely sober. There's a genie living in my cell phone." In fact, he was probably listening to her conversation.

"This is a new marketing campaign, something you're trying out on me before you release it on the unsuspecting public. Right?"

"No. It's Jim."

"You've found a new man? That explains everything. Why didn't I pick up on it? You never make sense when you're in love."

"No, no. He's not a new man and I'm not in love with him." A prickly sensation skittered across her shoulders and warmed the pit of her stomach. She tried to rationalize her body's physical reaction to her words. Clearly, she'd eaten too many shrimp.

But as much as she would have liked to deny it,

Meredith realized that she harbored more than simple feelings for Jim. He was larger than a project, more important than a marketing plan. They shared a kinship of a sort, an offbeat approach to the world, a determination not to fail. Jim was a lot like her. He understood. The fluttery feeling in her stomach increased.

It wasn't the shrimp.

If she didn't find a man who loved her before the end of the month, Jim would be . . . She couldn't force herself to think it. Without any fanfare at all, her focus had changed from getting the promotion to helping Jim survive. "What am I going to do?" Meredith asked.

"What you always do with your hot projects. You worry them to death and then they turn out fine." Meredith heard Janice yawn.

"Death?"

Meredith wasn't sure of the djinni equivalent to death, but the bottom line was the same. World without Jim. Amen.

"You know you do. You fuss over every little detail. Of course, that's what makes your work so good. Look, Meri, bring your materials with you to dinner on Friday and let the family look at them. They've been a pretty good barometer for your crazy ideas before."

"Friday. Dinner." Her sister hadn't heard anything she'd said. Or didn't believe her.

"You've got until the end of the month, right?"

"Right."

"Then, talk to Mom and Dad on Friday and make changes over the weekend. That still gives you plenty of time. You'll be fine. You always are."

"You're right, Janice. Thank you. Go back to sleep,

and hug the girls for me. I'll see you Friday. G'night." She carefully set the phone down.

She hoped she'd be fine.

She reached for the phone once more. "Jim? I need you." She waited. Nothing. Not a whiff of spice. "Jim? We have to talk." Empty room, the ornate clock ticking away. "I'm sorry I snapped at you. Please come back."

The air beside her shimmered and two dark eyes, complete with cocked eyebrows, appeared.

"Good, you're here." Meredith reached toward the handsome face coalescing before her. As her genie slowly formed, her heart caught in her throat. "What's wrong with you?"

Jim had appeared, but he was faded, almost transparent in spots. And there was a definite blue tinge to his otherwise tanned skin.

"The Chairman of the Board was not pleased."

# *Chapter Seven*

## *"Djinn Rummy"*

"Jim!" She touched his arm. Still solid. "You need to sit down. Here." She led him to the sofa. "What happened?"

Jim leaned back, staring at the ceiling. "My boss. He doesn't appreciate my unique skills. You know, a little on the stuffy side. A stickler for the rules." He coughed. "Can't deal with new ideas."

"Are you going to be all right?"

"Sure. Don't worry about me. Djinni are very resilient. Have to be to last as long as we do. We might be panting but we go on granting." He closed his eyes.

"I am worried. We've got a deal, Jim. I'm good at marketing, but I've never tried working with expired clients." She sat beside him and took his hand. "You're cold." She felt his forehead. "I think you're going into shock." Assuming genies did things like that. "Here, lie down." She pulled out a pillow and

135

maneuvered Jim into a horizontal position. "Put your feet up."

"Better. Much better." He opened his eyes slowly. "I've got to go before the ERB."

"What's the ERB?"

"Ethics Review Board."

"Why? What have you done?"

"I told you this wish of yours was going to be tough."

"You also said you could handle it."

"I can. I can. I just need to recharge. Get the ol' genie circuits firing on all cells again." He propped himself up on his arm. "It isn't your wish so much as my liberal interpretation of the number-three. Plus, the Chairman of the Board was not amused by my intervention with your pal Glenn. He wants the ERB to give me a refresher course." He squeezed her hand. "Not to worry."

"Right." She took a deep breath. "I take back my wish. I'll wish for something else entirely." It wasn't that she didn't really want true love, but it seemed excessive to spend a life making a wish come true. Even if that life belonged to an infuriating, sexy genie. Especially if that life belonged to an infuriating, sexy genie, her mind corrected.

Jim shook his head. "I wouldn't let you do that, even if you could. I'd never be able to hold up my head at reunions if I gave up now." He shrugged. "Anyway, you'd probably wish for simple things, like a better wardrobe, or an original O'Keefe to hang in your garage. I kinda like taking on difficult wishes. Besides, I'm having too much fun giving you a hard time to quit now." He raised the corners of his mouth in a wicked grin.

Jim squeezed her hand lightly, and then began to massage the hollow of her palm with his thumb.

Meredith felt heat steal through her body. She closed her eyes and reveled in Jim's tender ministrations. He was definitely not cold anymore, a part of her brain noted in wry amusement. Another part of her, a less cerebral part, longed to stretch out beside him, to feel his warmth all along her body. Bad idea. Meredith extracted her hand gently. "Look," she said, "this suite is available for the whole evening. Why don't you stay here and rest, and we'll talk about the ERB tomorrow."

"Thanks, Meredith. The ERB will be finished with me long before tomorrow. But, I would like to relax." He grinned mischievously. "You could rub my tummy. It would help me recharge."

Meredith cocked her head. "Really?" Jim had lost his transparency, and the blue had been replaced by his normal healthy tan. "Are you sure you're not just looking for more sympathy?"

"Aw, you caught me." He smiled, blinked and disappeared. "It was worth a try."

"Well, there you have it." Genies bounced back rapidly, she was glad to know. She looked around the suite. Without Jim it seemed very empty and impersonal. She yawned. Home. Sleep. Mere mortals needed more than a tummy rub to revive.


"Stanley, for a small cat, you take up too much room. I'm putting you on a diet." Meredith turned over in bed, nudging the warm lump beside her. "Move over."

The lump shifted and opened its eyes. "Sorry."

"It's okay," Meredith mumbled, looking at the warm, brown eyes luminous beside her on the pillow, but not registering their presence.

She closed her eyes.

She opened her eyes. "What are you doing in my

bed?" She slid to the edge of the mattress, almost falling on the floor for her efforts, and grabbed the blankets to her.

"I couldn't sleep. The ERB was hard on me."

"Jim, what am I going to do with you?" She saw several possibilities flit through his warped, genie brain.

"I don't suppose you'd . . ."

"No."

"What if I . . ."

"Don't even think about it."

Jim leaned on his elbow and reached toward her. His strong, warm hand rested gently on her shoulder. "I only wanted company. It gets lonely in that phone." He blinked slowly.

"I don't doubt it, but you could give a girl some kind of warning."

"Sorry. The ERB wasn't just hard, it was horrible— the worst I've ever been through. I wanted to be close to someone who cared."

"Me?" She thought about the series of sketches she'd drawn. They all featured a certain genie. She couldn't seem to get his image out of her mind.

"Right on the first guess. Except you were sound asleep, dead to the world. Down for the count. Guess I got drowsy watching you and thought I'd catch a few winks myself. Listening to you snore lulled me right to sleep."

He knew she cared. This might complicate things. Especially since she didn't seem to be able to focus on finding love even *with* Jim's agreement to accompany her to Hertzenstein. All she seemed able to concentrate on was Jim. And now, with him so close . . .

"Thanks. I appreciate your not mentioning my less ladylike qualities." She tried to use sarcasm to put a little distance between them. "Speaking of which, if

I don't get a full eight hours, I'll snore through my own presentation."

"I thought your snoring was cute." Jim trailed a finger along her collarbone, stopping at the base of her throat. His touch *was* soothing. "You know, I can think of some things more relaxing than sleep."

She narrowed her eyes. "Are you making a pass at me?"

"For a human woman, you're very appealing. By the Soul of the Flame that created me, I swear I can't figure out why all these men keep leaving you."

She sighed. "It's simple. They're threatened." She had to turn this conversation away from the all-too-appealing possibilities of what to do with Jim in her bed.

"That's too simple."

She thought a minute. "They don't want competition?"

"Doubtful. These are all very successful men. Competition should spur them on, not run them off."

"I'm difficult. I demand instead of ask. I'm not demure and quiet and feminine." She smoothed her hair out of her eyes and tried to ignore the sensuous tango Jim's fingers were completing down her arm. "I'm not merely decorative."

"And you think men want that? The merely decorative?"

She shrugged. "I suppose."

"I think you don't give men enough credit. Take a look at things from their point of view."

For the briefest instant, Meredith was sickeningly dizzy. Then, her head cleared and she saw herself lying on the bed, the blanket and sheet pulled severely up under her chin. Her/Jim's fingers stopped at her wrist, picked it up and brought it to her/Jim's lips. Whether it was the sensation of looking out of

Jim's genie eyes or the shock of seeing a frightened Meredith huddled beside her/him, she/he closed her/his eyes tight.

"Make it go away. Please." Vertigo washed over her and she was in herself again. She shuddered.

"I think you're afraid of being vulnerable with a man. Afraid he'll stomp on your heart with steel-toed boots and then leave it, flub-dubbing on the floor."

Tears stung her eyes. How could someone she'd known less than a month know her so well? Understand her so accurately? She'd fought and clawed and battered her way into a position of relative equality in a man's world. She was afraid to be soft and feminine. Afraid she wouldn't know what to do, she'd spent so much of the last ten years competing.

"Of course you'd know what to do." Jim finished her thoughts.

"You read thoughts, too?"

"Only under very special conditions."

"Well, butt out. These thoughts are mine and only mine." Slowly, she slid out of her bed and put on her silk robe. "I'm going downstairs." She'd finally found a man who understood her and didn't mind that she had a demanding job. A man who cared about her enough to watch her sleep. A man whose existence depended on her falling in love with someone else. Too much reality was not what she needed.

"Don't go. Please. Stay here with me." Jim took her arm and gently guided her back into bed. "Let me make the fear go away. You can trust me. We're a team, remember?"

She was shaking. With cold or with anticipation, she couldn't tell. She allowed Jim to pull her into his strong arms and hold her against his broad, muscular chest. Her shivering back pressed against his warm skin. He pulled the sheet and blanket over them both and held her, his touch light but searingly hot, his lean muscular body spooning hers. He kept insisting that he wasn't a man, but her body couldn't tell the difference. He felt male, sounded male.

Suddenly overcome by vulnerability, the events of the past week finally catching up with her, she turned in his embrace, buried her head in his shoulder and wept.

He stroked her hair. "I knew there was something more going on than worry about a simple meeting." He kissed the top of her head.

"Jim," she sniffed. "What are we going to do? It's Monday again, already. I've run off a man with perfect teeth and a man with a perfect family. Not to mention my cat. Where are we going to find someone who wants to fall in love with me?"

"Ah, you're worried I can't grant your wish because of my energy fluctuations. Don't. Being close to you, like this, restores my powers."

Great. She had a future as a battery-charger for limp genies. "You're still coming with me, aren't you? To see the duchess, and then to the Gala?" She pushed away from him. "You're not going to abandon me, too?"

"What? A genie leave his post of duty? Never. I'd be shot at dawn. Or boiled in oil. Or forced to listen to Abba for an eternity. I never leave a job incomplete." Not until the final curtain falls.

Meredith sniffed and reached for a tissue. "Good. It's too bad the men in my life aren't as trustworthy as you are."

"Well, we've been looking in all the right places for a man. Perhaps we should look in some of the wrong ones."

"What do you mean?"

"You've spent your adult life linked up with career

# Karen Lee

builders. Maybe what you need is a fully successful man whose career tends to itself. Someone who can, actually, appreciate just you."

"I suppose it's possible. Only, I don't know any men fitting that description who aren't already attached or who don't have legions of bubbling beauties hanging off of them."

"Or, you might be happy with a bad boy," he speculated. "You know the type. Black leather on taut muscles and a powerful motorcycle between their legs. They scoff at rules. They're exciting, dangerous. Unpredictable."

"Like you?" Meredith grimaced. "I have enough unpredictable events in my life, thank you." She smiled at the thought of introducing a renegade to Horton and his cronies. She cocked her head, trying to imagine Jim in black leather. It wasn't difficult and it made her hot with excitement.

"What's this I detect? An unspoken fantasy?"

"No. Definitely not." It was too easy by half, envisioning her genie decked out like Marlon Brando, and twice as appealing. She shook her head. "No."

"Okay. We'll work on the first one, then." Jim leaned close and kissed the tip of her nose. "Stick with me, babe."

She looked at him and, without thinking, reached up and ran her hand through his tousled black hair. Before he could react, she pulled his face to hers and kissed him. A quick, electric meeting of two sets of lips—one human, one fantastical. Realizing with a start that she'd been wanting to kiss Jim for days, she deepened their contact carefully, slowly.

For his part, Jim matched her enthusiasm, his free hand molding the back of her head, his long fingers tangled in her hair. His was more than simple friendly comfort. The kiss sang of passion promised.

Her brain danced with vivid images of bodies mingled, of shining, bright silks, of spangled stars blasting through ebony skies. Of genie and girl, together in a brilliant cloud of sensuous cinnamon.

She broke the kiss, suddenly overwhelmed by the possibilities that lay stretched beside her. She would not let herself fall for this thief of Baghdad. That way lay failure. For both of them. Her heart hurt with the knowledge that this graceful, kind man would leave her at the end of their month together, one way or another. If she got involved with her genie, she'd never find her true love. "Jim."

"It's okay, Meredith. I understand." He cradled her face, stroking her brow with his thumb. "Sleep. We'll talk in the morning. Sleep now."

She closed her eyes, settled back into Jim's comforting embrace and fell into a deep, contented sleep.

Her alarm announced the dawn. Meredith stretched and reached for Jim. She found instead a sleepy black and white cat who didn't appreciate the early hour and let her know it with short meow. Stanley stretched, looked at her with slitted eyes and curled back into a fuzzy pile.

"Jim?" Where was he? She shook her head as she reached for her workout clothes. He had been there. She remembered his kiss too vividly to have imagined it. And she was fairly confident it hadn't been Stanley's shoulder she'd wept against. "Jim?"

She finished tying her sneakers and stretched again. She needed to focus on the meeting with Horton. A solid workout would clear her mind and allow her to concentrate better. Sweat always helped. She'd missed too many mornings, lately. It would be good to get back to the gym, chat with the regulars, check in with her personal trainer.

She wandered down the curved staircase, flipping

on lights and wondering where her genie was lurking. There were no signs of him, though, no spice scent, no blue aura. She shrugged. He must be sleeping. She'd kept him up late. "Sleep tight, djinn."

At the gym, Meredith chose her favorite stationary bicycle and started pedaling. She selected a program designed to prod her red blood cells into a brisk gallop. As her heart rate increased, she sipped water and sopped perspiration.

And thought about Jim.

He'd been so understanding and calm in the face of her emotional breakdown. Just the qualities she'd always looked for in a man. He'd listened to her rant and not tried to talk her out of it. He'd been comforting and gentle, with just the correct amount of passion and no more.

Lying close to him, she'd known immediately that his human form was completely male, and yet he'd respected her need to be close but not physical. Although she was certain he would have complied with her wishes—wasn't that what genies were for?—if she'd wanted him to.

Kissing him was unlike anything she'd experienced. He was focused totally on her. He didn't have last week's football scores rattling around in his head, or thoughts about rotating the tires, or nagging strain about unpaid bills. His whole being was hers, dedicated to her pleasure.

The sheen of sweat she toweled away didn't come entirely from the exercise. *You can't fall in love with a genie. Remember that.*

A thrum of excitement made her look up. A cluster of gym babes in black and pink spandex giggled around the free weights. Meredith sat up, straining to see who they were encouraging. All she could see was the occasional flash of male muscle encased in blue. She shook her head.

"Excuse me, Meredith? Meredith Montgomery?"

She gave up watching the tangle of feminine curves and swung her attention to the man standing beside her. "Yes, I'm Meredith. Do I know you?" She'd seen this man around the gym, but couldn't put a name to his sweaty brow.

"I was hoping you'd remember me. We met at an Internet conference last month." He tossed his towel casually over one shoulder, and Meredith couldn't help but notice that the black muscle shirt he wore certainly earned its name on this man. "I'm sorry to interrupt your workout, but I wanted to make sure it was you." He extended his hand. "I'm Karl Tiburon."

"Oh, Mr. Tiburon. You gave a presentation on the expanding market opportunities. I guess I didn't recognize you without your clothes." How could she not have remembered him, the single most successful man in the Capital region, president and CEO of a conglomerate of companies that expanded almost daily. He wasn't as wealthy as Bill Gates, but what was a few billion among friends?

Tiburon chuckled. "Look, I'm sorry I disturbed you. I don't want to interupt your workout, but I am looking into a new project and your name has come up a few times as someone I should talk to. I was hoping to meet with you about it, and when I thought I recognized you across the room, I figured there was no better time than the present. Do you have any free time in the next few days?" His smile was sincere.

Meredith smiled. "I would love to get together." That didn't come out right. "How about tomorrow

145

afternoon? I don't have my calendar with me, but I believe I'm free around three."

"Good. See you then. Your office." He nodded ever so slightly and departed, his stride balanced and feline.

"Well." Maybe Jim was right. She needed successful rather than climbing. Her workout interrupted, she mopped perspiration from her forehead and neck and headed for the locker room. What a pity he had seen her in this state, sweat-soaked T-shirt and straggly hair.

Although he hadn't seemed to mind. Her heart danced a step or two. Jim would be safe after all.

She longed for a hot shower. Fortunately, it was early enough that the showers were empty. She picked the largest one and stepped in, dropping sweaty T-shirt, bra, panties, socks, shoes and shorts on the floor.

The water pummeled her back as she stretched and thought about Karl Tiburon. What could he need her advice for? She squirted shampoo into her hand and began washing her hair. She'd have to wait until tomorrow afternoon to find out.

As she rinsed billowy suds from her hair she realized that the fragrance of her favorite shampoo had changed subtly—it definitely had overtones of cinnamon.

"Jim, you promised never to interrupt me in the shower."

His darkly handsome face emerged from the steam. "It's okay. I'm blindfolded."

"Right. Like I believe that makes a difference." She turned off the faucets and grabbed her towel, winding it around her slim frame. "I was done, anyway." She snagged a second towel and dried her hair.

"Ready for the big meeting this morning? I assume you've read the presentation?"

"Why else did I drag myself out of the phone and spend an hour levitating circular hunks of iron, impressing the women and amazing the eunuchs in this quaint seraglio."

So, it had been her genie causing the commotion this morning. "Oh, Jim, you're priceless." Meredith chuckled into her towel. "This isn't a harem."

"Could have fooled me. Lots of lovelies, muscular guys guarding the entrances. The only thing missing is the sultan himself—and an explanation of why you're part of his brood." Jim had fully materialized at this point, sans blindfold and lounged on the bench in the changing area of the shower stall. Since he wore only a towel wrapped around his waist, Meredith couldn't help but notice what an enticing picture he presented. Water dripped from his black hair and ran in rivulets across his muscular chest, making sensuous patterns in the hair that covered it.

Meredith cocked her head. "Am I the only one who can see you?"

"If you like. Why?"

"Because this is the women's locker room. No testosterone allowed." She laughed as Jim blushed, then disappeared. "See you at the office."

Jim thought briefly about making all the chairs in the conference room disappear. That would make for a short meeting. He still couldn't understand why humans insisted on all these stupid meetings. This was the third one Meredith had been to in a week and a half—all of them too long and all of them about the contest between her and Griffin. For once, though, Jim admired Meredith's fashion sense. It baffled him how such a talented artist could have such a blind side as to how to showcase her coloring and beautiful features with clothes. But today, she had gotten it right. Her rich, plum-colored wool suit set off the highlights in her red hair well, and the conservative off-white scarf arranged carefully at her throat gave the whole outfit a distinguished, pulled-together look. Meredith looked like the perfect image of a corporate executive; she radiated confidence. Jim enjoyed seeing this side of Meredith. Although, he'd also liked seeing another side of her in the shower this morning. He hadn't lied about being blindfolded; it had just slipped a little—before she'd had a chance to cover herself with the towel, he thought with a satisfied grin.

"Darcie, you remember Jim." Meredith brought Jim back to the present.

"Darcie. Good to see you again." Jim bowed low over Darcie's hand, not quite kissing it. "How am I doing so far, taking care of your Boss Lady?" He raised an eyebrow.

"You must be doing fine. She looks relaxed for once." Darcie's eyes twinkled. "Not herbal tea, I assume. What kind of magic are you using?"

Jim decided to cut back on the charm. "Oh, you know. The old-fashioned kind."

Meredith had turned to greet someone else, but now she had her head cocked at them, as if she wondered what they had been chatting about so quietly. "Darcie, do you have time for lunch, or is Francis keeping you too busy to spend time with your former boss?"

"I think I could sneak away for a while."

Meredith nodded as Darcie piled Griffin's presentation on the table and turned to greet Bill Horton as he entered the room. William Peterson Horton had presence. It wasn't that he was overly tall, Jim decided. It was more in the way he carried himself, he had a proud and confident bearing. He reminded Jim of the kings he'd served in centuries past. His steel-gray hair and neatly trimmed mustache added to the aura.

Francis Griffin, a full foot shorter, was right on Horton's heels. Jim detected irritation in Meredith's expression and knew Griffin was up to no good. He extended his hearing and listened in on the end of their conversation.

"So, of course those problems, having gone undetected for so long, are what will cause difficulty between Meredith and the duchess. Insurmountable, I'm afraid."

"Thanks for the heads-up, Francis. I'll be sure to ask about that."

*Hmmmm.* Why did Griffin have details about Meredith's meeting? Wasn't the duchess supposed to be her assignment? What had happened to Wyoming? He was confident Griffin and Meredith hadn't switched prospective clients.

"Meredith, good morning." Horton shook her hand, smiling. "And this must be your new assistant I have been hearing so much about." Horton turned to shake Jim's hand. "I am glad we finally get to meet. Meredith has been hiding you away, not letting you come to any of our other meetings."

Jim reached over to grasp Horton's hand. "Pleased to meet you, sir. Working with Meredith has been an experience."

"She's a delight, isn't she?" Horton glanced sideways at Griffin. "A powerhouse of energy is our Meredith. Let's get started. I've got another meeting in an hour." Horton sat at the end of the long table and folded his hands.

"Please, Meredith," Griffin said. "You go first. I be-

# Karen Lee

lieve you've got more material to cover." He smiled. Darcie, seated beside her temporary boss, raised a shoulder in a "Sorry, I can't control him" kind of shrug.

"And how would you know that, Francis?" Meredith asked.

"Just trying to be friendly. No need to snap." Out came the handkerchief.

Meredith looked to Horton for confirmation. When he nodded, she stepped to the laptop and began her presentation. "You know the background of the assignment in Hertzenstein and the challenges." Meredith clicked on her first slide and stepped back. "So we're not going to spend time on that." Deftly, she moved through her presentation, highlighting the promising results of her approach. "I should tell you, Bill, Darcie helped with the research for this part of the presentation."

Darcie smiled. And Jim grinned. How like her to share the credit for a job well done. What a shame the Chairman couldn't adopt that management style.

Griffin raised his hand, the class troublemaker looking for attention. "Ah, what about your revenue projections for other European locations? Could you break those down for us?"

Meredith narrowed her eyes and moved to the white board. "Do you want those by country or by tourist group?" She smiled sweetly, making swift columns of numbers.

Jim watched her commanding presence and licked his lips. He'd used those lips last night to excellent purpose. She was the single most extraordinary woman he'd met in his centuries of existence, and he'd met many. She was strong, yet vulnerable. Focused, yet confused. Challenging. A puzzle to be solved, a riddle looking for an answer. He, the djinn she'd named Jim, had an answer. He needed just the right moment to . . .

"Dr. Goodman? Jim? What are your thoughts on this market-penetration strategy?" Meredith pinned him in his chair with a sea-green stare. "Jim?"

"Huh? Oh, yes. I'm sorry. I was reconsidering the packaging options for first-class airfare. What was the question again?"

"Bill was wondering if the market strategy was too aggressive for our main target group, the British. With your expertise on English affairs, I thought you might want to field this question."

"Ah. Yes, of course. Excellent question, Bill. Quite perceptive. The British generally prefer a cautious approach, but with the program Meredith has outlined, it is my belief that the target market will eagerly put aside their traditional reserve and spend their hard-earned pounds." Jim smiled at Meredith.

"Hmmm. I see. Fine job, Meredith." Horton shuffled his papers into a tidy pile.

"I have one more question." Griffin smiled, but Jim could detect no humor behind his eyes.

Meredith shook her head. "I wish I knew what you were up to, Francis. Why are you asking questions when Bill is obviously satisfied with my progress so far?"

Wish. Wish? She'd made a wish! He didn't bother to ask her if it was a real wish; the emotion underlying her statement left no doubt in his mind as to the veracity of her request. Jim shifted into action, moving to stand behind her. He opened her mind, letting Griffin's life play out in front of her eyes. Black and white images of Griffin appeared against a blue background: Griffin playing three-card monte in the school yard; Griffin copying answers from a cheat sheet while taking a high school final; typing up a false resume. All his foibles, all his mistakes, all his compromises. Everything that brought him to where he was today—sabotaging her project so he'd get the promotion.

"How could you?" Meredith could barely control her voice. "Is the promotion worth that much to you?"

"What are you talking about?" Griffin began to gather his papers. "Bill, I think we should postpone my presentation to give Meredith a chance to calm down." He pulled out his ubiquitous handkerchief once more to catch the trickles of sweat on his face.

"Calm down? I'm about as calm as I can be, given what I know about your sleazy life."

"Meredith, what's wrong?" Bill Horton stood, clearly shocked. "What are you saying?"

She faced Griffin. "Tell me about your meeting last week with our top competitor, Gordon-Stern. Getting pointers for your trip to Wyoming, or selling secrets?" She was shaking. Jim stood behind her, supportively close.

"How in the world? What would cause you to concoct such an outlandish story?" Griffin leaned toward Horton, his handkerchief damp in his hand. "I told you she was under too much stress with this duchess thing."

"So you did. Meredith, how do you know that Francis has been giving confidential information to Gordon-Strunk?"

"Because Jim . . ." Jim realized she couldn't tell Horton how she knew. He'd never believe her. He owned a whole company; he was more technology-bound than she.

"Because your new assistant said so?" Horton looked questioningly at Jim.

"Exactly, Bill," Jim said. "I was working late several nights in the conference room next to Francis's office and I overheard a couple of phone conversations."

"He's right, Bill," Griffin admitted. "I did talk with Gordon-Stern, but only because the head of their systems group is a friend of mine. We set up a golf date, that's all. In fact, you're welcome to join us if you're available." The perspiration threatened to turn into a flood.

Oh, he was smooth, this viper in their midst. But Jim was no stranger to the sneaky ways of the wily, and he knew there was more than one way to catch a snake. It was time to take a different tack.

"I'm sorry. Perhaps I was hasty in my conclusions. It is possible that I misunderstood the content of the call." Jim tried to ease the tension in the room as he pushed another piece of information into Meredith's head.

"Thank you," Griffin said. "Meredith, I know we're rivals for this promotion, but accusing me of selling company secrets? I didn't think you would stoop so low." Griffin leaned back, a satisfied smile on his face, his nervous flush fading.

Meredith took a deep breath. "Bill, I apologize. My outburst was very unprofessional. However, you should talk with Francis about potential mergers with Gordon-Stern. I'm sure you'll find his ideas most enlightening."

Francis sat up straight, glared at Meredith and sputtered, "She doesn't know what she's talking about, Bill. Why can't I use my relationships in the industry? They have valuable contacts in Wyoming. Gordon-Stern is a partner in a deal, that's all." He grabbed the stack of papers in front of himself with a shaking hand.

"Really? And what deal might that be?" Horton returned to his seat and leaned back, waiting. "I'd be very interested in how our biggest competitor has turned into our partner."

"I'll leave you two to discuss this in private. If you need me, I'll be in my office." Meredith gathered her presentation, smiled and left the room.

Jim bowed slightly, arched an elegant eyebrow and followed her into the hallway. He hated leaving Darcie with the piranha, but he had no choice. Meredith leaned, shivering, against the wall. He swept her into his arms. "I think that went rather well, all things considered," he said.

"Thanks."

He released her as Darcie came out of the conference room. "Whew! After this, I'm going to need that lunch, Meredith." She scurried away.

Loud voices erupted from inside the conference room. Griffin could be heard protesting his innocence and trying to place the blame on Meredith. "How could she know if she's not involved?"

"I trust Meredith implicitly. It's you I'm worried about. My office, ten minutes." Horton did not sound pleased.

Both men exited the conference room and brushed past Meredith and Jim. "You're not out of this yet, Montgomery. I'll see you fired for interfering with my plans," Griffin threatened once Horton had moved out of hearing distance.

"You made a wish," Jim said as they entered Meredith's office.

"So I did. And you granted it. In spades."

Jim cocked his head. Slang phrases were so difficult to keep up with. "Spades? As in digging implements?"

"No, as in cards. You know, hearts, diamonds, clubs, spades? You filled in my royal flush."

He shook his head, thoroughly confused. "I know England has a queen, but I thought the United States was a democracy. How can royalty be flushed?"

"Never mind. Now that I know about Francis, I've got to be especially careful with this project."

Jim hurried to keep up with her. "That bad?"

"Worse." She sat at her desk. "He knows about my desperate search for true love and plans to hold it up to Horton as a primary example of my inability to handle the promotion."

"That's rubbish. One thing has nothing to do with the other." Jim sat on the desk next to her and took her hands. "Trust me. I've got a plan."

"Instant love, just add water?" She radiated complex, confused emotions. First, satisfaction that the presentation had gone well. Then, frustration that she couldn't pin Francis to the wall. Then, sadness. It was the sadness Jim couldn't reconcile. "It better be fast-working, whatever it is." She picked up her office phone and listened to her voice mail, and then closed her eyes as if in pain.

"The duchess's secretary called. Someone told the duchess my proposal was simply recycled from last years' Iceland project and that I was too busy to be original. I'm supposed to call her back tomorrow so we can talk. It was Francis, of course, but I can't fix that now." She sat down and put her head in her hands. "I don't know what to do now, and we're running out of time."

# Chapter Eight

## "Djinn Sing"

"Boss Lady, you look terrible." Darcie frowned at Meredith, who sat toying with her chicken Caesar salad, dressing on the side, hold the anchovies. Today Darcie had her copper hair pulled back from her face, gathered in a clump of curls behind one ear.

"I've got a lot on my mind." Like a duchess who was very real and a true love that didn't seem to exist.

"I don't know what Horton said after the meeting this morning, but the Cookie Dough Troll is not happy."

"Cookie Dough Troll?"

"It fits, don't you think? Francis is shaped like a lump of cookie dough and has an attitude like a troll—without a heart." Darcie sat back. "It helps me keep a balanced perspective on life in general, and working for Griffin in particular."

"Can I ask you a sticky question?" Meredith squinted one eye over her forkful of romaine lettuce.

*Meredith's Wish*

"And I want an honest answer, please." On the way to the restaurant, she'd had the beginnings of a crazy idea.

"Sure. Ask away. The only questions I can't answer are ones that might be construed as spying on the Troll, or tattling out of class."

"I respect that. The question doesn't have anything to do with Francis Griffin and his malodorous management ways. It's about Jim."

"The excellent Dr. Goodman?" Darcie chortled. "His name sure fits him. He is fine, fine."

"He doesn't appear odd to you? Different?"

"Different as in handsome, strong, intelligent, articulate, attentive, gorgeous—different from any man I've ever met or would hope to meet? That kind of different?"

"No. Different as in, well, unreal."

"What are you talking about, Meredith? Your Mr. James is a fine specimen of male pulchritude, with a generous serving of gentleman on the side." Darcie folded her arms on the table, abandoning her Death by Chocolate dessert, momentarily. "Are you sweet on your assistant?"

"Well, I don't know that I'd label it 'sweet,' more like spicy." Meredith held up her hand. "Don't say it. Darcie, sit down."

"I am sitting down."

"Jim Goodman isn't a doctor."

"You mean he's not a medical doctor."

"He isn't any kind of a doctor."

"Could have fooled me. I can surely see him as a Doctor of Love. I know he's a genius. I filed the briefing papers from this morning's meeting with Horton. I could see your work, but Jim's efforts were brilliant."

157

"No, he's not a genius. Well, yes, he is in some ways."

"Anyone who can make the Troll scowl-o-meter peak for over an hour has to be a throwback to Einstein."

"Really? What made him scowl the most?"

Darcie described several graphics. "But the marketing model irritated him more than anything."

"Thank you, Darcie. That was my work."

Darcie nodded. "I thought I recognized your signature ruthlessness. But Jim, ah, he's, well . . ."

"He's charming, lovely to look at, delightful to hold."

Darcie's eyebrows shot up.

". . . and I have to return him at the end of the month."

Darcie frowned. "You make him sound like defective software. Pity. I thought you two made a nice couple."

*Me, too.* "Sorry. This assistant came with an expiration date." She paused. "He's agreed to come with me to visit the duchess and he *is* coming to the Gala. Please try not to drool on him." What were the penalties for falling in love with your genie in this race for the corner office? She didn't know.

But she so badly needed another head, another opinion. She was falling under the djinn's spell. And that wouldn't do at all. In her mind, true love should last longer than the end of the month.

"What am I going to do?"

"About the Troll? I wouldn't worry overmuch." It was Darcie's turn to lean forward. "*I* think he's planning to leave the company."

"Really? Who would have him?"

"He's been very secretive, but I think that's why he's been talking with Gordon-Stern."

"They're welcome to him. Then I get the corner

office and the new title, and you get the office with a view next to mine." She'd need all the help and understanding she could find once Jim left—especially if he failed to grant her wish.

She was beginning to wish she'd never spoken the infamous "I need a man" speech. But not quite.

She wondered if there was an outside chance that Karl Tiburon would fill the bill. How much maneuvering would that take? And, could she be convincing with images of Jim dancing in her head. Only one way to find out.

She shoved back her salad plate. "Darce, it's been great talking with you. I've got an important meeting tomorrow afternoon with, well, with a man who is almost as charming as Dr. Jim, and a good bit more stable." She signaled the waiter. "Lunch is on me."

"Thanks. I knew I liked working for you. Who's this man of mystery?"

"I'll let you know if, or when, it works out." She fished money from her bag and stood. "Let's walk back. It's such a lovely day."

When she returned to the office, there was voice mail waiting for her from the mystery man himself. She dialed Tiburon's number.

"Karl Tiburon, please. This is Meredith Montgomery returning his call." She waited while his secretary connected them. "Karl, hi. It's Meredith Montgomery."

"Meredith, thanks for calling back so soon. Listen, I can't make it tomorrow. The board of directors has some claim on my time. I'm really sorry. I was looking forward to talking with you. However"—she could hear him smile—"my evenings are my own. What would you say to dinner tonight at Morton's. Around eight?"

Even better than a business meeting. Dinner

would be more relaxed. "That would be fine. I'll meet you there."

"No, let me pick you up. E-mail me directions to your house. I'll be there, say, seven-thirty."

"Sure. That works. Give me your e-mail address." After she'd hung up, she sat quietly for a moment. Here was a man who was definitely his own person, someone confident with his achievements in life. Needing to share her latest news with Jim, she retrieved her cell phone from her briefcase. She hadn't heard from her genie in too many hours. She knew it didn't take long for him to find mischief and that she'd be in the middle of it.

She dialed. And waited. A second, two, ten.

"You called, oh, wondrous one?" Jim's voice was blurred and imprecise.

"Are you all right? You sound funny."

"Just tired is all. Your wish wore me out."

"I thought it would revive you. Don't you get credit for granting wishes?" This energy-drain thing was getting serious.

"Normally, yes. However, the ERB decided that your case was special. No out-of-order wishes. Your first one is unfulfilled still. Numbers two and three will actually subtract energy until number one is completed." He sighed. "It's the djinni way."

The djinni way didn't make sense. But then, not much in her life did these days. "I see. I called to tell you that the answer to number one may be in sight."

She felt Jim shift. "That's good news. Who is he?"

"I thought you knew. Didn't you steer Karl Tiburon in my direction this morning at the gym?" The multimillionaire certainly fit with their earlier discussion about searching out men who were successful rather than men who were still climbing.

"Tiburon? Not I, said the little blue djinn."

She paused. "Will the wish be considered granted if I find the man on my own?"

"Technically, sure, the wish is granted. I mean, you've got your man, the answer to the wish."

"I hear a catch."

"Nothing that would impact you, of course."

"But it has lasting ramifications for my djinn, right?"

"I don't get total credit for it is all."

"But the Chairman of the Board wouldn't hold you responsible, would he?" This was beginning to sound like a classic catch-22. He couldn't grant the wish because it was against djinni rules, but if the wish were to come true and he hadn't helped, he didn't get credit.

"The All-Powerful Chairman of the Board is an unpredictable force, Meredith. And, as his name implies, all-powerful. He might decide to take pity on me."

"But you doubt it."

She could feel Jim shrug. "I've worked for His Powerfulness for too long to anticipate the kindness required to let this slide past."

This was silly. "Let me talk to him. I deal with chairmen on a regular basis. Perhaps I could—"

"Absolutely not. Your role in this is to make wishes, not try to manage the process."

But she was good at managing. "I just thought it might help. If it won't, of course I wouldn't want to upset things." Jim had sounded slightly frightened, mixed with equal amounts of chagrin and stress. "Perhaps he needs some tangible evidence of your ability to add value to the djinni. Can you appear? It's easier talking to you in person. I've got some dynamite ideas for your marketing plan, all designed to soothe the savage djinn."

# Karen Lee

There was a slight popping sound and Jim stood before her in diaphanous, billowy pants, a jeweled belt supporting a sinister-looking scimitar. His head was swathed in an elegant turban, a single blue topaz hanging in the middle of his forehead. His arms, wrists banded in wide gold, were folded across his chest. Which was barely covered by a short, red vest.

She swallowed, her throat suddenly desert-dry, all thoughts of plans, marketing or otherwise, vanished. "Is this a new look? My cultured assistant might sport a goatee, but an earring?" If he'd been handsome in a suit, this costume-party outfit really emphasized his best assets.

"You mentioned a marketing plan. I thought a traditional look would fit the public's preconception better than tweed and a pipe." He turned around slowly. "What do you think?"

Meredith stood up. He was wearing funky pointy slippers. She could barely breathe, so strong was her impulse to throw her arms around him and kiss him all over. "This is great," she managed to croak. *Control, Meredith, take control.* She opened a desk drawer and extracted a camera. "Let me get a picture or two to give to the art department. They're working on some ad copy and this will set their minds ticking." She focused the lens. If the guys in design didn't like them, she could use them as refrigerator memories when this was all over. That thought dampened her sudden infatuation. "Shouldn't you be holding your lamp or something?"

"I live in a phone, remember? How about a magic carpet?" A miniature version of her red Turkistan rug wove into existence and floated next to the genie.

She moved across the office, snapping pictures. God, he was gorgeous. "Turn sideways and give me one of your raised-eyebrow looks. Great." She paused. "Does that thing really work?"

"The carpet? Absolutely. Of course this isn't the latest model. The Chairman of the Board hasn't released the turbo version to mere field operatives yet, but this baby can deliver." He waved his hand and the carpet lowered itself so he could step onto it. As it rose, he sat, legs folded, slipper points almost touching his knees. "Want to take her for a spin around the city? You haven't seen Washington and the monuments until you've seen them from a magic carpet."

She glanced at her watch and set down the camera. Well, why not? "Let me get my coat. Whoa! Urfph. Oof." She was seated in front of the genie, his arms strong around her.

"You don't need a coat. I'll keep you warm."

That was what she was afraid of.

They floated around the office. "How are we going to get out? We can hardly slip past reception undetected."

"Not to worry." He spread his fingers toward her window and the glass disappeared. They sailed through the opening into the afternoon sun.

Dipping down over the Roosevelt Bridge, the carpet headed up the Potomac, gliding along at treetop level. "Don't we need clearance from the FAA or something? What about violations of airspace?" Meredith leaned back against the solid chest of her genie.

"All taken care of, my dear. They think we're a weather balloon," Jim murmured into her ear, his warm breath hinting of spice and adventure.

"Are you sure?"

"Have I let you down yet?" He straightened. "Don't answer that—I'm working on the wish thing."

"But, that's what I was trying to tell you in my office. Oh, my. Look at that." Meredith pointed to the crews of Georgetown students rowing enthusiastically down the river.

"Duck!"

"Where?"

"No, duck down." The carpet banked right and swept an elegant turn under one arch of Key Bridge. They came up above the bridge and hovered, watching traffic build on its way into Virginia. "Isn't this a better way to navigate jams?"

Meredith nodded and snuggled into the genie's arms. "Definitely. Once around the park, James."

"All part of the standard genie tour package. Designed to bring the client the maximum experience with her djinn."

She raised one eyebrow. She had an idea of what her "maximum experience" might be, and she was sure it didn't include touring D.C.

They skimmed the top of the Lincoln Monument, pausing in front to view the great man in his chair. They turned loops around the Washington Monument, chased pigeons along the Mall, sideswiped the Air and Space Museum ("This is one flying object they don't have," Jim exclaimed) and coasted along the front of the Capitol Building itself, dipping a bow at both houses of Congress. They swept past the White House and headed out over the Tidal Basin.

The famous cherry trees were a riot of pink in the April afternoon. Above their branches she could see the white marble columns of the Jefferson Memorial. Its gentle, domed shape always reminded her of Monticello. Jim circled the monument, giving her a glimpse of the framer of the Declaration of Independence, frozen for all time in bronze. The carpet came to a gentle rest on top of the graceful building.

"Whew." Meredith held tightly to Jim, worried that he might let her go and she'd slip down the dome, then worried he wouldn't let her go and she would melt into a slithery puddle from the sheer excitement of his arms wrapped around her, his chest pressed solidly against her back. She thought her heart would pound clean out of her body. Magic-carpet riding with Jim was akin to flying in her dreams, only significantly more erotic.

Why couldn't *Jim* be the one to fall in love with her?

"So, you liked my tour?"

*Liked it?* It was only the single most exotic, sexual, sensual thing she'd done up to that moment. The undulating motion of the carpet slipping effortlessly over the air felt, well, intimate. She leaned back into Jim's embrace. "Yes."

She'd been up in a hot-air balloon once, floating free and silent, but flying with Jim was more intense, more exhilarating. With Jim, the responsibilities of her job, her worries about the duchess, indeed everything that weighed her down, were gone. Jim's strong but gentle arms offered sanctuary from the stresses of her daily life.

Sitting between his outstretched legs, she rested comfortably against his chest. The soft hairs of his goatee tickled her neck as he whispered in her ear, "I'm pleased. I've felt lately that I have been more trouble to you than help, what with the Glenn incident and all. I wanted to show you another side of me."

"So far, I like this side of you." She twisted at the waist and reached up to place her hands on his shoulders. "And this side." She knelt between his legs, brushed her lips against his. "And especially this side."

# Karen Lee

She traced his eyebrow, allowing her fingers to slip around his neck and pull him to her. She closed her eyes as their lips met once more.

He matched her pace, hesitant at first, then more insistent, as though resisting the temptation of her kisses and then finally giving in.

As their kiss deepened, Jim lay back on his carpet, bringing Meredith with him. She slid her hands under his vest, exploring by touch the muscles she'd admired since the day they'd met. "You're all the man I'll ever need," she whispered, "no matter how often you tell me you're just a djinn."

He trailed kisses, soft as sunlight, across her forehead and down her cheek. "You realize this will never work," he murmured.

"It's working now." She rolled onto her side, running her hand across his shoulder and down his arm. She caught his hand in hers and kissed his palm, the gold cuff cool on her cheek. She saw passion in his eyes. Passion tinged with hesitation.

She couldn't do this. If she fell in love with Jim, she guaranteed his total failure.

The mood spoiled, Meredith straightened. "You're right, of course. I shouldn't have . . . I'm sorry."

"No apology necessary. I could have stopped you." He pushed a wisp of hair off her forehead. "I wanted to kiss you—I want to do a lot more than just kiss you." His eyes moved away from hers, looking off into the distance. He was silent a few moments, his expression more serious than Meredith had ever seen it. Then his eyes returned to her face and he gave her a small smile.

"I shouldn't have taken you away from your work."

"Oh, no. I loved it. I needed something to break up my day. You know I get too intense about my work.

166

It was wonderful. I enjoyed it immensely." Truth be told, she'd enjoyed it too much.

Jim smiled, his white teeth a startling contrast to his tanned face. "I'm glad. I like making you happy." With that, he enclosed her in his arms again. The carpet executed a vertical takeoff the Pentagon would have been proud of and flew back to Meredith's office.

Standing once more on solid floor, Meredith swayed slightly. Jim caught her, looked deeply into her eyes and drew his thumb along her eyebrow and down her cheek. "I'll be sad to leave you, Project-Meredith."

For an instant, Meredith saw more than mischief, more than physical passion in Jim's eyes. Just behind their intriguing darkness was a flicker of caring.

"You can't leave without your marketing plan." She went to her desk and picked up a blue folder. "It'll make good reading tonight. It's not complete, of course. I'd like your input. Then we can make changes, tailor it to your exact goals, and, of course, there's the layout from the ad people to be included. You can plan for your triumphal reentry into the good graces of the Chairman of the Board."

"You're cute when you talk marketing."

"Why, thank you."

"What are you going to be doing while I'm slaving over your brilliant scheme to reintroduce magic to the world?" He thumbed through the pages, paused at the graphs and smiled.

"It's what I've been trying to tell you all afternoon. Karl Tiburon, self-made millionaire, has invited me to dinner. He wants to get my thoughts on some new product ideas for one of his many companies."

Jim closed the blue folder. "Tiburon. I guess you'll want to try this one solo?"

# Karen Lee

"You mean, no helpful genie suggesting menu items and offering advice about beds and pillows?"

"Yes. Well, it was the thought that counted." He held up the folder. "I want to spend some time with this at any rate. You can handle things with Ol' Karl and I'll learn about product endorsements."

Meredith slipped up beside Jim and put an arm around his waist. "Not to worry. I'll be fine tonight."

He sighed. "Better to get half credit and not meddle than to meddle and get none at all, I guess. Still . . ."

"Half credit for Karl and a full-blown, well-conceived marketing plan will fix all your troubles."

For a long moment, Jim locked gazes with her, his brown eyes growing darker by the heartbeat. "I doubt this will be as interesting as your evening, but"—he bowed low—"I wish you love." He swirled into a brief cloud of blue smoke and disappeared.

She wasn't certain, but she thought she detected a twinge of sadness in his voice. It was possible, she conceded, that Jim's feelings were as strong as hers. For an instant she allowed herself to imagine that there was a happily ever after in their future, then stopped. "Forget it, Montgomery. The only way you can give Jim any kind of ever after is to find true love. Someplace else."

Jim paced the small confines of the cell phone, the blue folder with Meredith's marketing plan abandoned in a corner, next to the extra memory chip. He was behind on his reports to Headquarters and his energy was low. Again.

He remembered a lecture in Advanced Conjuring about severe energy drains and their causes. It had nothing to do with wishes out of order, or retracted

168

wishes, or wishes at all. Severe depletions of djinni power were a result of only one thing.

The diminished djinn had begun to care about his human. To be sure, all red-blooded genies were expected to dally with their humans, and he'd had no trouble encouraging his djinni libido where Meredith was concerned.

Involvement with humans wasn't discouraged. Given their long and glorious history of mischief, djinni frequently took advantage of tangled human emotions, human sexual drives. In practice, such activities came under the heading of General Nuisance. Actual caring? That was definitely unacceptable.

The ERB had spent considerable time questioning Jim about his *feelings* for Meredith. Not about his tricks, his jokes, his amusing scampishness. Those qualities they had no quarrel with. It was his *feelings* for this person.

He'd begun the job with a well-honed contempt for all things human, just as any good genie would have. He'd followed it with pranks and general deviltry, all standard operating procedure. It was the way he'd begun to actually *care* about Meredith that worried the ERB.

He'd had the temerity to *understand* that she needed art in her life. And, she wasn't bad, either. He'd peeked at her sketch of himself. She'd managed to get the devilish gleam in his eye just right, and even Leonardo hadn't been able to capture that.

The ERB didn't care. They were concerned. How about the designer dress? He could just as easily have let her wear any of the ones in her closet, but *he* wanted her to feel special. *He* wanted her to be beautiful. For *him*.

And the kissing? The caressing? The very real desire to consummate the relationship? All these were acceptable djinni practices. As long as these actions were precipitated by healthy djinni roguishness, they supported the eons-old reputation of djinni as Master Rapscallions. The ERB was certain to suspect their brief encounter atop the monument this afternoon. He'd begun to have very real, very deep human feelings for Meredith.

Jim sat on a chip and held his head in his hands. What was he going to do? He wished he could just turn the "I care" switch back to off. His buddies had always warned him it would happen one day. He'd never believed them because no one had ever seen a genie fall for a human. Oh, there was the legend of the genie who took on so many human emotions that he turned into one, but that story had been invented to scare young genies, to keep them in line. Lately, however, he'd begun to wonder if there wasn't a kernel of truth in that tale. Just look at him—energy siphoned off with increasing frequency as his feelings for Meredith increased.

He was a one-genie energy crisis.

"The solution is obvious. If I stop caring, I run at full power. If not, the Chairman won't have to worry about snuffing me out. I'll have done it myself." He stood and paced once more. "I'll just have to quit caring about her."

If only it were that simple.

# *Chapter Nine*

## *"Dry Djinn"*

Meredith sat at her vanity, putting the finishing touches on her makeup. It was Thursday evening, the middle of week two in this nutty soap opera that had become her life. She had three days to stoke the fires of love with the good Mr. Tiburon, decide whether or not it was love of a true kind and save her djinn from a fate worse than living in a cell phone.

"What a crazy week this has been, Stanley. I haven't had this much social life since I can't remember when. And after tonight I've got to face the family—with a genie who claims mothers love him." She zipped her skirt and straightened it. "I'm going to have to talk to Jim about Mom and her fixation on my getting married. It wouldn't be fair to unleash her without prior warning."

She wondered briefly whether or not to warn her mother about Jim.

She looked in the mirror, tipping her head to one side and then the other, evaluating the impact of her new shade of lipstick. She normally didn't worry about this kind of thing, but with Jim's life on the line, she couldn't overlook any effect that might help. "Passion Spice." Should work.

Then, of course, there was Francis. What should she do about Francis? She'd made an appointment with Horton for the next morning. She had to learn the outcome of his meeting with her rival. And fill in the details Francis would most certainly have neglected to mention.

"Well, Stanley, what do you think?" She stood, circled slowly in front of her cat and watched his gold eyes. "What, no comment? I just spent the better part of two hours fussing over my appearance and you have the temerity to simply lounge on the end of the bed and clean your face?"

Stanley's pink tongue stopped momentarily as he regarded Meredith. He closed his eyes and began washing himself once more, as if to say, "You're on your own."

She really wanted Jim to be there. To tell her she had no taste in clothes. To joke with. To talk to.

She looked back in the mirror, half expecting him to grin out at her. Once more, she reviewed the sable-colored suit she'd chosen for the evening. It still said "business meeting" more than "could you love me," but she was comfortable with that approach. Besides, the V-necked, green silk T-shirt with a touch of lace at the neckline made the ensemble less stark, more approachable.

She heard a car stop in front of her house. "Too late to change now, Stanley. We're cleared for launch. Or dinner." She chuckled, gathered her evening bag and went to answer the door.

Tiburon hadn't sent the typical black Cadillac. It was a classic Rolls Royce almost the same color as her suit. *Good choice, Meredith. Always thoughtful, dressing to match the transportation.*

As Tiburon's chauffeur walked up to her door, she ducked back in. "Forgot something. Be right back." Seconds later, she emerged. "Can't go into a business meeting without my phone." *Or without a genie, just in case.* She smiled and peeked into the backseat.

"Where is Mr. Tiburon?" Meredith looked closely at the chauffeur, trying to see through his obligatory dark glasses. He was about the right height to be Jim.

"Señor Tiburon's meeting is running late. He told me to assure you he will be waiting. Is there something wrong, Señorita?" He held the door, motioning her into the car.

"No, you reminded me of a friend that's all." Perhaps Jim really meant it when he said she'd be going solo. She climbed into the luxurious Rolls.

The chauffeur nodded, tipped his cap and slid behind the wheel. Meredith settled into the deep, leather seats.

The phone embedded in the armrest rang. "Please answer it," the chauffeur directed. "It will be Señor Tiburon."

She picked up the receiver. "Karl?"

"Meredith, forgive me. My business frequently eclipses my personal plans. I trust you are comfortable and Enrique has seen to your needs?"

Enrique? Ah, the chauffeur. "Everything is fine, Karl. This is quite the automobile."

"I prefer classics. So often the modern is merely slick. Classics retain a charm I find pleasing."

"It is elegant, to be sure."

"Because of this meeting I have decided it would

be preferable for us to dine at my home. I hope that is acceptable."

Warning bells went off inside her head. A change of location to something more personal might be good, or might spell trouble. Still, desperation fueled bravery. "That will be fine. I've always wondered how business moguls lived."

Tiburon chuckled. "Just like normal folks. You should be here in about twenty minutes. There's wine in the refrigerator if you want some. Bottled water if you prefer."

She heard the phone click, the connection broken. *Well, there you have it. Normal indeed. Normal people didn't have antique Rolls-Royces and drivers.* She took a bottle of expensive water from the cooler, opened it and then leaned back and decided to enjoy the ride.

The interior of the car was expansive. Plenty of legroom Meredith realized as she stretched out. Plenty of room for Jim to come popping in, offering advice, warning her about Tiburon's less-than-honorable intentions . . . Where was that dratted genie? He'd made so many appearances at her other "dates," this evening seemed somehow empty without him. She hoped he was feeling better.

She thought about the last two weeks. It had been one of the most unorganized, unplanned periods of her carefully structured life; she held on to her sanity with calendars and clocks, anticipating every eventuality. Not recently though. With all the twists and turns and unexpected surprises that had wreaked havoc with her schedule lately, she should be a nervous wreck. She wasn't.

Jim had somehow changed her ability to deal with chaos. He introduced quirky thoughts, unstable events and an otherworldly humor that disarmed her. She noticed that the tension in her shoulders, which was standard this far into a week, had not developed. Maybe she should try relaxing more often. Maybe genies were good for the soul.

Or the heart.

When they arrived at the Tiburon estate in the horse country west of Manassas, Virginia, tall wrought-iron gates swung open to admit them. A long, winding drive lined with blooming dogwoods marked the way to the house. Through the growing dusk she could see mares with their newborn foals, grazing peacefully in the verdant green fields. The car rounded one more curve and the house came into view.

*House, ha! More like mansion.* Meredith tried not to stare at the tall columns of the building Tiburon called home. It didn't work. The house sat on the crest of a hill that provided a sweeping view of the valley. As she exited the Rolls, Meredith could see stables and what she assumed were guest quarters to the left.

"This way, Señorita." Enrique guided her to the front door.

The entrance was palatial, with high windows and a jungle of green, growing things—tall palms, orchids and bird-of-paradise carefully placed in nooks and niches. Outside, the Tiburon digs looked like antebellum South; inside, they held the warmth and mystique of the Southwest. She stood on terra-cotta tiles and held her breath. "Wow."

"Most people have that reaction." Karl Tiburon emerged from his leafy bower. "I thought adding plants would make it less imposing, friendlier."

"The tropical forest exhibit at the Baltimore Aquarium should be envious. I keep expecting parrots to swoop down." She paused. "Butterflies at a minimum."

Or an AWOL genie.

"I thought about that, but there's no way to restrict the wildlife to this part of the house. Besides, the floors get so messy." He tucked her hand into the crook of his arm and led her through the foyer into the main part of the house. "I'd be delighted to give you the ten-cent tour while we wait for dinner." A proper butler emerged from the shadows and took her coat.

"A tour would be delightful." She nodded, her hand warm on his arm. An opportunity of immense importance, this evening was one she'd only fantasized about, walking through an extraordinarily elegant mansion on the arm of a successful, wealthy, handsome man.

She waited for the bells and fireworks. For that flutter in her stomach that indicated the first attack of chemistry between two people. Nothing. Question was, did she need chemistry if her goal was saving Jim? Did true love announce itself with clanging gongs? Or, did it sneak up and tickle your ear with cinnamon breath? Maybe after dinner things would be clearer.

"You know, you are a remarkable woman, Meredith. I've watched your career with great interest." He swept her along the broad hallway. "This is the library."

Meredith entered what was clearly a man's room— deep forest green leather chairs flanked a matching wine-colored sofa. A huge bowfront curio cabinet revealed a collection of antique Pueblo pottery.

"I didn't know anyone but me was interested in my career."

"You might be surprised by the impact you've had in this industry."

For a second Meredith stopped, trying to judge the

accuracy of his statement. Impact? She'd have to think about it. She gazed around at the shelves of books. There were thousands. She walked toward a display of oversized volumes and ran her finger along a binding. "May I?"

"Certainly."

She pulled a book from the shelf and opened it. Lush illustrations greeted her. She turned a page and jumped. Jim's face grinned out from the figure on the color plate.

"There you are. I've been worried about you." Meredith whispered into the pages of the book.

"You enjoy Burton?" Tiburon stepped closer to Meredith and looked over her shoulder. "His *Thousand and One Arabian Nights* is one of my favorites. It's a first edition." He turned a page, revealing another exquisite rendering of Jim. "The illustrations are especially elegant." He pointed to the genie forming out of the spout of a gold lamp. "This one, for example, is representative of the fanciful imagination that created the magical stories."

"Yes, isn't it?" Snapping the book closed, Meredith was sure she heard a muffled "Ow!" reverberating across the binding. "The genie's so lifelike, he almost jumps off the page." Was he here? Or had he posed for the illustrations some hundred years ago? She returned the volume to its place and continued to study the different titles, her heart fluttering wildly.

Typical. *Now* she got palpitations. When she looked at an illustration in a book. Not when she needed to capture a real man's heart. What had her genie done to her?

A library ladder leaned conveniently against the shelf, offering easy access to books higher up. "I've always thought it would be fun to ride around a room on one of these wheeled ladders."

# Karen Lee

"My daughter tried it when she was about five. Crashed into the edge of the fireplace and broke her arm. She's had a solemn respect for ladders ever since."

"I didn't know you had a family."

"Only Estelle." In answer to Meredith's inquiring look Karl said, "Her mother died several years ago."

"I'm very sorry. Will your daughter be joining us for dinner?"

He chuckled, a low, sonorous sound. "She likes to keep track of her father's female guests, to be sure, but she's in Barcelona studying art at the University."

As he spoke, they walked through the library and into a sitting room. The walls were hung with an eclectic collection of paintings, ranging from cubist to art nouveau and back to romantic. The place had the feel of a museum.

"Are you happy in your position at Horton Consulting?" Tiburon's voice was low and friendly. "I wonder sometimes if they know what a talent they have in you."

"Lately it's been challenging. But, there are rewards to be had for hard work." If he was her true love, she should probably turn this conversation away from careers and toward caresses.

"Indeed." He took her hand. "It is a shame, isn't it, that our careers leave us so little time to develop the relationships that bring true happiness." The man was a mind reader—surely a characteristic of her true love.

She looked into his chocolate eyes. They reminded her of another set of brown eyes. The ones that belonged to a genie who seemed to be ever present, at least in her mind. Nervously, she motioned to a painting. "That looks like a Picasso." She moved closer. "It is a Picasso."

"I hope you don't find my collection pretentious."

"That old thing? Heck, no. I've got a Monet hanging in my bathroom." Of course, it was a print from the National Gallery and not a signed original. She looked at another painting, a portrait. She couldn't be sure, but the somber Spaniard seemed to wink at her and raise a Jim-like eyebrow. She thought of the sketch she'd started of Jim in full genie regalia. It would never hang in a gallery, but it would always be close to her heart.

Karl put his hand on her elbow. "You have such a delightful sense of humor." They moved from the gallery. "This is the morning room. It's situated to catch the sunlight when it's fresh and new."

"Does it have a matching afternoon room?"

Karl laughed. "Yes, actually. The solarium across the hall."

They wandered from room to room, Karl providing a warm tour-guide commentary. Finally they stopped at the base of a sweeping staircase.

"Up there are the family quarters and my private office." He led her to the dining room. "If you wouldn't mind waiting here while I let the kitchen staff know we're ready to eat."

"No, not at all." Meredith sat and glanced at the clock. Eight-thirty. She hadn't seen Jim since their wild carpet ride around four, if you didn't count the book and the painting. She'd expected him to at least masquerade as the butler or something. But he was seriously absent. Karl was charming, but she was worried about Jim. How could she know if Karl were her true love if she couldn't keep her mind on her subject?

She took her cell phone from her purse and dialed.

"Hi. You've reached the House of Djinn. We're not

home right now. Please leave a message after the beep. Beep."

"Jim, stop playing around. I need your advice."

"Jeez, can't a djinn catch forty winks in peace? I thought you had it all under control. After all, you found this one."

"Yes, but . . ." What was she going to say? She'd grown accustomed to having Jim around? Missed his quaint quips and quibbles? Wanted to see him grin at her, wanted to breathe the fragrance of a djinn at work?

"But what?"

"I'm kind of out of my element here and I wanted your wise counsel."

"Wise, am I now? Well, three things. One, he's a man. Two, you're a woman. Three, do what comes naturally. Good night." There was a click and then dead air.

"Jim, you rat, don't desert me." Fine. If that was the way he wanted to play it, she'd show him.

"Business call?" Tiburon entered the room. "See what I mean about careers interfering? Put the phone down, Meredith, and enjoy your evening. We'll talk business after dinner."

She smiled up at him. "If we have time for business." He drew away. Great. Now she was blowing a career opportunity, too. "I only meant that to successfully discuss new products and new markets, we really should get to know each other better."

"Of course. Forgive me. It's just that so many beautiful young women see me simply as marriage material. I sometimes forget that it's possible for beauty to be backed by brains and talent." He pulled out her chair for her. "Shall we?"

Throughout the meal they laughed, talked, exchanged ideas and enjoyed themselves. Meredith relaxed, deciding to let things take their course, and forgot about Jim.

Almost.

Until Karl talked about his last trip to Saudi Arabia, the wonderful coffee he'd brought back with him, not to mention the luxurious carpets. She could guarantee his didn't fly.

She forgot about Jim until she tasted the saffron rice with shredded carrots, raisins and cardamom. The subtle fragrance brought his image vividly to her mind and teased her nose with his scent.

Except he wasn't there.

She didn't think about Jim at all after the main course was completed. Then Karl offered her dessert—sopaipillas with honey and cinnamon. She could taste her genie's lips, feel his presence, and yet, Jim was in hiding, disguised as an electron.

"Meredith? I asked if you'd ever been to Buenos Aires." Karl rose from his chair. "Let's talk in the library." They carried their coffee with them and settled on the soft leather sofa.

"No, I've never traveled in South America. I'm sorry I seemed distracted. I was just thinking of a friend."

"He must be a special person to command your thoughts." He set his coffee down. "And a lucky one."

"He's a business associate, nothing more." She smiled. "You said you had ideas you wanted to discuss."

"Yes. Actually, ideas and people. I'm spinning off a division of my company into its own corporation and I'm looking for a consultant to review the marketing strategy. I wonder if you know Francis Griffin."

Unfortunately. "Yes, he works at Horton Consulting with me. He heads up our consumer markets practice."

"Tell me about him."

And spoil a perfectly decent evening? What to do? She knew Francis was dealing under the table with several competitors and that he was a lying, cheating snake, but she couldn't really tell Karl that. "I don't know Francis that well. We've been friendly competitors for about eighteen months. I know his group always comes in under budget and generally exceeds revenue projections." But only because he hires the cheapest labor available and underestimates sales.

"I see. How does he handle pressure?"

From his reaction this morning, not well at all. "He tends to react quickly by asking for more information if he's not sure of his position. He stands by his people." As he watches them being consumed by lions. "I know Bill Horton has been spending a lot of time with him lately."

"If you were me, would you want him analyzing one of your companies?"

"I'm not really in a position to say, Karl. I'd need to know a lot more about your company and your expectations."

"Such poise. You know more about this man than you reveal. For instance, I expect you know he left his last position under cloudy circumstances that could have resulted in his being fired." He settled back in the cushions. "I also know his qualifications are overblown. And so do you. However, you manage to handle my questions deftly."

It was not information most prospective clients could discover. "You flatter me, Karl. You know so little about me." A silent butler moved to refill their cups with coffee.

"I know more than you might expect. I know, for

instance, that you have supported your mother and father through some financially troubling times. That you put yourself through college and graduate school. That you are one of the most creative marketing minds in the region." He smiled modestly, "I know a little about you. And I like what I know."

Meredith studied her coffee cup, running her finger around its delicate rim. "You've done your homework." Very few people knew she'd financed her own education. Karl must have great sources. If you had the money, you could afford private spies.

"I like to be informed when I'm contemplating a business relationship with a person. Or a company."

She frowned slightly. The evening had been so promising, yet confusing. Every time she thought he was warming to her in a personal way, he turned the conversation back to business. When they discussed work, he always managed to color his comments with hints of interest beyond just work. Well, it was simply going to take more time. There were no singing choirs, but she was comfortable with him. She'd have to figure out how to turn the conversation to more personal topics. To save a genie, think like a genie.

"You find that objectionable, Meredith? I expect you do the same when you're analyzing opportunities."

"Yes, of course I do. I know you own two dozen companies outright, have controlling interests in a dozen more and are probably looking at a small Internet venture to round out your portfolio." And you're a cool operator, smooth and charming.

He raised his eyebrows. "Very good. I'm pleased, although I expected nothing less. I wonder, however, if your tact in talking about your colleague Mr. Griffin isn't hiding something. Be frank with me, Meredith."

She could hear Jim's taunting whisper in her head, "How in the world can you be Frank? You're Meredith."

"Not to avoid the question further"—Meredith gave a small, self-deprecating smile—"but could I freshen up in the powder room and then we can talk?"

"Of course. You remember where it is?"

She nodded and left the library. *What to do?* Karl was charming, patient, considerate, handsome, and obscenely rich. If she encouraged him she was certain she could move his interest to a more personal level.

Jim would be safe, sound and back in the djinn business, assured of a place in the new djinn hierarchy. She was doing precisely what she had promised him she'd do.

So why did she feel so lousy about it?

*Finally,* thought Jim. *She's going to be alone.* He'd cooled his heels in this cramped phone for the entire evening, mostly behaving himself, pledging again his support for all things djinni. It hadn't been much fun. A genie without mischief was a genie without purpose.

On the other hand, a genie without a job was, well, not.

His last conversation with the All-Powerful Chairman of the Board had been memorable down to the last and finest detail: Don't interfere with Tiburon, stay out of Meredith's way, allow these simple humans to come together naturally or suffer the consequences.

And so, he'd been very busy not interfering, staying out and allowing. He hated every second of it.

# Meredith's Wish

He paced between VLSI chips on the printed circuit board, alternating between boredom, worry, and moments of sheer panic. What if Meredith actually succeeded with this Tiburon person? Jim knew he'd spend eternity wondering. Wondering what it would have been like to be with her. Wondering if she was happy. Wondering if she cared as much as he did.

What kind of name was Tiburon, anyway? Spanish for shark. She'd better watch herself. Sharks had a nasty bite.

Had a djinn ever had to choose between two such agonizing alternatives? First, let Meredith fall in love with Tiburon and lose her forever, but save his own useless being. Or, second, blow up the blossoming relationship and claim Meredith for his own, but cease being altogether. He clenched his fists in frustration as he sat on a yellow capacitor and bounced along in Meredith's purse. He bumped his head against the back of the battery when she tossed her bag on the counter.

Ouch! She must be really aggravated. He needed to be sure that she was okay. He closed his eyes and disappeared.

He could see Meredith clearly from his vantage point on the antique vase where he posed as an ancient Greek athlete. He hefted the short but deadly javelin carefully. If he aimed it just right he'd be able to catch her attention.

Meredith sat in front of the mirror and snatched a tissue from the gold box on the vanity. She dabbed at the corners of her eyes. Were those tears he could see glistening at the edge of her lashes?

He reached back with the javelin and heaved it. The weapon, life-sized compared to Jim's diminished stature on the vase, was actually about three inches long. It sailed across the room, glinting in the mirror, hit Meredith's bag with a tiny *ploink* and clattered onto the marble surface like an overlong needle.

"What?" Meredith picked up the tiny missile and turned it in her fingers. "Where did this come from?"

"Psssst. Over here," Jim whispered from the surface of the pottery.

"Jim? Where are you?"

"Here. On the Grecian urn."

He watched her puzzled reaction as she walked toward the terra-cotta pot next to the bronze Etruscan helmet. He shivered when she touched the rim of the vessel he decorated, and exhaled in frustration when she looked inside.

"Not in, *on*. I'm busy winning the first Olympics here." He stomped the painted ground with a resulting dull thud.

Meredith leaned to get a closer look. "On the pot."

"An indelicate phrase, but accurate." He leaned back against the figure of a lion and crossed his long legs. "How are things going?"

"Things are fine." She stared at the black figures on the ancient vessel. "Why are you imbedded in pottery?"

"There haven't been a lot of openings for extra help in the Tiburon staff. Your Karl has a keen sense of security. Besides, I needed to recharge."

"I can't talk to terra-cotta. It'd be a lot easier face-to-face rather than squinting at a stick figure."

*Stick figure? Rather cheeky, and thoroughly insulting.* "Whatever you say, Meredith." Jim stretched, reached out to the lip of the vessel and pulled himself out of the clay. Immediately he expanded, like a sponge soaking up water, and stood in front of her, arms folded across his broad chest. "Better?"

"Good God, you're naked."

"Well, yes, I am." He posed, looking at himself in the mirror. "Absolutely appropriate for Olympic athletes in 776 BCE." He flexed his biceps, moving from one weight lifter's pose to another. He gave Meredith a half smile. "Not bad for an old geezer." He tossed his head and his tightly curled hair barely moved.

Meredith pulled her gaze back to Jim's laughing eyes. "Not bad for a young geezer, either. No wonder you caused such a stir at the gym."

"It's what I do best." He coughed slightly, and leaned back against the counter. "You wanted to talk."

Meredith appreciated tanned, developed muscles as well as the next woman, and Jim's were especially outstanding. With him standing there looking like Adonis ready to pounce on Aphrodite, she was finding it difficult to remember why in the world she wanted to talk. There were so many other tempting options.

"Uh, right." In fact, she couldn't think at all, looking at his body. Maybe if she concentrated on his lips, her head would clear. But that brought Technicolor memories of his kisses and flustered her even more. "Talk. Yes." Perhaps she should focus on his eyes, or the end of his nose.

"Meredith?"

"I'm fine."

"Liar."

"Couldn't you put on a towel or something?" She pushed the box of tissues toward him. "I can't think around all this skin."

Jim looked at the box, extracted a tissue and held it in front of his most intimate anatomical feature. He shook his head. "Obviously, this won't work."

She turned away, closed her eyes and took deep breaths.

"You can look now, I'm as decent as a djinn can be under the circumstances."

She pivoted. The black Speedo bathing suit just barely qualified as decent and left nothing to the imagination. "I've seen more fabric in a package of dental floss," she said.

"You don't like it?" His smile faded, replaced by a hurt, lost-puppy look.

Her emotions were frayed at best. What she needed was understanding, not pouting.

Jim stepped forward, turned her so they were both facing the mirror and enclosed her in his arms. "I'm sorry. I know you're under a ton of pressure, and that you're trying very hard to save me." He rested his square chin on top of her head. "I was only trying to add a bit of levity. You look so serious." He kissed her hair, nibbled on her ear. It was obvious that his pledge to stop caring about her had failed.

Meredith relaxed back into his embrace. "And I enjoy your antics."

"But not tonight."

She looked up at Jim, pulled his head down and kissed his cheek. "Whatever will I do without you?" It was what she wanted to do with him that clouded her normally sane judgment. She moved the kiss from his cheek to his lips and he responded.

Just when she thought she couldn't stand it anymore, he pulled back slightly and gazed at her with undisguised longing. He ran a trail of kisses along her forehead, moved down her cheek and whispered, "I think you're doing quite well. Without me."

"I'm not sure. Karl is a delightful man, sophisticated, articulate. He likes music, art." Her breath caught in her throat.

How could something as simple as a kiss on her neck be so damned devastating? She looped her arms around Jim's neck, pulling herself closer to him, hip-to-hip.

She'd been right. The black Speedo hid nothing.

"He's attractive and wealthy," Jim murmured in her ear. "I'd say damn the torpedoes." His hands trailed down her back and caressed her fanny. "Head him off at the pass and close the deal." Slowly, he began to push his hips against hers.

She gasped. A tight coil of red-hot desire unwound in the pit of her stomach. Then she remembered: She couldn't do this. Not with Jim. She wouldn't compromise his very existence for the powerful sensations he stirred. With a great deal of effort she pushed herself away from him. "We can't do this."

"Why not?" His cinnamon breath tickled her neck. "I've tried it before and I know you won't be disappointed." He caught her earlobe in his teeth.

"Stop. Please." Oh, how she wanted him to drag her to the floor and have his way with her. But there were priorities. His life. Her wish. His life.

Abruptly, Jim stood away from her, dropping his arms to his sides. "As you wish." Passion smoldered in his eyes, barely under control. He took a deep breath. "You're probably right. We shouldn't do this. It always leads to trouble." He stepped away and leaned against the wall.

She coughed. "You were saying something about a deal being closed?"

"Right. Tiburon. He could be the one, you know. But you've got to make the moves. There is your promotion to think about."

"And your own career, don't forget. But there doesn't seem to be a deal to close. I'm not sure where Karl is headed with this evening. It's been a quasi-social, mostly business kind of time." She felt her heart slowing.

"He's not interested in a personal relationship?"

"Right. My sense of the evening is he's been conducting an in-depth interview. I think he may want me to consult on a business venture." Which would give her more leverage at Horton Consulting.

"That would just about seal my fate. I hope this marketing plan of yours is as good in execution as it reads on the page, because we're going to need a series of minor miracles to keep my head out of the soup."

She smiled up at him. "You read my plan?"

"Every word, comma, chart and graph. I especially like your ideas for the series of media ads." He paused. "I wonder if I could get the Chairman of the Board to let me come back and pose for the print ads."

"It has to be you. Who else could pull it off?"

"Indeed. I can see me now, reclining on my magic carpet, adorning the sides of city buses across the world."

She saw Jim reclining on her bed, adorning her life. The powder room was still fresh with cinnamon and passion. She cleared her throat. "Interesting thought."

"I figured you'd like it." He kissed her forehead. "You have yet to sample the rest of my powers, you know."

Meredith tried to pull herself back to the present. "I have to go or Karl is likely to send out a search party. I am off to see if there's business with Tiburon Associates in my future. And you should begin preparation for dinner with my mother."

"How tough can that be?"

"You don't know my mother."

# Chapter Ten

## *"Djinn Haze"*

Karl drove Meredith home in his red Mazerati. In a neighborhood populated by BMWs, Lexuses and Mercedes, Meredith still felt very conspicuous in such a luxurious car.

"Forgive me for being personal, but you seemed distracted this evening. Is something wrong?" Karl draped his arm across her seat after he came to a stop in her driveway.

"Nothing I thought I couldn't handle." She watched the digital clock on the dashboard throw away seconds. "Horton Consulting is, at heart, a family owned company with family ideas." Her mother, for instance, would fit right in. "You know I'm in line for a promotion. What you don't know"—unless his spies were really good—"is that I'm the only unmarried executive in the company."

"Is that a detriment? From what I know about you, you're doing just fine on your own."

# Karen Lee

Yes, that was true. Why hadn't there been brass bands and angel choirs tonight? Why did she seem to have more in common with her genie than the men around her? She'd tried so hard not to be the proper businesswoman this evening, but it hadn't worked. "I suppose that's true." Didn't he understand that she wanted more out of life?

Karl was silent for a moment. "Perhaps this will help." He paused. "I was serious about wanting someone to consult on my new division. I want you to take it, Meredith. Write me a plan." He touched her arm gently. "I want Horton Consulting, because I want you."

She'd already put her heart in a plan. A plan to save Jim. But a sign, any sign that there was a spark, a hum, a bit of static of feeling on Karl's part would make her so much happier. Meredith opened her mouth to speak.

"Don't make a decision quickly. I'll send the details to your house tomorrow. You review it and, when I return from my trip to Sydney at the end of the month, we'll talk. I've spoken to two other firms, but I really want you to handle this for me."

Next month would be fine for her career, but with true love trotting to the end of the queue once more, it would be too late for Jim. The seconds on the clock piled into minutes. "Okay. I'll read it over."

"Good." Karl got out and opened her door. "I'm hosting a reception for some close business associates when I get back. I'd like you to come and meet these people. It won't hurt your career."

Meredith closed her eyes and saw her bridal bouquet go up in flames. No amor, por favor. "Thank you. I'd love to meet your friends."

"Good. I predict you'll do very well on this project, Meredith. I also predict that Horton Industries will

192

do substantial business with Tiburon Associates." He walked her to the front door, ushered her inside and gave her a quick kiss on the cheek. Then, he smiled and went back down the steps.

Meredith watched as he drove away, wondering why she wasn't more upset that his very proper kiss hadn't sent bolts of lightning up her arm. Any relationship that developed with Karl Tiburon would take time, lots of time. It was the one thing she didn't have.

She had until Monday and she was fresh out of candidates to swoon at her feet, declaring their undying love. Truth be told, Meredith knew there was only one man she wanted to hear declare his love, only one man who made her even believe in the possibility of true love. She shivered as she walked slowly through her house, listening for signs of life. In her treasure hunt for true love it seemed all paths led to Jim. For his sake, she sure hoped his boss was as impressed with her marketing talents as Tiburon had been.

"Meredith, pass your young man some more lasagna. He's hardly eaten a thing." Mrs. Montgomery beamed across the table at Jim. "Can't have him leaving hungry, now, can we?"

Meredith and Jim sat at her family's maple dining room table, covered now in her mother's best linen. Meredith groaned inwardly. Trying to impress the various men Meredith dragged home was a lifelong pursuit for her mother. Meredith knew she kept hoping for a proposal and a happily-ever-after marriage for her eldest daughter. It occurred to Meredith that the duchess and her mother had a similar reverence for marriage. She hoped they also shared a penchant for Jim. In fact, if her mother's reaction to Jim's charm was any indication, Meredith had little to worry about with the duchess. Jim had stormed the home front successfully, and Meredith suspected that the duchess's defenses stood little chance as well.

"Of course not, Mother." Meredith gave Jim her sweetest "Here you go again" smile and handed him the lasagna.

"No, thanks. Really, Mrs. Montgomery, I'm so full that there won't be room for that peach pie I heard you talking about if I eat any more. And if it is anywhere near as good as your lasagna, I definitely don't want to miss out." He sat back and stretched, filling the room with his presence.

Jim had been right. Mothers, or at least *her* mother, loved him. To be sure, her mother's lasagna was a neighborhood legend, rivaling Nona Mangione's as the most requested dish at summer potluck dinners, and complimenting her cooking always won a person points. With Jim, however, there seemed to be something else.

"I knew I liked you, Jim. Never quarrel with a man who likes peach pie." Meredith's father leaned over and confided, "The secret's in the crust. It has to be flaky. Georgia's melts in your mouth."

"Sam, don't bother the boy."

"Really, Mom. You'd think Meredith had never brought anyone home for dinner before the way you two are carrying on." Meredith's sister, Janice, began to clear the table, pausing to wipe tomato sauce from her youngest daughter's chin. "Lend a hand, won't you, Meri?"

Anything to hurry the evening along. "Sure. I'll take that, Dad." Meredith stacked a small pile of dishes and followed her sister into the kitchen.

"I'm glad you left your project at home this time.

It gives Mom and Dad a better chance to know Jim. He's really nice. He's even better than you described in your phone call." Janice ran hot water in the sink and added the dishwashing liquid guaranteed to give you smooth, lovely skin. "You know, I don't remember much from that call, other than your obvious enthusiasm for Jim. Now I can see why you're so impressed."

"Don't get too excited just yet. Jim's been doing some work for Horton. He was there when Mom called to set up dinner and agreed to come with me. There's nothing serious going on here, so put away your 'something blue' because you won't need it."

"You work too much."

The second favorite topic of conversation in the Montgomery household after Meredith's lack of a husband was her grueling work schedule. "I know. It pays the bills."

"Meredith, you know I appreciate what you did for the folks as much as they do, but you don't have to work so hard now. They're back on their feet and doing well." Janice scraped plates into the disposal. "Whatever happened to your art? You know, I'd really like you to do portraits of my girls. And the new baby when he gets here."

"A boy this time, huh? Harry will be happy. Speaking of people who work too much, when's he getting back from Cleveland?"

Her sister wrinkled her nose. "He'll be back tomorrow." She flicked suds at her sister. "As for the baby, we don't know for sure if it's a boy, but Harry calls him 'Zeke.'"

"Great. You'll have an Ezekia to go with Georgia, Roberta and Maxine." She grinned. Every time her sister got pregnant, she was certain it was going to

Karen Lee

be a boy. "I'll do a portrait of your girls. And their new sister."

Peals of laughter trickled into the kitchen from the dining room. "Do it again, Unca Jim. Do it again."

"Whatever is he up to?" Meredith leaned into the dining room just in time to see Jim pull a quarter from her niece's ear. And then one from her nose. He coughed and handed her two more quarters. As he dribbled the coins into her hand, they disappeared.

"Me next, Unca Jim. Me. Me." Jim repeated the trick for each of the three little girls, taking them gently into his lap one at a time to perform the feats of magic.

"How old are you girls? Seventeen, eighteen, and nineteen?" Jim grinned at the trio of small faces.

"Nooo." Georgia giggled at Jim's mistake "I'm seven. Maxine is five. And Roberta is three."

"Seven. Five. And three." As he spoke, Jim pulled sparkling quarters from the air. Seven for Georgia. Five for Maxine. And three for Roberta.

Nothing like a genie to keep the troops entertained.

Mrs. Montgomery entered the kitchen and began cutting the pie. "He's wonderful with the girls, Meri. I think you should option him before he decides to move on."

"You say that about all my boyfriends."

"Jim is special." She nodded to her daughter.

"Mother, please." Meredith blew a stray hair out of her eyes and picked up another dish to dry. "Jim and I are just friends. He came with me tonight as a favor. We don't even know each other well." At least her mother had waited until Jim had swallowed his first bite of dinner before she'd started her Standard Boyfriend Questionnaire. How serious are you? Are you gainfully employed? Do you like children?

"Nonsense. I know a perfect match when I see one. Just like I knew your father was perfect for me when I met him. He was standing there, at the counter in that little coffee shop, staring at me over the rim of his cup, and I just knew." Her mother took the dried plate and put it on the stack with the others. "Jim looks at you that same way."

"Don't faint, but I agree with Mom," Janice chimed in. "Haven't you noticed how he watches you? He listens to what you say. Harry never pays that much attention to my ideas."

"No, Harry is always distracted by your other charms." She smiled at her sister's trim figure. Three children and a fourth on the way and she still wore a size six.

"There are days I'd prefer he noticed my ideas." She patted her just-beginning-to-show stomach. "Face it, sis. You two fit."

"How did you two meet?" Mrs. Montgomery wiped the counter for the tenth time.

*Well, Mom, Sis, I wished him up and he appeared in a cloud of blue smoke, with his trusty flying carpet at his side.* "I told you, we met at work." Not entirely a fib.

She'd known him for two weeks and during those days she'd laughed more, been out of her office more, than she could ever remember. She was comfortable with Jim, and it was obvious enough that her family had noticed.

Yesterday, she'd taken the afternoon off and gone to Georgetown, where she'd sat on the banks of the Potomac, watching the people wander by. The time hadn't been wasted. She'd taken her sketch pad and had half a dozen scenes set down that would make satisfying paintings. She'd thoroughly enjoyed the sunny day, and had realized that she wasn't worried about the duchess anymore. Jim would be with her, and that meant almost as much as the contract.

"Tell us about his family," her sister prodded as she finished with the plates and turned her attention to washing the crystal.

Her sibling was famous for sticky questions. "He's an orphan." It was the easiest way to avoid that snake pit.

"All the more reason to welcome him to our family. He needs all of us." Janice handed Meredith a goblet to dry. "Just look at how he plays with the kids. He's a natural father."

She thought about Karl. Given time, she was sure she'd be able to break that businesslike coolness. Problem was, she didn't have time. Funny how she hadn't really needed time with Jim. In a few short weeks they had easily fallen more and more into sync. She could feel when his energy was up and knew what was bothering him.

Karl was a blank page. She knew a lot about his business posture but virtually nothing about his personal goals. He was stable and successful, but there was no zing.

Jim was unexpected, the squirt-gun shot between the eyes. With Jim, life was exciting. She never knew quite what to expect next. Increasingly, her physical reaction to her genie tended to pounding pulse, cold sweats, hot passion—all the bells and whistles. But no future.

"What was that you said?"

"Meredith, honey, you should learn to listen. I was saying how your father and I appreciate all you've given up to help us. But, now that our life is on track once more, we'd like to see you happily married as well."

"Mother, really. I thought we agreed that was a taboo subject." Meredith finished drying the wine-glasses. "If I meet my true love and he asks me to marry him, you'll be the first to know."

Jim thought dinner had been an unqualified success. "I told you mothers loved me."

They sat at her kitchen table, trying to recover from Friday night at the Montgomerys'. "More coffee?" Meredith refilled her cup.

"Nope. I've got a lot of work to do before this trip of ours. I'm not out of tricks yet, you realize. I'll find your true love." He gazed forlornly into his cup. "I hope."

"You know, it was weird tonight. Janice didn't remember the details of our conversation about you."

Jim sighed. "It's all very nice when they think I'm your faithful assistant at work, but people get weird when they find out you've got a genie in your pocket. They want to borrow your phone, like Griffin does, or help you formulate wishes. It's a drag."

"So you erased her memory?"

"More like clouded that part of it. She did remember me as Jim, after all."

Meredith shook her head and finished her cup of coffee. "I wanted to talk to her about our trip to Hertzenstein. I need some sisterly advice." She ran her finger around the rim of the cup.

He looked at her, a deep sadness in his eyes. "I've been thinking about that."

"Whoa, there, cowboy. You aren't going to bail on me, are you?"

"No, I wasn't planning to. But, I'm worried about the trip." He paced her kitchen, stopping to load the dishwasher with coffee mugs and spoons.

"What's to worry about? What's a Grand Duchess

or two for the man who charmed Mr. and Mrs.
Please-Marry-Our-Daughter Montgomery?"

How could he explain that posing as her husband
would mean he'd have to act like he loved her, like
he wanted to protect her and care for her? And that
was too darn close to how he actually felt. "It isn't
that." He came back and sat beside her.

"What is it, then? Do I need to make a wish to
satisfy some arcane djinni rule?"

"If you did, it would be a wish wasted. No, you'd
better hang on to the last one. You never know when
you might need a wish. It might take that to get the
duchess to sign your contract."

"Don't you worry about her. Heck, I've dealt with
bigger challenges than some old lady stuck in the
nineteenth century." She reached across the table
and stroked his hand. He jerked it back.

"Meredith. This isn't a good idea." More than anything he wanted her to touch him. But the Chairman
had lectured him on breaking off his growing fond-
ness and suggested in unpleasant terms that he'd
best do it *now*.

"Fine. If you want to abandon your project, that's
your choice, but don't expect me to try to explain it
to the Chairman of the Board when he comes asking.
If you'll remember, customer satisfaction was a big
part of my marketing plan."

He sighed. "Of course I remember." He stood and
sketched a bow. "As you command, oh, Mistress
Mine. I'll be your boy toy on this trip. Just be careful
what kind of games you play and don't break it." He
disappeared in a cloud of blue cinnamon.

Well. She definitely preferred the mischievous Jim
to the worried, silent one. And, once more he'd
avoided the topic of her talking with the Chairman.

But, she reminded herself with a smug grin, he had agreed to go. She'd have plenty of time on the trip to lay down a plan of attack for the djinni management team.

She hummed happily as she emptied the coffeepot and wiped the counters. Besides, she thought she'd figured out a way around the true love problem. Once she'd talked Jim into letting her meet with his All-Powerful Chairman of the Board, she'd dazzle him with the marketing plan, get him to agree that Jim was perfect to implement it, and, voila, Jim would be saved. Her contract would be secured and she'd be worrying which way to place her Turkistan carpet in her new office. And, she wouldn't need that ever elusive true love.

She went up the stairs to her bedroom with Stanley trailing at her heels. "You like him, don't you, Stan? He's very sweet and he's funny." The cat jumped onto the bed and curled into a ball. "Well, I think he's quite marvelous. I just need to explain to the Chairman of the Board that I was under extreme stress when I made that first wish. He'll understand." She checked on her image in the mirror. She hadn't met a chairman she couldn't charm into changing his mind. Jim's boss couldn't be much different.

As she prepared for bed, Meredith let her mind concentrate on her upcoming trip. She'd already made reservations for two, so that wouldn't be a problem. He'd probably want to ride along in her phone, but she needed him in the flesh. That word sent her thoughts careening off into an entirely different, and not unpleasant, direction.

If she had to have a bogus husband, Jim wasn't a bad choice at all. Her research on the duchess indicated she liked her men tall and dark. How could she not approve of Jim? After all, she wouldn't know he was a genie and she would think he was married. Signed, sealed and unavailable for comment.

They'd been invited to tea the day after their arrival. Tea with a duchess. It was a pleasant thought. Afterward, she would offer her formal presentation, and the duchess, having found Meredith happily married, would gleefully sign the contract. Meredith would hop on a plane and be back in time for golf on Friday. A whole two days early.

Wouldn't that frost Griffin?

She snuggled into her bed and patted her trusty cell phone, a satisfied feeling in her heart. First, she'd fix things with Jim's boss, and then pick up the prize from her own.

"Face it, Meredith, there's no way you can mess this up."

# *Chapter Eleven*

## *"Coffee, Tea or Djinn?"*

"How could I have messed this up so badly?" Meredith dumped the entire contents of her briefcase onto the airline counter, dribbling pens, paper clips and other paraphernalia all over the floor. Her cell phone fell onto the floor. "I know that ticket is in here somewhere." Why did all of her Mondays have to be like this? She looked to Jim for help.

He adopted an air of innocence and picked up the phone. "I told you, darling, that you needed to be careful with the tickets." He looked over Meredith's head to the exasperated ticket agent. "We're newly-weds off on our honeymoon. You understand. She gets a little rattled by all the emotion."

"Emotion my Aunt Patty's Pig! Someone took those tickets. They were right here in the pocket of my . . ." She reached into the zippered opening once more and pulled out two tickets. "Oh. Here they are." She began packing her briefcase once more. "Sorry."

She tried to smile at the long line of passengers waiting to check in, and was rewarded with a chorus of
scowls for her efforts. She was momentarily grateful
that the airline had segregated the first-class passengers from coach. That line was ten times as long and
looked dangerous.

"No problem, ma'am." The clerk took the tickets
and fiddled with the computer keyboard. "Any bags
to check?"

"Yes. These five." Meredith struggled with her
matching set of Louis Vuitton luggage, catching the
hem of her pale-yellow silk dress on the corner of
one. She quit fighting the recalcitrant garment bag
and looked at Jim. "You could help, you know."

"Sorry. I thought you were doing rather well all by
yourself." He winked at the leather luggage and,
piece by piece, it hopped onto the scale. "There."

"Stop that," Meredith whispered. He'd promised to
save the genie tricks for private moments.

"Hey, you asked for help. I helped. You can't expect me to actually, physically, lift something." He
murmured and cocked an eyebrow at her, his devilish grin well in place.

"Is that all?" the agent asked. "Are you certain you
haven't forgotten the spare tires or the ton of hay for
your racehorse?"

"Are you trying to tell me that my luggage is over-
weight?" Meredith demanded.

"Yes. It is significantly over the limit. I'll have to
assess a charge."

The scale sighed in relief as Jim touched the top
bag, magically lightening the load. "I think you
should check your measurement once more, sir," he
said kindly, pointing to the stack of bags. "I believe
you've read it incorrectly."

The clerk walked around the heap of leather and

squinted at the number on the scale. "I was certain it read three hundred pounds over. Forgive me, ma'am. I was mistaken." He slipped luggage tags on each piece and handed the folder with the claim slips and boarding passes to Jim. "You had better hold these." He glanced nervously at Meredith. "Enjoy your flight. Next." He waved them away with a quizzical look at Jim, as if to ask why he had married such a demanding scatterbrain.

"He was the door prize at a charity event I organized. I wanted the box of Girl Scout Cookies but I wound up with him," Meredith said, answering the unspoken question, snatching the ticket folder away from Jim and stuffing it in a pocket of her briefcase. "Not that it's any of your business."

"Now, darling. Temper, temper. This is supposed to be a joyful time," Jim admonished. He smiled at the flustered ticket agent. "Thank you for your patience. This way, dear." He steered Meredith toward the gates.

"What did you do to my luggage?"

"I assumed you wanted all of it to accompany us on this trip, although I can't figure out why you need five bags for a simple three-day trip. What do you have packed in there?"

"Things. A variety of outfits. Extra shoes. You never know what you might need and it is a foreign country. I might not be able to purchase what I need."

He chuckled. "I think you brought your entire wardrobe. If I were to pop back to your house would I find your closet and your bureau drawers empty?"

"Not quite." She glanced over at her genie. "Thank you, anyway. I appreciate your putting my luggage on an instant diet."

"Of course. No problem. Whatever you want, my

# Karen Lee

dear. I live to serve. Your merest desire is my life goal."

She wrinkled her nose. "I wish you'd quit being so solicitous. This goody-goody routine is getting on my nerves."

"Is that an official wish or are you simply expressing your true feelings about your hardworking husband."

"No, it wasn't an official wish." She was on edge. "And you know perfectly well you aren't my husband. I'd appreciate it if you'd keep that in the forefront of your mind on this trip. You're here as a place-holder for the man who'll bring me true love. The one neither of us seems to be able to find. Nothing more." She looked around nervously, hoping neither the duchess nor Griffin had any ears lurking nearby to overhear their conversation.

"Meredith," Jim stopped and pulled her around to face him. "You've got to stop this. You've turned into a first-class shrew."

She sighed. "I'm sorry. I got an e-mail from Griffin this morning before we left. He's gloating over how well his first meeting with the East Overshoe, Wyoming, city council went. He might actually close the deal, and I'm worried I might not. Plus the fact that you don't seem to understand the logic of my talking directly to the Chairman of the Board and explaining about the mess-up with the true-love wish." They'd spent the entire morning, and all the way to the airport, arguing about it.

"We've already been through this. It isn't going to happen. Concentrate on your curtsy for the duchess and let me worry about my boss."

"What if the duchess does a background check and finds out this is all a lie? What if . . ."

"Slow down. Take a breath. A deep breath. I told

206

you I'd take care of it. Don't worry. Trust me."

"Last time I trusted you, you pirated Glenn away from his wife."

"That was the old Jim. This is the new, improved model." He smiled broadly. "See? No tricks up my sleeves."

"Of course not. You're wearing a short-sleeved shirt." It was a Hawaiian print with large pink flowers on a yellow background. Any other man would have looked silly in it, but the bright, flamboyant colors seemed only to accent Jim's dark good looks.

Maybe it wasn't the contract that was bothering her. Spending any amount of time this close to her picture-perfect genie was bound to be stressful, especially after their encounter at the Tiburon mansion. She tingled all over at the memory of his touch.

Still, he had agreed to this whole crazy plan just so she could have a corner office.

Hormones. She'd blame it on hormones. It couldn't possibly be the prospect of meeting minor royalty, or Griffin's e-mail. No. "Once we get off the ground and I've got a scotch in my hands, I'll calm down."

Jim narrowed his eyes. "No alcohol. It isn't good for you and it isn't good for me."

"What is this built-in bias you have against drinking anything stronger than coffee?"

He sighed. "Remember the Hindenburg? The lighter-than-air thing was a wish I granted. Of course, I wanted to help pilot it." He coughed slightly. "Alcohol impairs judgment. I should never have tried to land the stupid blimp."

"Oh." Maybe flying with a genie wasn't the smartest thing she'd decided to do. "You just need a little practice is all."

His hand was firm on her elbow. "No alcohol."

They arrived at their gate and sat in standard-issue airport seats. Meredith had decided long ago that the airlines made the waiting area seating as uncomfortable as possible so passengers would be grateful for even the cramped airplane seats.

"Hmmmm. We'll see." Meredith pulled a file folder from her briefcase and thumbed through the dossier on the Grand Duchess one more time. At seventy-one, the duchess had been married, happily Meredith assumed, for fifty years. She had six children, three sons and three daughters, who were also all happily married. Or so her limited information on the royal family indicated.

Meredith gazed at a candid snapshot of the duke and duchess in one of the brochures. The Grand Duke was still a handsome man, even at the age seventy-five. He wore his gray hair swept backoff his forehead, revealing a long, thin face with strong features. He had his arm wrapped around the duchess's shoulders and she fit well into the crux of his arm. They both wore happy, relaxed smiles, and Meredith thought she could detect the glow of new love on their faces. New, after fifty years. How did they manage that? she wondered. She shook her head slightly. Maybe all this talk about true love was making her read too much into a publicity photo. She put the brochure away. The state of the duchess's marriage was not her concern. Her mission, and she had accepted it, she thought ruefully, was to convince the duchess that Horton Consulting was the only company that could help her launch a major tourist campaign, complete with electronic kiosks in airports around the world. Meredith traced the Horton logo on the cover of her presentation. She was very pleased with her work. The whole concept, the entire approach had come to her more easily than usual. Absorbed in how she would approach the duchess, Meredith didn't realize their flight was boarding.

"Must be really interesting reading." Jim took her elbow, and the heat flowing from his hand snapped her attention to his face. "Time to go."

"Already? Oh, yes. The duchess. Fine." Why was it that his simple touch turned her into a complete, stammering idiot. "Do you have the tickets?"

He reached around her and pulled the boarding passes from a pocket in her briefcase. "Now I do." He guided her to the gate and down the gangway.

She smiled at the flight attendant who showed them to their first-class seats. "Does your prohibition on alcohol extend to champagne?" He nodded. "Not even a spot of the bubbly to celebrate our marriage?"

"Not one bubble. It's a bogus marriage. Remember?"

"Spoilsport." She settled into the spacious leather seat and ordered an orange juice without ice. "There. Is that better?" She pulled the latest Catherine Abbott novel from her briefcase and opened it.

"Much better." Jim ordered water. "What are you reading?"

She shrugged. "It seems that since I met you, my tastes in literature run to the magical. This one's got a disappearing mountain in it."

"Humph. A simple task, I assure you, for any advanced magical being." He sipped his drink. "If you had wished me to move mountains, instead of locating elusive true love, I wouldn't be in such trouble with the Head Office."

"If you'd let me talk to the Big Djinn, you wouldn't be in such trouble."

"If I let you talk to the Chairman, I'd be in worse trouble."

209

"I don't understand. You've been on your very best behavior. What's bothering them now?"

"Too much good behavior is bad for djinni morale. We tend toward mischief, you know."

She could think of a lot of mischief the two of them could get into, once they were settled in the suite of the five-star hotel she'd selected.

"Everything will turn out just fine. Trust me." She pointed out the window. "We're about to take off. I'm actually headed for my biggest promotion yet." On the wings of a huge lie. What had happened to her? She used to pride herself on her ruthless, but ethical, business practices. Now look at her. She'd lied to a client, something she'd never done before. And why? To get a promotion she deserved anyway.

And then there was the problem of Jim and his business practices. He'd been having more and more frequent conversations with the Chairman of the Board, and she knew his decision to pose as her husband had cost him a lot. She had managed to convince herself that she would be able to talk with the Chairman of the Board, despite Jim's conviction to the contrary. She only hoped she was right.

"Fasten your seat belts, ladies and gentlemen. Place your seat backs in the full upright and locked position. Be sure any carry-on items are stored securely beneath the seat in front of you." The flight attendant droned on about water landings, flotation devices and oxygen masks. Meredith watched out the window as the plane taxied to the end of the runway. Takeoff was her favorite part of flying.

She felt Jim move next to her. "This would have been much simpler if I had handled our travel plans." His skin had turned a questionable shade of green. "I don't know how something this big can actually stay in the air."

"Maybe there are other kinds of magic in the world besides yours." She watched as his face got more and more pale. "Are you feeling okay?"

"I feel fine. I just hate airplanes."

"Have you ever been in one before?"

"That's beside the point. It isn't seemly for a genie to use human transportation when a simple flick of the wrist"—he illustrated the move—"would have us where we're supposed to be instantly."

"Ladies and gentlemen, we've started our descent into Hertzenstein International Airport. Be sure your seat belt is securely fastened low across your lap and your seat back is in its full upright and locked position." Jim gave a relieved sigh.

"What have you done?" Meredith shot a panicked look at Jim, then glanced out the window of the airplane. They were definitely landing. She looked at her watch. "How did you do that?"

"I'm a genie, remember?" All around them, passengers were stretching, waking up from their naps. Flight attendants collected used glasses and other garbage just as though the flight had taken eight hours rather than five seconds.

"Rats," Meredith said. "I've missed the warm chocolate-chip cookies, not to mention the in-flight movie."

"Cookies. I perform a colossal feat of legerdemain and she's worried about cookies." Jim smacked his forehead with his open hand. "What was I thinking?" He reached into the seat pocket and withdrew a chocolate-chip cookie so warm the chips oozed into the napkin. "Your wish is my command."

Meredith took the cookie and glared at Jim. "Aren't you causing more trouble for yourself with these little tricks? You told me the Chairman of the

Board was nearly apoplectic the last time you talked with him."

"That's *my* problem."

Maybe. But she felt it was equally hers. It had been her impossible wish, after all, that had practically sealed his fate. "If you'd just reconsider letting me . . ."

"Meredith, the All-Powerful Chairman of the Board does not speak with mere humans. Period. He will not manifest himself for a quick conversation with you no matter how badly you want him to. Geniedom doesn't work the way Corporate America does. Period."

"But, if . . ."

"Period." The plane had landed, and Jim took their one carry-on bag out of the overhead compartment. "If you care anything at all for me, Meredith, you'll drop this ridiculous idea right now. Unless you want me to fail?"

She patted his arm. "Of course I don't want you to fail. You're supposed to be finding me my true love. What woman wouldn't want that?"

He narrowed his eyes and smirked. "Right."

One thing at a time, she counseled herself. First, get the contract with the duchess, and then figure out how to force the Chairman of the Board to appear.

All the way to the hotel, Jim was silent. The limo didn't impress him, neither did their suite. When she tipped the bellman for delivering their luggage, he didn't say a word. She suggested a stroll along the river, and he merely nodded.

"Jim, you have to talk to me."

Nothing.

"Please? I'm sorry I brought up the Chairman of the Board. It won't happen again. I promise."

His natural cinnamon scent, which had been absent the entire trip, came back. She breathed it in, warm and fragrant, and a familiar calm settled around her shoulders. Her old Jim was back.

"Let's say we skip the stroll along the river and try something new and fun."

"Sure. I've always wanted to take a carriage ride through the old part of the town. It would be quiet and relaxing. What do you say?"

"That wasn't quite what I had in mind, but if you want to, then that's what we'll do. You're in charge."

"You make it sound so official."

"It is."

"You sound tired. Are you certain you're all right?"

"I'm wonderful, couldn't be better. Quit worrying about me as if I mattered to you."

Midstride, Meredith stopped and stared at her genie. He sounded just like a boyfriend she'd had in college. The closer he got to telling her he loved her, the nastier he became. Was that what was going on here?

Jim shook his head, apologizing. "Long flights wear me out. You're right. A pleasant carriage ride through the park is just what the doctor ordered. Lead on, Meredith."

Long flights indeed. "Wait here while I change my clothes."

"Ah, yes. The tons of luggage. I knew there was a purpose for them after all."

"Don't be snotty."

He'd been warned. More than several times. The Chairman of the Board had been explicit and direct. Under no circumstances was he to develop any further feelings whatsoever for his project person, Meredith.

# Karen Lee

And he'd tried. Really he had. Jim wandered around the expansive suite, admiring the gold- and peach-colored wallpaper. He sat at the harpsichord in the corner. He fiddled with the keys, making an awful racket. He didn't care. The disharmony coming from the antique stringed instrument suited his mood. He'd been telling himself she meant nothing to him. She was just the latest in a long line of Masters of the Djinn. Sure, she was beautiful, but what woman wasn't, seen in the correct light?

Meredith was funny. He generated enough funny on his own to suit him. She had long, shapely legs, a stunning body and full lips. So did many women he'd known. No, the problem he was having didn't relate to the physical. If it had been just that, the Chairman wouldn't have his fez in a fuss.

She cared about him.

No one ever had. In all his centuries of service to the Order of the Djinn, no one had cared about him beyond his ability to grant whatever greedy wish they wanted. He was good for getting things. Period.

Meredith seemed to think he had some innate worth beyond his magic. She liked his company, for Djinn's sake! She laughed at his jokes, argued with his rules. She . . . somehow she had wiggled her way into his heart.

"Ready?" She stood in the doorway of the large bedroom, dressed in a stunning white linen outfit, her arm stretched up the doorjamb in a Hollywood pose that had worked for sultry women since the species had been invented. The slacks clung to her trim hips, the gold knit top revealed perfect breasts and the gold chain around her delicate neck fairly cried out to him to rip it off and kiss her all over.

He stopped breathing. Great Djinn, she was magnificent! He swallowed, trying to find his voice. "I'm

214

ready," he croaked, and bowed toward the door.
"Shall we?" Next to her, he felt positively dowdy in
his gray slacks and navy sweater.

She walked to him, stood on tiptoe and planted a
chaste kiss on his cheek. "Relax. You'll have fun."

Little did she know. Relaxing within five miles of
Meredith Montgomery was the most dangerous
thing he could contemplate. The Chairman of the
Board had made that very clear.

Even though it was late spring, the midday breeze
was chilly. The carriage driver covered Jim and Meredith with a beautiful, hand-crafted quilt. Delicate
pieces of colored cloth formed interlocking rings
that danced across their laps. Meredith snuggled
closer to Jim, absorbing his natural warmth. She
smiled up at him. "Comfortable?"

"As much as a genie can be in these extreme circumstances." A hardening of certain male features
threatened to overwhelm his better genie judgment.

She chuckled and spoke words far more apt than
she realized. "Loosen up. It isn't going to take off. In
fact, it isn't as perilous as that taxi you drove the
night of the Toothman Disaster."

Perilous wasn't the half of it. If she snuggled any
closer, well, he wouldn't be responsible for his actions. "Perhaps. But I was doing the driving then. I've
never trusted humans and look, now we've got one
in charge of this wild animal." He indicated the
horse hitched to the front of their carriage, resting
his hind leg, snoozing in the afternoon sun. "Looks
like danger to me."

Meredith laughed, a crystalline sound that sparkled, glinting off and then echoing down the cobble-
stone street. "Isn't this just the most wonderful place
you've ever been?"

He looked around the square, studied the

centuries-old buildings with their gilt trim and ancient statuary. It took his attention off his uncomfortable condition. Temporarily. Boxes of gaily colored flowers festooned the porches and hung from windows. Truthfully, he'd been a lot of places more magnificent. But they paled in comparison because they hadn't had the added attraction of Meredith.

In his head, he heard the Chairman of the Board clear his throat. "Careful, Djinn. You are on the brink. The decision is entirely yours, of course. If you come back to me now and renounce your emotions, I'll restore you to your former position." Like that was any incentive. Jim had gotten used to his cell phone.

"I could replace you, you know. Send in a substitute to finish the job."

Not likely. If finding true love was verboten for him, how would any other djinn be able to grant her wish?

*I'll be fine. I can manage this assignment.* He hated being reminded he was a failure, hated it even more than being told what to do all the time. Come to think of it, that was the definition of being a djinn— being instructed what to do. He took a deep breath, relishing the taste of air in his body. He'd had about enough of taking orders. Defiantly, he put his arm around Meredith. He'd show his boss who was boss.

Meredith leaned into his light embrace and he felt his very human body tighten in response. He should have been wary, should have been concentrating on how much djinni mischief he could create. What occupied his mind was how to get Meredith out of her perfect outfit without ruining it altogether. What was the point of being a handsome man with a beautiful woman if you didn't enjoy it?

"Look there." Meredith pointed to the fountain of stylized fish spitting water into the air. It occupied the center of the small square they'd just entered. "Isn't that beautiful? I wish I'd brought my camera."

Jim pulled back from her and watched her gazing at the sights. It couldn't have been an official wish. Even Meredith wouldn't have been that foolish. Still, he had to check. "You really want a camera?"

She shook her head. "I need to remember not to begin sentences with 'I wish,' don't I?" She gazed at the tall, brick row houses they were passing. "It would be nice to capture all this on film, to remember our time together, but no, it isn't a real wish. I should have remembered my camera, that's all."

"In all that great mountain of luggage the bellman struggled to make fit in our suite there isn't a camera?"

"No. I completely forgot to take it from my desk after our impromptu photo shoot that day you showed up looking like an escapee from Scheherazade's imagination."

"That was fun, wasn't it? We could do the same tour of Hertzenstein if you want." He flexed his fingers, ready to summon the magic carpet.

"No." She snuggled closer. "This tour is just fine. If you've taught me anything in the past weeks, it's to relax. So, relax. You need to enjoy your life, too."

The tightening around his heart grew. He knew he'd never survive this trip by following all the Chairman's demands. In a flash of genie clarity he made a decision. If he was going to be downsized out of existence, he decided, he was going to enjoy every last moment.

# *Chapter Twelve*

## *"Djinn on the Rocks"*

"Straighten your tie." Meredith stood in front of Jim appraising his appearance. "You're meeting minor royalty and you need to be at your best. Here"—she brushed a stray wisp of hair off his forehead—"let me help."

"Now I'm perfect, is that it?"

"Absolutely." Actually, he'd been perfect from the instant he'd entered her office. Had it been only two weeks ago? Well, two weeks and a day, she amended. In striped pants and dove-gray tails, he looked elegant. The duchess should be very pleased. They were off to take tea.

"How do I look?" Meredith checked her posture.

"Softly professional. You look great."

She walked to the mirror and adjusted her hat. "I feel silly. I'm not used to being soft. Firm business-woman is more my style. But, this is what tradition calls for, so this is what Her Grace, the duchess gets."

She twirled around, feeling the sweep of layered lavender silk against her legs. The flared skirt of the dress fell to just above her ankles in an A-line. The wide fabric belt of darker purple set off her small waist, and the fitted bodice with its scalloped neckline and three-quarter sleeves made her look entirely feminine. She decided she liked the effect.

Jim stood behind her, his hands on her shoulders, looking around the enormous hat she'd perched on her head. "If you tip it like this"—he moved the brim slightly—"it gives you a mysterious air."

She tilted her head. "You think so?" She angled her neck the other way and looked up at him out of the corner of her eye. "Is mysterious good?"

"Oh, yes. It's always worked for me." He stepped from behind her and offered her a gloved hand. "My lady?"

"You're really getting into this, aren't you?"

"Hey, that's what you wanted, I thought."

"Well, yes. But I'm not used to you being so co-operative and I'm just a little suspicious."

"You're a difficult woman to satisfy, Meredith Montgomery. Most people would be delighted to have a compliant genie to do their bidding. But you? You question everything. You would prefer me like this?" He snapped his fingers and his formal attire changed to ratty jeans and a white T-shirt that strained across his broad shoulders and chest. A half-smoked cigarette dangled from his lips.

"Or this?" Another snap. He was dressed in a karate gee, complete with black belt. He dropped into a ready stance and looked dangerously competent.

"Perhaps this is more to your liking?" He spun around in a perfect dancer's twirl and was dressed in a seventies-style brown polyester suit with a loud shirt and an impossibly wide tie.

"Enough. I understand this genie assignment might be a little unusual."

"That's one way to put it." His brown polyester melted away and he was once again dressed for tea.

"Could you just be serious for a few moments, so we can go?"

"Whatever." He was taller by half a foot when he set the gray top hat on his head and opened the door for her.

Well, ask a genie to be dignified and this is what you got—cool, aloof, reserved. Almost immediately, she missed the mischievous genie of moments before. She wanted the fun back, not this stuffed-shirt creature at her side. However, she didn't want the fun back in the middle of tea, and she'd asked him to be somber, so she should probably just keep her mouth shut.

"An excellent idea."

"You're reading my thoughts again. Admit it."

"Hard to tune them out when they're so loud." He held up his hands in protest. "I'll try. I'll also behave myself for now. Remember? Mothers love me."

He took her elbow and escorted her out of the suite, down the stairs to the lobby, where the duchess's chauffeur waited to take them to the castle.

And what a castle it was. Fairy tales couldn't have concocted a better one. With tall turrets and flying flags, the grand chateau stood at the top of a gradual incline, surrounded by green fields and sculptured gardens. Meredith felt as if she'd fallen into the middle of a Cecil B. DeMille movie set. All that was missing were the knights on white chargers swooping in to defeat the dragon and save the maiden fair.

Boy, was this a universe away from her normal life.

The stretch limo pulled slowly into the yard and

stopped at the tall, arched entrance of the enormous white stone structure, and the chauffeur opened the door and let Meredith and Jim out.

"Whew! I was in a castle just like this in the mid-fifteen hundreds. I'll bet it's got a dandy dungeon." Jim gazed up at the imposing edifice and the huge clock, which bonged the hour in honor of their timely arrival.

Hoping they wouldn't have occasion to find out about the dungeon, Meredith ignored him and walked up the wide, inviting steps and into the castle's foyer. Assuming that was what the room was called. She'd never been in a castle before, although this one certainly matched her preconceived notions of what one would look like.

The entrance hall was wide and long, walls sporting an assortment of really ugly and very old portraits of previous dukes and duchesses engaged in dukely and duchessly pursuits—mainly sitting in uncomfortable-looking chairs, gazing with almost pained expressions off into the distance. Under the large, dark paintings, huge wood chairs lined the walls. Each chair had a maroon damask cushion on it bearing the duchess's crest of two white unicorns standing on their hind legs, holding a red heart between their outstretched horns. Beneath the beasts' feet was a banner that stated *Amor omnia vincit*. Love conquers all, if she remembered her high school Latin correctly.

Positioned between the depressing paintings were empty suits of armor standing guard. It reminded her of her office building, full of empty suits.

"This way, Madame, Monsieur." The butler motioned for Meredith and Jim to follow him. With his gaudy and glittery uniform, he reminded Meredith of the guards in the castle of the Wicked Witch of the West. However, since she didn't think the duchess was going to melt, it seemed they had little choice but to walk after him, through the doorway just to the left of the long hall, and up a broad circular staircase that wound up and up and spilled them out into an anteroom of some sort.

"Please be seated. The duchess will receive you momentarily," the butler announced, and he disappeared.

"Well, there you have it." Meredith sat on the edge of a wooden bench that was at least five hundred years old, if one believed the date carved into its back. "This place is so old." She gazed with distaste at their surroundings. The castle decorator obviously didn't have much imagination. The anteroom looked much as the hallway had, dark and depressing. The bulky furniture and low lighting did little to make the atmosphere inviting. Although, she had to admit that the crossed swords—she estimated fifty or more—adorning the wall behind her, might have had something to do with the ominous feel the room projected. She prayed none of the weapons would come loose while she and Jim stood under them.

"Nah," he said. "It's practically brand-new. Now, if you want old, let me tell you about this sultan and his harem. It was, let's see if I remember it correctly, around the year three hundred twelve. I recall that date because that was the number of women the sultan had in this particular harem. Oh, and such a variety of beauties they were." Jim sighed.

"I don't believe you. I think you're making all this up." Meredith gazed up at the twenty-foot-high ceiling and marveled at the paintings she saw there. Angels and cherubim, or at least junior angels, gazed down on them keeping a close eye on their actions.

Meredith hoped they would keep the swords at

rest. Or maybe their disapproving frowns were a warning that they knew she was here to lie to royalty. For personal gain.

"I told you I'd been around for a very long time. You don't think I've been in a seventeen-hundred-year-old harem?"

"No."

Jim stood and walked to the leaded-glass windows across from Meredith's bench. "Watch." He waved his hand and the transparent surface grew cloudy. Soon, a motion picture of sorts began playing out on the panes of glass. Meredith stared as ornate doors opened onto an immense room filled with pillows and fountains and barely clad women. Frolicking in the pool with two amazingly beautiful specimens was Jim. He didn't look exactly like he did today, but there was no mistaking the glint in his eyes.

She was about to ask him a question when the doors to the sitting room opened. Immediately, Jim's home movie stopped and the windows returned to normal. He took Meredith's hand as she stood. "Show time."

Together they walked into the duchess's private rooms. Jim whispered into her ear:

> I sat with the duchess at tea.
> It was all that I hoped it would be.
> Her rumblings intestinal
> Were not infinitesimal
> And everyone thought it was me.

Meredith was smiling widely as she curtsied to the duchess. Trust Jim to calm her nerves with a silly limerick.

"Come in. Come in, my dears. You must be Meredith." The Grand Duchess of Hertzenstein stood and came toward them, her bejeweled hand out-stretched. "It's very nice to meet you at last. I've so been looking forward to our little visit. It's nice to get to know the people you might do business with, don't you think?" She motioned Meredith to take the large armchair beside her own.

"And you." She indicated with a wave of her hand that Jim should sit on the couch across from them, as she resumed her own seat. "You must be Meredith's new husband." After looking him up, down and all around, she turned to Meredith. "A good choice, my dear. Very good-looking. And so tall."

Yes, he was, but anyone would have towered over the duchess. Standing just five feet, even with the heels on her shoes, the duchess's hat didn't reach the middle of Jim's chest. In fact, it barely made it to the first button on his formal vest. Her milk-white hair curled around her friendly round face and her dark eyes sparkled out from under white brows. She looked like your typical, garden-variety fairy god-mother, minus the wings.

"So nice of you to invite us. This is a lovely room." Not normally at a loss for things to say, Meredith struggled to find appropriate conversation topics. Although she could hold her own with the best in a business setting, dealing with Hans Christian Ander-sen's great aunt was a bit unnerving.

"This old place?" said the duchess. "I guess it is rather comfortable. If you don't mind the odd ghost popping in unexpectedly." She smiled broadly. "The castle is renowned for its haunted rooms. This one, fortunately, isn't graced with a ghost."

It certainly didn't look spooky, Meredith thought as she took in her surroundings. A warm and cheer-ful fire lent the sitting area a cozy feel. Unlike the other parts of the castle Meredith had seen so far, this room felt inviting, homey and lived-in.

The duchess arranged her skirts over her short legs. "Come, come, dear. You mustn't be shy. Tell me about yourself. And, don't worry about the ghosts. I thought it would be a nice feature to attract tourists." The duchess rang a small bell and a uniformed servant appeared out of nowhere, carrying a tray laden with assorted goodies. Cakes, cookies, tiny crustless sandwiches. And tea. A great pot of steaming tea.

He set the delicacies in the middle of the table and began to serve. The tea smelled wonderful and, although she was a dedicated coffee drinker, Meredith sipped the hot liquid with what she imagined was obvious enjoyment.

"I agree completely about the tourist angle. There are ghost tours in every major European city. It's a natural extension of a country's personality, its history."

"Our country is small, but it has a lot to offer. Take this castle, for instance."

"You know," Meredith said, "I've never really been in a castle before." She smiled at the duchess. "Is it overwhelming, living among all this history?"

The duchess stood up, all five feet of her springing easily out of the chair. "Would you like the ten-pfennig tour?" She nodded to the servant to hold the tea. "Of course, there are no lifts, but you young folks shouldn't have any trouble with the stairs. Let's start at the beginning. Back in the main building." She opened the door and swooshed into the hall.

"All of this"—she swept her hand in a wide arc, indicating the hall and the rooms leading from it— "was added in the early nineteenth century. The real castle was a simple keep, square, solid and very plain." She led Meredith and Jim back the way they had come, past the circular staircase and into a narrow passage.

Meredith felt cramped, while Jim had to stoop to fit through the space. "When was this part built?" she asked.

"Tenth century. It connected the duke's dining room to the guardhouse." The duchess chuckled. "I expect the prisoners didn't appreciate being housed where they could smell the sumptuous dinners the duke frequently held for his friends. Especially when their own menus were somewhat limited."

"See?" Jim whispered. "I knew there were dungeons."

"Not just dungeons, my dear boy, but nasty holes where the worst of the Duchy's enemies were simply dropped and left to starve to death."

Great, thought Meredith. I sincerely hope those holes have been filled up so the duchess won't be tempted to shove me down one if she finds out I'm not married.

"Of course, Duchess Julianna put a stop to that practice in 1297." The miniature tour came out into a large, rectangular room with a barrel ceiling. "This used to be the main room of the original castle. Dukes and duchesses conducted all their business here, in front of the fireplace." She pointed to a huge stone structure with a wide hearth. Above it hung five shields.

"What's behind there?" Meredith pointed to a wall that looked like it had once been an arched doorway.

"Ah, the famous hidden room." The duchess chuckled. "The story goes that in the fourteenth century, a visiting emmisary from Denmark refused to talk with the duchess. He didn't believe in dealing with women at all, much less married ones. So, the duchess, Thalia the Thin, challenged him to a game of cards. If he won, then she would allow the duke to represent Hertzenstein. If he lost, however, he would relinquish Denmark's claim to a small piece of land the two countries were squabbling over and kiss the duchess's hand in public, prostrating himself before her."

"So, what happened?" Jim asked.

"Of course the duchess won, didn't she?" Meredith prodded.

"The emmissary and Thalia were so evenly matched that they played, nonstop, for twelve days and twelve nights. Pages brought food and drink and still they played. Some say they're still in there playing. But, in truth, the emmissary finally gave in."

"Then, why is it closed up?" Meredith asked.

The duchess tilted her head and smiled. "Once he lost, the emmissary refused to uphold his end of the bargain and bow before Thalia in public, so she had him walled in."

And I thought I was a tough businesswoman, Meredith thought.

The duchess chuckled at Meredith's horrified expression. She patted Meredith's hand. "Part of later renovations, my dear. There are no skeletons bricked into walls here. At least not in this part of the castle."

Meredith's heart slowed to a more normal beat as they crossed the great room and peeked into several other rooms. She wasn't entirely certain the duchess was kidding about that hapless emmissary being walled in. It was obvious that Hertzenstein revered both its history and its traditions. She began to have second thoughts about her little fib.

They finished their tour back in the sitting room, where the tea had been kept hot for them. The duchess returned to her previous perch on the large armchair that easily dwarfed her, while Meredith and

Jim both sat across from her on the couch. "I understand you've created the definitive solution to our tourist worries and, if you're successful in persuading me to sign a contract, you're in line for a promotion at your job" The duchess's dark, intelligent eyes appraised Meredith as the younger woman choked on her mouthful of tea.

"Why, yes. How did you know?" And how much other information had this old busybody been able to glean? She hoped Jim had indeed taken care of everything—especially the document trail required to represent a marriage. She felt her stomach clench. Maybe their hoax hadn't been such a good idea.

"I make it my business to know the people I invite to tea." She lifted a plate of goodies. "The ginger cake is quite good, you know." Meredith couldn't tell if the duchess was making small talk or if the comment held an underlying massage. How much did the she really know about Jim and Meredith?

"Thank you." Meredith selected a piece and set it on her plate. Perhaps she'd underestimated this woman. "It's true. I'm being considered for the position of vice president."

"How very wonderful for you. Now, enough business talk." She smiled charmingly at them. "Tell me, how did you two meet?"

Saved. Momentarily. But even as Meredith launched into a laundered description of how Jim had come into her life, she felt a rush of guilt she hadn't expected. She had never lied in a business situation before. And it was one tradition she didn't like breaking. Back in D.C. she had told herself a little white lie was no big deal. After all, she was qualified for the job, so why should some silly tradition prevent her from helping the duchess—and securing herself a promotion? Somehow, though, this rationale offered her little comfort as she met the duchess's frank gaze.

Meredith had not expected to like the duchess very much. She had imagined her be a pampered old woman mired in antiquated traditions. But so far she had found the duchess to be smart and charming. It was hard not to like a woman who seemed to be able to step away from the trappings of her position and view her country and its traditions as an outsider might. Meredith knew from experience that not everyone, especially people in powerful positions, had such an ability.

The duchess laughed upon hearing how Jim had delivered Meredith her new cell phone when the receptionist at Horton Industries had mistaken him for a messenger—not a consultant meeting with Meredith to discuss work possibilities.

"Well, I was dressed in ripped jeans and a baseball cap. I had planned to change before the meeting, but I was running late due to a flat tire."

A flat tire. Meredith had to suppress a grin. Jim had a talent for this white-lie stuff—must be all those years of djinn mischief. The only time she'd seen Jim use a car for transportation was when he had masqueraded as the taxi driver.

"Anyway, I was carrying a package of coffee for Meredith, so it was an easy mistake. I delivered her the phone, got the job working as her assistant-slash-consultant for this project, and the rest, as they say, is history." He smiled lovingly over at Meredith, as though fondly remembering their first meeting. "You might say, I came with her cell phone." He grinned broadly now, gently patting Meredith's hand.

He is really good at this playacting, Meredith thought, as her heart accelerated under his warm gaze. "Of course, by the time he made it to my office he was perfectly turned out in an Armani suit," Meredith said with a laugh.

"Ah, I always aim to make a good first impression." Jim shrugged. "You never know who you might meet." He put his arm around Meredith and gave her shoulder a quick squeeze. Then he raised his eyebrows at the duchess. "I made a quick stop in the men's room to change clothes." He leaned forward and stage-whispered, "Good thing I did, too. She might have hired me with my Ph.D. and all, but she never would have fallen for a guy in ratty jeans and a grease-stained shirt."

Meredith elbowed him in the ribs, "*I* didn't fall for *you, you* fell for *me.*"

Jim sighed and leaned back against the couch again, looking suitably downtrodden. " 'Tis true, 'tis true. Nothing I could do about it."

Meredith couldn't help the smile that plastered her face. Jim was really hamming this up. And, as long as he didn't jam it up, all would be well.

The duchess laughed again as she stared at the seemingly happy couple before her. "So, Jim, what are you a doctor of?"

"I hold a doctoral degree in literature and mythology."

"Then you must be familiar with the legends surrounding the Duchy of Hertzenstein."

"Quite a fascinating set of tales, Your Grace. I came across them during my undergraduate studies and they are some of my favorites."

The duchess settled back in her chair. "You must know of the magical qualities of our tower rooms, then." She peered at Meredith over the rim of her teacup. "We didn't visit all the towers on our tour. Too many steps for these old knees, I'm afraid."

Meredith certainly hoped Jim wasn't faking this

*Meredith's Wish*

knowledge because she hadn't heard of Hertzenstein until two weeks ago. Her reading had included economy, exports and imports, the tourist trade, pertinent customs and such, but no legends. And certainly not of towers in castles.

"Of course," Jim continued. "It's said that a man and woman who spend their wedding night in the tower of Hertzenstein Castle will have true love throughout their lives." He reached for a cookie. "I've always wondered if the legend were true, or if, like kissing the Blarney Stone, it was simply something for tourists."

The duchess ducked her head, smiling. "Your husband is not only handsome, he's also very charming, my dear Meredith." The duchess sipped her tea and smiled. "As a matter of fact, Jim, the castle tower does contain magic. My husband, Edgar, and I spent our wedding night in that tower. And we've been happily married for fifty years."

"I thought I recognized the glow of a well-loved woman about you, Your Grace," Jim said.

Meredith listened to their exchange in bemused silence. She couldn't remember why she had ever doubted that Jim would be able to win the duchess over. Whether Her Grace believed in their marriage or not, she certainly liked Jim.

"Oh, listen to you!" The duchess winked at Meredith. "I can see why you couldn't resist this charming rogue." She smiled at Jim. "The Heartstone of Hertzenstein Castle is like the alchemist's stone, only for lovers. Edgar and I occasionally return to that room and that bed. It makes us feel young again. Our love has grown throughout the years, providing us protection from the ills of the world. We've always had each other to rely upon."

"I know the history behind your tradition of

231

having only married women negotiate contracts," Meredith said, trying to regain control of the conversation.

"I rather thought you'd be interested in that, my dear." The diminutive woman reached for another piece of ginger cake. "This is excellent cake today. Hans, our chef, has outdone himself." She pushed the plate toward Meredith. "You really must have some more.

"The tradition began with Hermione, of course. I'm a direct descendant of hers, you know. The custom was strengthened a century or so later, when noblemen in the surrounding fiefdoms still exercised the *droit du seigneur* or the right to take any peasant maiden to their beds. One of my other ancestresses, the Grand Duchess Eglantine II, didn't like this practice at all. She felt it was often unhealthy for the maidens, and that it ruined perfectly good marriages inside the castle as well. Specifically, the story goes that she was concerned her husband would stray. However, she couldn't ban such a time-honored tradition outright, so she formalized the rule of only dealing with married women by signing a royal document and affixing her seal. She knew that by working solely with married women, she would cut down drastically on the number of unmarried women in the castle, specifically the number of maidens to whom the duke was exposed. You can see the legal document she had created in the castle museum if you like."

She signaled for more tea to be poured. "Of course, Eglantine took her duke, Chauncey, to the tower on their wedding night, so it's entirely possible that he wouldn't have strayed. In any case, the policy worked out so well, and Eglantine's marriage was such a happy one, that the subsequent duchesses followed the practice until over the years it became a sacred tradition. As mothers passed the title of Hertzenstein to their daughters, they also passed on this custom. Some view it as a good-luck charm, if you will, a way to ensure successful business dealings and happy marriages."

"And the titles of Hertzenstein always pass from mother to the daughter. No men allowed. Correct?" Jim was obviously well informed about the various mores of their hostess's culture. When the duchess nodded, he asked, "Would it be possible to see this famous tower room?"

"Of course, of course." The duchess stood. Then paused as a satisfied smile came over her face. "I have a better idea. Why didn't I think of this before?" She signaled the servant, whispered something in his ear and turned to her guests. "According to the *Washington Post*, it's been several weeks since you took your wedding vows, but the room still has magic to offer. Would you two be my guests during the rest of your visit? I would very much like you to have the tower room." The duchess cocked a snowy eyebrow and smiled at Meredith and Jim. "Although I think you've found true love without it."

Meredith tried not to let her mouth fall open. Jim really had covered the paper trail in documenting their fake wedding. "But, we couldn't impose, Your Grace."

"Nonsense, child. I insist." The duchess seemed to grow in stature as she organized the matter in an authoritative tone befitting her royal status. "I'll have your luggage transferred from the hotel this afternoon. This arrangement will also make it more convenient for us to work together, Meredith."

Oh, boy, oh, boy, oh, boy. How had this gotten out of control so quickly? One minute they were talking about a potential tourist attraction and the next, the duchess had her and Jim sleeping together! She begged Jim with a panicked look to help her out.

He ignored her discomfort and put his arm around her shoulders again. "Thank you, what a lovely gesture. Meredith and I would certainly never pass up a blessing for true love." He grinned down at Meredith to see if she caught his double meaning.

She could only stare back at him in shock. A whole night with Jim in a room designed just for lovers. She had definitely lost control of the situation.

Jim turned back to the duchess and continued. "But Meredith and I would prefer to pack ourselves. We left quite a mess in the hotel suite. You understand." Jim smiled in his wonderful way.

"Of course, if you think it necessary." The duchess clapped her hands together, her jeweled bracelets making more sound than her hands. "I'll expect you this evening, then, first for dinner and then as our overnight guests." She nodded to them and said, "I must make the proper arrangements. You'll excuse me?" Meredith dropped a sloppy curtsy and Jim bowed with a flourish as the Grand Duchess of Hertzenstein left the room.

Meredith grabbed Jim's arm and pulled him back onto the couch. "I'm not sure this is such a good idea, sharing a tower room that's clearly possessed." Wide-eyed, she looked at Jim. She'd had fantasies about having her way with him, but she was definitely not ready to make those dreams real. "And what did she mean about true love?"

"She's an old woman, steeped in the legends of her country. I expect she'd see true love between"—he looked around the room—"those silver lions on the table if she thought it would enhance the story. As to staying in the castle, I don't see that we have any choice. If we insult the duchess, you'll never get your contract or your corner office. Besides"—he kissed her hand—"I promise I'll do whatever you want me to."

There was that sexy grin once more. She was doomed. Doomed.

Meredith was beginning to think that she didn't really want that corner office. The sun came into that particular room very strongly after two o'clock and ruined the view. She'd have to have entirely new furniture, and her Turkistan carpet, well, it was too small for the new space.

"Don't give up now, Meri. This is what you've always wanted, isn't it? The corner office, the title, the respect."

"Yes. I guess so. I'm just surprised that she'd be so gracious." *And I didn't think I'd have to sleep with you to get it.* "I presume it will be more difficult to say no to a guest than to a simple saleswoman." Meredith gathered her handbag and the butler, hovering just outside the doorway, escorted them down the winding stairs and back outside.

Once they were seated in the duchess's limousine, Jim cleared his throat. "What's wrong? You're as white as a sheet." He cocked an eyebrow. "Don't you want to spend the night with your husband?"

"Will you promise to stay in your phone?"

Jim laughed and sat back in the seat. "Meredith, Meredith, what fun would that be?"

It wasn't the duchess that was bothering her. It was the prospect of spending the night in some haunted room designed to reveal true love with a genie she couldn't be in love with. How ironic that she was spending the night in a room guaranteed to help the occupants discover true love with the only man she couldn't possibly fall for. In fact, she needed to fall for someone else to save him. The whole thing was such a tangled mess, it made her head ache. Perhaps she wasn't destined to have true love after all; the deck certainly seemed stacked against it.

She thought about it as they started back to the hotel. What if she really wasn't supposed to find true love? What if fate had decreed it—a somewhat successful career, but no true love for Meredith Montgomery? It would be a wonderful solution to Jim's dilemma. How could the Chairman of the Board argue with destiny? If she wasn't supposed to find true love, then her wish would be void and Jim wouldn't be responsible. He could go on doing genie things in the Reorganized Organization.

Satisfied that she might have found an answer to Jim's problem, she relaxed a little. Now she just had to worry about spending the night with one unbelievably sexy genie. "I'd like to do something with the rest of the day, Jim. Something different. Something outrageous." Something like wading in the fountains of the town, or throwing confetti from the hotel windows. She was beginning to realize that being a stuffy businesswoman all the time was boring. And this afternoon, she didn't want stuffy at all.

# *Chapter Thirteen*

## *"Djinn With A Twist"*

"You specified outrageous." Jim straddled a power-ful, black motorcycle, his white-T-shirted torso draped in a black leather jacket. "Hop on."

"Yes, but a motorcycle?" Meredith looked skep-tical.

"Not just any motorcycle. A Harley Soft-Tail, babe." Jim took off his aviator sunglasses and smiled broadly. He had a cigarette stuck behind one ear and his hair had somehow grown longer. It brushed the collar of his jacket.

"This is a new look for you. I'm not sure it's a good one." It wasn't just good. It was perfect. If Jim had been her ideal man before, this bad-boy persona he'd picked up was so potent and virile that she wanted to rip off his jacket and have her way with him. Whew! She felt her forehead to make sure she wasn't perspiring.

"Hey, you love it. Admit it." He looked her up and

down. "Your outfit doesn't quite work, though, does it?" He dismounted and walked around her, the heels of his tall, black leather boots clicking on the pavement as he moved. Silently, he studied her clothes.

"Everyone is staring at us, Jim," Meredith whispered. "This isn't good. We need a low profile. We're in a foreign country, for heaven's sake."

"Heaven doesn't care about where we are, babe, as long as we're together." He'd completed his circuit around her and stood, arms crossed, pondering. "Come with me."

He pulled her through a small, arched doorway and around a corner. "No prying tourists here." He cocked his head, scratching one temple with a contemplative finger. "I think this would work better." He snapped his fingers and her wool camel slacks, off-white cashmere sweater and Hermes scarf changed instantly into skin-tight black leggings, short boots with a zipper up the side, a red crop-top and her own black leather jacket.

Running a hand down her hip, she realized that the leggings were all she had on and, clearly, the top didn't allow for a bra. She touched her hair. No longer smoothly hugging her face, her auburn locks felt like they'd been through a wind tunnel. All big and tangled. She probably looked like she was auditioning for a local revival of *Grease*.

"Much better." Jim guided her to the Harley and picked her up. "Hop on." Over her protests, he set her on the seat and mounted the bike in front of her.

"What, no helmets?" Not that one would fit over this hair.

"Trust me. I'm an expert carpet flyer. How difficult can a motorcycle be?" He turned the key and revved the motor. "However, if you insist." Two helmets that looked like something from the Sci Fi Channel appeared. "There you are." She pushed one over her huge hair and fastened the strap while Jim stuck his sunglasses in his shirt pocket and donned his own space-age wonder. He climbed back on the bike and put it in gear. "Hang on."

They peeled out of the drive in front of their five-star hotel and roared down the street. People stopped and stared as they flew by.

Meredith found herself holding on to Jim like a drowning woman, the wind snatching her objections away before they got to his ears. Once she realized he really did know how to drive a bike, she relaxed just enough to relish the erotic combination of speed, wind whipping her jacket and Jim's muscular torso in her grasp.

She rested her head against his back, and thought she could hear his heartbeat through her helmet. Or maybe it was her own heart that was beating so loudly in her ears. The mixture of unchecked acceleration and the smell of leather combined to ignite a set of feelings she had trouble identifying. Her former corporate-climbing beaus had never come close to producing the intimacy she felt at this moment, her thighs tight against Jim's, her breasts pressed against his back. Through two layers of leather, she felt exposed, open.

She shivered. This was a man she could love. This man excited her beyond all reason. This being from somewhere else was somehow able to draw her out of her normally constrained, fettered self and show her that there were adventures to be had in this world. The pursuit of career seemed oceans away. Jim had reduced them to their elemental essences: man and woman.

Jim rounded a tight curve and pulled the big bike into a wooded park. Carefully, he parked the machine, pulled off his helmet and twisted around to see how Meredith was doing. "I told you I could manage it," he said. With a movement that was pure seduction, he slid his sunglasses on.

Smiling at him, she removed her own helmet and hugged him. She traced his top lip with her finger. *What the heck.* She kissed him, tasting his faint cinnamon flavor and relishing it. She felt the breeze against her face, their lips, and shivered.

He broke their contact. "Slow down, Meredith. Just because I can manage a raging machine between my legs doesn't mean you can take advantage of me." He threw his arm around her shoulders and kissed her forehead. "Come with me."

She shrugged and got off the bike. "Okay. I wasn't trying to take advantage, Jim. I was just trying to . . . It doesn't matter." She put her arm around his waist and walked with him into the trees.

They stopped beside a little stream where sunlight hopped from wavelet to wavelet like diamonds on caffeine. Clumps of purple irises decorated the banks, surrounded by groups of pink rhododendron and yellow daisies. She'd fallen into a Monet painting. Jim sat on top of a picnic table and took off his sunglasses.

"I like it here. It's soothing, the sound of the water, the birds sharing gossip, the breeze playing tag with the leaves. It's peaceful."

What was going on here? Meredith sat on the picnic table seat and leaned against Jim's leg. It might be a good time to just be quiet and listen.

"I remember being a very young djinn, sitting beside a stream not unlike this one. There was a couple on the opposite bank, getting very friendly with each other. As I watched, I wondered why genies never made friends, never got close to any other being."

Meredith looked up at him. "Why?"

He looked across the stream and watched squirrels dart in and out under the bushes. "It took me centuries to figure it out." He took her hand. "Djinni are the essence of mischief, of practical jokes, of trouble in all shapes and sizes. In the great pantheon of otherworld beings, we're cousins to demons. Borderline evil." He began to stroke her hair. "That's why the Harley, these boots, the black leather are so appropriate. An icon of rebellion against rules of any kind—that's what djinni are, Meredith."

"Why are you telling me this now?" Her hand was warm in his, comfortable and secure. His fingers toyed with her hair and she badly wanted him to drag her up to his level and cover her face with kisses. Instead, he continued to explain.

"I'm telling you now because I'm committing the ultimate act of rebellion and I'm going to suffer the consequences."

She gasped. "No."

"It's okay. Really. I'm very practiced at breaking and suffering. It's what I seem to do best and I'm used to it." He stopped talking and sat quietly, her head against his knee. "I only wish I could give you the true love you want." He shook his head. "It's the one rule I can't budge."

He hopped off the table and pulled Meredith to her feet. "And it's the one rule that will bring me down in the end. But, I'm not going to go without memories of you." He held her head in his hands and kissed her. It started soft, moved swiftly into firm, and on to insistent. His tongue slipped between her lips and teased her. He deepened the kiss, pulling her against him.

Meredith thought she would faint.

Then she was afraid she wouldn't, and she knew

she couldn't go on feeling what she did without getting out of all this leather and down to basics. Her
skin. His skin. You know. Basics.

She ran her hands up his chest and across his
shoulders, pushing the heavy leather jacket out of
the way. He shrugged out of the coat, and it fell away
to rest forgotten in the long grass. Cinnamon, mingled with the fresh fragrance of green growing
things, surrounded their embrace. She loved his
body, its solid strength, the way it pressed against
hers.

Almost involuntarily, her hands slipped under his
white T-shirt to explore him more thoroughly. She
felt weightless, formless, like someone had boiled
her bones into soup. She sagged against him and he
held her up, lifting her into his arms and carrying
her to a grassy spot beside the stream.

"I'm allergic to grass," she managed to gasp.

"I've taken care of that," he answered. "And all
those annoying little bugs are gone, too." He chuckled as he laid her down. "Sometimes a genie can use
his magic for comfort." He kicked off his boots,
stripped off his shirt and lay beside her. "I want you,
Meredith. I've never wanted a woman so much before."

He leaned down, his hair brushing her forehead,
and nibbled on her neck. The sensation of his touch
raised goose bumps all over her body. She shivered
beneath him. "You're wearing entirely too many
clothes," he said softly.

She tried to sit up to shed her jacket, and it disappeared. She should have known. Genie mischief
focused on passion was bound to make impediments
go away. She pushed off her boots and reached for
her magic man. The ground was soft beneath her.
The sun shone warm on her legs, which were mys-

teriously missing their leggings. It had been Jim's
choice of attire, and he'd obviously known exactly
what the afternoon held.

She felt Jim's hands stroking the outside of her leg,
and she responded by wrapping it around his waist.
His solid weight felt good against her.

His hands explored higher, bypassing the pulsing
need between her legs, sliding up, under the brief
crop-top to tickle her breasts. Tight coils of heat cen-
tered between her legs, and she thought she would
cry out if he didn't relieve that wanting immediately.

Instead, he slipped the top up and slowly lowered
his mouth to her breast. His tongue was hot against
her erect nipples. She pressed herself into his kiss as
her hands went to the buckles on his leather pants.
She had to get to him, release her genie for better or
worse.

He'd moved from her breasts to her belly button,
which he kissed as he stroked her hip.

"This isn't fair," she panted. "I'm practically naked
and you've got . . ."

"Don't be in such a rush, Meredith. We've got all
the time in the world." He continued his downward
trail, coming to rest just above the patch of curly red
hair that was wet and hot, waiting for his touch.

"You're beautiful," he said, kneeling between her
legs. "I could look at you like this forever."

Meredith groaned in longing as his heated gaze
swept over her. Fine. He appreciated the female
form. He could go to an art gallery if he wanted to
look. This particular female needed tending to, not
staring at. "Please?" She wanted him, needed him to
stop looking and finish what he'd started. "Now,
please. I need you now."

"You business types, always in such a hurry." He
grinned devilishly and kissed her stomach once

more. This time his descent didn't stop until he'd discovered her center, her most intimate core, where passion that had built up over the short time she'd known Jim had gathered, waiting for this very moment.

She grabbed his hair with insistence and arched into his embrace as she exploded like fireworks on a short fuse.

"I see that works well," Jim murmured as he returned to minister to her breasts, his leather pants miraculously and decidedly gone, his mouth working its magic again. His exquisite male anatomy was rigid against her.

She gasped. "Oh, yes, that works." Once more she arched her back, wanting more and more of him. All of him.

"I wanted to wait until we were in the duchess's magic tower, but I don't think I can," Jim whispered.

"You'd better not wait," she returned. The release of moments before had been merely a prelude to what she felt building up inside her now.

"As you wish." He entered her swiftly, found their rhythm and took them both flying again. The sensation of him inside her was almost too much to bear. Every molecule of her being cried out to match every molecule of his.

And then the molecules joined and her world spun off its axis in a shower of shooting stars so bright, so stunning, that she cried out with amazement at the glory of it.

Slowly, they came back to earth, a perfect two-point landing. Two beings, two bodies joined in a two-part harmony as old as creation.

"You are so incredibly beautiful, Meredith. So incredibly sweet." Jim breathed the words to her through air that had grown still and thick with their shared passion. "I will miss you dreadfully."

He was saying good-bye. He couldn't go. Not yet. She needed him, needed his quirky view of life, his passionate lovemaking; she wasn't willing to let him go. "Your fate isn't sealed, yet, djinn." She lay in his arms, beside the gurgling stream, sated and happy. "I don't have my contract and you haven't presented your marketing plan." She pushed his hair off his forehead. "We've got time. You said so."

"Yes, I did." He surrounded her with his strong arms, pulling her close. He kissed the top of her head. "All the time we'll ever have."

"I haven't wished my third wish." She paused. "If I never wish it, what happens?" Maybe they did have all the time they needed.

"Theoretically, I have to stay in your service until all three wishes are accomplished. But, practically, with the downsizing going on and the Djinn Reorganization Board anxious to report successes, there's no way the Chairman will let me get away with that. Not considering how far I've bent the rules this time." His finger traced the tops of her breasts, then changed course and dipped into her belly button.

She laughed and pulled him down. Holding his face in her hands, she looked into his eyes. "I really wish you'd quit eavesdropping on my private thoughts and just kiss me."

"As you wish."

Great Djinn, he was in trouble now. He'd half expected the Chairman to turn up in the middle of their lovemaking, spouting management maxims and handing him you're-outa-here papers. Maybe the Chairman had a heart after all. No, not likely. He was probably just waiting for Jim to tell Meredith exactly how he felt about her. Then the final gong would sound and the Big Man would pronounce Jim's death sentence.

He'd been mostly truthful with Meredith when he'd told her he was breaking the rules. What he hadn't told her was how serious it was for a djinn to refuse to do what the Chairman ordered. How devastating it was to become emotionally involved with one's human master. Paramount to mutiny on a British sailing ship, or treason against one's government, emotional attachments were not something the Chairman of the Board would forgive or overlook as mere mischief. And Jim's feelings for Meredith definitely went far beyond simple, physical lust.

At the moment, however, Jim didn't care how the Chairman punished him. Meredith lay snuggled against him, asleep in the afternoon sunlight. Her auburn hair glinted cinnamon in the sun. Cinnamon. His signature scent. Her fair skin was sun-dappled in cinnamon and honey. He kissed the spot between her breasts.

She moved, opened her eyes and smiled.

"It's time we returned," he said. "The Grand Duchess is expecting us to move into her magic tower tonight. I think we can accommodate her." Instantly, their clothing returned, unwrinkled and clean.

"My own personal laundromat," she whispered. "Just what I always wanted in a man."

Her jest made him sad, because it reminded him he could never be the man she'd always wanted, the man he longed to be.

He took the long way back to the hotel, not wanting to break the connection he'd made with Meredith. Over the centuries he'd taken a few human lovers. It was almost expected that djinni mischief included sexual exploration. When he'd originally thought about making love to Meredith, it had been with that expectation in the back of his mind. Pure mischief, acceptable, approved of. When he had actually decided to follow through on his desire, he had known he felt more than just physical attraction to Meredith, a lot more if he was honest with himself. But the actual experience had far surpassed his expectations.

He should have known it would. There wasn't a selfish breath in Meredith's body. A lot of unfulfilled passion, yes, but she'd given herself up to the act without demands. Her arms tight around him even now, as he swung the big bike into a slow curve, made him hard again. She had given him the ultimate gift of herself, and what had he given her?

Worry, trouble, unfulfilled wishes.

He vowed their time left together would only be filled with fun and carefree abandon. He would show her how much he appreciated her faith and trust, how much he really cared.

He stopped in front of a group of small shops on a narrow, cobbled street. "How about some coffee?" He swiveled on the motorcycle seat. "You do want to see a little of the country before we go, don't you?"

Slowly, Meredith released him. "Couldn't we just go back to the hotel and spend the rest of the trip in bed?"

"That is one option, I suppose. But, your new best friend, the duchess, is expecting us this evening for a rousing game of ten-pin after dinner. And, you'll never get that contract signed flat on your back in bed with me."

"Maybe I don't want a signed contract."

"Meredith."

She slid off the bike. "Okay. Coffee it is. And maybe we could stop in that little chocolate shop?"

Putting his arm around her shoulders, he led her

into the chocolate shop. Ten minutes later, they emerged carrying a sack bulging with an assortment of sinful sweets.

"You should try one of these," Meredith said, offering him a dark chocolate covered with chopped nuts of some sort. "Like a tiny orgasm in your mouth. I promise."

"I should never have taken you to that stream. Now you've got sex on the brain." He accepted the tempting candy, using his tongue to capture the sweet from her outstretched fingers. Of course, *he'd* had sex on *his* mind since the day he'd first met her.

"Once I managed to scrape through all that attitude you've been packing around with you, you were simply irresistible. It's your own fault." She popped a candy in her mouth and closed her eyes with obvious enjoyment. "You should never have opted for the rugged, sexy look."

She was probably right about that.

"However," she continued, "you know and I know that we're on a short timeline." She drew a finger from his sideburn to his chin, making his leathers fit a bit too snugly. "I plan to enjoy it all."

He might not be able to grant her wish, but he'd certainly succeeded in changing her attitude about fun.

# Chapter Fourteen

## "Djinn Soaked Hearts"

Meredith found herself humming as she waited for Jim to wish their luggage up the zillion steps to the infamous Hertzenstein Tower Room of True Love. In a castle with no elevators, there was a distinct advantage to having a genie as a bellman.

She walked around the room, peeking out of the slitted windows, bouncing on the bed, looking behind the tapestries. She was sure there were hidden doors and other secrets to be discovered.

She and Jim had a week of nights to spend together, here and back in Virginia. She flopped back on the bed and hugged herself. He was so tender, so strong, so considerate. He'd definitely spoiled her for normal men. Briefly, her heart hurt with the knowledge that these few nights of pleasure would likely be their last. She would have to savor these last days together—moments like the one this afternoon beside the creek—they would have to be enough.

# Karen Lee

Until she had time to talk with the Chairman of the Board, that is, and then she could wish her final wish. She smiled. Jim would be so surprised.

"There. That's the last of it." Jim wrestled the final pair of suitcases through the arched doorway. He dropped them at the foot of the bed and looked around. "So, this is the famous room." He sat on the end of the bed. "It isn't much to write home about, is it?"

"It'll do. It doesn't have all the amenities of the five-star we just left, but it has all I need." She knelt on the bed and put her arms around him. "You."

He grasp her hands and kissed them. "You're dangerous. The more I hang out with you, the more human I become. You'll ruin my career. I have a reputation to uphold, you know."

"Jim, we need to talk about that. I have a plan that may save us both."

"Later, my project. Later. Right now we need to find the Hertzenstein. The Heartstone." He stood and walked slowly around the circular room, pausing every now and then to touch the wall.

"The duchess mentioned that, didn't she?"

He nodded. "It's part of the legend. Hertzenstein means heart of stone. The story goes that when the masons built this tower, one chunk of rock, a particularly stubborn piece of pink granite, refused to split properly. The more they tried, the more the rock resisted. When the masons finally gave up, they found they'd created a stone in the rough shape of a heart. They embedded it in the walls of the bedroom of the future grand duke as a good-luck piece." He continued searching the walls.

"So, what happens when you find this heartstone?" Meredith began to look as well.

"It's part of what makes the love celebrated in this

250

chamber true love." He looked over his shoulder and
smiled. "It's probably the closest I can come to actually granting your wish." He took a step toward the
head of the bed. "Ah, here it is." He pushed aside the
pillows piled against the wall and touched a jagged
pink stone in the rough shape of a heart.

Meredith joined him next to the heart. She
touched it tentatively. "It's smooth."

"Probably from all the people who've rubbed it
through the centuries. Like kissing the Blarney
Stone, anyone wanting true love will seek out the
Hertzenstein." He took her hand and kissed the
palm. He placed her hand over his heart. "My own
heart of stone, Meredith. A genie's heart. I'm sorry I
couldn't grant your wish."

A single tear slipped down her cheek. He caught it
with his finger. "Don't cry. Genies melt when they
come in contact with tears."

She jerked away from him. "Are you kidding?"

"Of course I am. Nothing harms a genie. We're in-
destructible, which is why you don't need to worry
about talking with the Chairman of the Board. I've
got it all figured out."

"Tell me. Tell me what you've got planned. I want
to help."

"You already have. Your marketing plan is excellent. I see no problem at all with adopting it in prin-
ciple. The Chairman will be most pleased."

He was lying. And he hated himself for doing it, but
he couldn't have Meredith wearing herself out worrying about his life when she had her own plans to
fulfill. He'd already planted enough magic traps with
Señor Tiburon that he felt confident Meredith would
be getting a lot of attention from the man. It wouldn't
quite be true love, but it would be affection, and he

counted that as close enough for djinni work.

Of course the Chairman wouldn't see it that way, but Meredith would be happy and that was more important.

"You've gotten awfully quiet for a genie who used to talk nonstop." Meredith opened her smallest bag and pulled out her standard flannel nightgown and her bunny slippers. "Time for bed, don't you agree?"

Snatching the flannel from her hand, Jim raised one eyebrow and said, "Let's try something more daring." He wadded up the flannel and tossed it to her. She caught something black and lacy and downright naughty.

"Why, this is the negligee from that night with Glenn." She was so innocent, one of the qualities he treasured.

"Of course it is. You don't think old married man Glenn could have come up with anything that risqué, now, do you? I wanted to help him out a little."

"Here I thought he really had designs on my body that night and it was all a genie trick. You imp."

"Wrong genus and species. Imps are an entirely different, although related, order. The Chairman keeps them busy in grade schools, teaching little boys how to throw spitwads."

He loved teasing her. She lobbed a pillow at him and he had to retaliate. Of the half-dozen pillows left on the bed, four flew at her all at once. Meredith threw them back, and a general pillow fight ensued.

"I love it when a plan actually works." He snickered and gathered an exhausted Meredith into his arms. "Remember," he said, kissing the tip of her nose, "we're on genie time." He picked up the negligee from under the pillows. "I don't think we really need this, do we?"

"Are you kidding? I've been dying to try it on since

I saw it that night. If Glenn doesn't have sense enough to appreciate it, then you'll have to do." Laughing, she wandered behind the ornate screen opposite the bed.

He whistled his appreciation when she came out, dressed in his creation. "I should have been a designer, yes, I should have." The filmy garment was short, just covering Meredith's tempting hips. At that delectable spot between her legs, he'd designed a rising group of seashells that split somewhere around her belly button and just barely reached her breasts. The rest of the material was filmy and transparent, enticing and promising. Tiny straps of delicate lace held the whole thing up.

But not for long. He reached out toward her.

"Ah, ah, ah, Mr. Genie. No disappearing tricks tonight."

"I see. The strong-minded businesswoman has traded flannel for flimsy. I suppose you think that puts you in charge." He began to move toward her.

"What do you think you're doing, Jim?" She moved away from him, circling the bed.

"A little game of cat and genie, perhaps? Or genie and mouse?"

"You don't have to chase me. Just ask."

"Come to me, then, and make me forget who I am." She flowed into his arms.

He wondered briefly if falling in love with a human counted as granting her wish, but he rejected it out of hand. That couldn't be what he was feeling. Hadn't he told Meredith that genies didn't know how to love?

She grasped his shoulders and pulled him down into a kiss. Something about the room, the legend, heightened the sensations of being skin-to-skin with his sexy human.

In the open, exposed to the surprised glances of passersby, the bank of the stream had been a wonderful fantasy setting for making love. The tower room at Castle Hertzenstein was a different kind of fantasy.

It was like being surrounded by warm, gently scented clouds. Meredith didn't hear choirs. She didn't feel the earth move. She felt safe and loved. Secure.

And then she felt Jim. "What are you doing?"

He grasped her wrists and held them above her head. "You know how to bind a genie, right?" he asked.

"You say his name."

"Well, this is how you bind a genie's woman." He smiled, one eyebrow raised above a dark eye full of gleaming mischief of the erotic kind.

Without warning, she found she couldn't move her arms. She was bound by magic that felt like velvet ropes. Her heart shifted into high gear and pounded away in her chest.

Above her, Jim knelt, his knees between her legs. With one quick motion, he pushed her thighs apart, set his very skilled genie hands on the outside of her legs and began a slow, sensuous trip up toward her hips.

"Stop, wait." She wasn't sure this was what she wanted to do. She struggled against the magical bonds. "Please?" The invisible ropes loosened and fell away.

"It *is* a castle. I thought you might want to try something authentic." Jim kept his hands on her hips, but stopped moving. He grinned a heart-stopping grin. "Just a little something I learned from the late marquis."

"And which marquis would that be, hmmmm?" Meredith didn't know whether to be frightened, angry or aroused. The idea of being unable to resist Jim's advances had definitely brought a flush to her skin. Although the tower room had been cool enough just seconds ago, now even the gossamer garment she wore was too hot.

"Sorry, I thought it might go with the surroundings. All good castles have dungeons. So, I thought I'd create a little captive excitement here. Guess I figured wrong."

She narrowed her eyes and thought just a moment. "I suppose we could play a game, if you want." She sat up quickly. "But, I get to call the shots."

Surprise registered on Jim's face, as though he hadn't considered that she might want to be in control. Chains in a dungeon, indeed.

"You did tell me you'd do whatever I wanted," she reminded him. Slithering out from under her genie, she stood beside the bed. "You are wearing entirely too many clothes, genie of mine." She pretended to think about the situation. "What shall I have you remove first?" She grabbed his ankle and jerked. Jim toppled over in the pile of pillows and blankets, landing with a thud on the bed.

"I think the boots should go first, don't you?" Pointing to his lizard cowboy boots, she demanded, "Take 'em off, cowboy." Awkwardly, he tugged the boots off and dropped them on the floor.

"The belt next, pal. The buckle's much too big and you know what they say about men who wear overlarge belt buckles, don't you?"

"I don't have the slightest idea." He pulled the belt out of his jeans loops and it joined the boots on the floor.

"Well," she purred, "from what I've seen, you don't

need to wear one." She pushed him back against the pillows and straddled him. Carefully, slowly, she undid the buttons on his ersatz Western shirt. "Where'd you come up with the urban cowboy look?"

"I don't know. It seemed like a good idea at the time." He shivered under her touch as she slid the turquoise fabric of the shirt off his shoulders.

"Strip it off, pal." She felt shudders and explosions of desire gathering in her belly as Jim's muscular chest was revealed. He tried to sit up.

"Whoa, there, buster." One hand in the middle of his chest, she pushed him back down in the bed. "Not yet."

"Simon didn't say?"

"You're catching on."

With a dangerous smile on his face, he watched her struggle with the zipper on his jeans. "You're going to feel pretty silly, sitting there in your admittedly skimpy nightie and bunny slippers while I recline in all my male glory."

"Don't you worry your pretty head about that. I rather like the idea of being the only one wearing anything." She sat back on her heels and felt a quivering moistness between her legs. Her genie lay before her, his arms behind his head, his jeans unzipped and his body promising all kinds of unexplored magic.

The slow-burning embers that had been crisping the edges of her heart since their encounter by the stream rapidly blew into a raging forest fire of passion, complete with explosions and sparks spiraling into dense blackness. If she'd had any qualms about her feelings for her genie, they evaporated in a cocoon of sensations, forgotten before they were fully formed.

"Enough teasing." She leaned over and captured

his mouth with hers. "I need you. Now. Naked." She didn't even register surprise as his jeans and her nightgown disappeared together.

"As you wish." His voice was strained, ripe with longing and wanting. He rolled on top of her and began a long, slow dance of love, designed to bring her to a fever pitch.

He didn't have far to go.

As she arched into his body, she heard him inside her head say, "I promise you'll sleep tonight."

*You've done a lot of stupid things*, Jim told himself as he watched Meredith sleep. *But this one gets the highest honors*. Who would have thought he'd fall in love with his human. More to the point, what was he going to do now?

"You can't get to first base if you won't take your foot off home plate," the Chairman of the Board had told him on his first day on the job. He'd taken that advice and turned it into a glorious career. His reputation for trouble had earned him the nickname "Daredevil." Of course, that was usually followed by "screw-up," "hothead," "fool" and other terms less flattering.

Throwing caution in the Dumpster had always worked for him before. Why should he quit now? He'd just have to explain it to the Chairman of the Board in a way he'd understand.

True love was true love, after all.

Meredith awoke to the soft scent of cinnamon and hot bread. Shifting in the bed, she stretched a satisfied catlike stretch. As she opened her eyes, she saw Jim, dressed in a silk robe, pouring coffee.

"It's about time you woke up. You wouldn't want to be late for your big presentation."

She stretched again. After last night, she couldn't care less about her contract with the duchess. "That smells wonderful." She took the coffee from him and sipped. The hot liquid warmed her all the way down.

Not unlike the way Jim had warmed her last night. All the way down, inside and out.

"I suppose I should get going. Her Grace is expecting me at ten and she appreciates promptness." She rolled over. "What time is it, anyway?"

"Hmmmm. I'd peg it at quarter to ten."

"What!" Coffee slopped all over the bed as Meredith rocketed out of it and began looking through her bag. "I'll never be ready. How could you let me sleep so late. What's wrong with you?" She noticed him chuckling into his coffee cup.

"You keep forgetting I'm a genie." He shook his head, smiled, and she was completely dressed in an elegant black crepe suit, with a hot pink blouse peeking over the edges of the jacket. Matching shoes picked up the color, as did the hot pink piping on the sleeves.

"You've been choosing my clothes again."

"Yes. You planned to wear that dreadful tan outfit, with the yellow—not good. This is much stronger, more confident. Besides"—he grabbed her and kissed her—"it makes you look sooo sexy. Why don't we tell the duchess that you've lost your papers and she'll have to wait until this afternoon?" He pulled her to the bed.

"While that sounds much better than talking with our redoubtable duchess, I do have to do this. As soon as I'm finished, we can play. But not until." She smoothed the front of the jacket and admitted it did look stunning. "I like the effect, but I doubt it will impress Her Grace."

"I wouldn't be so sure. Not much gets past that old

girl." He touched her cheek. "She'll notice the bloom in your cheeks that matches the pink in the blouse."

Perhaps he was right. She felt so alive, so whole. Maybe there was magic in these old castle walls. At this moment, she believed she could conquer the world if necessary. And in retrospect, she supposed it was this confidence that led her to take one of the biggest and most important risks of her career.

"Before I start, Your Grace, I have to tell you something. About Jim and me." Meredith folded her hands in her lap and prayed the duchess wouldn't throw her out on her ear. She'd worried about this decision between bouts of lovemaking last night, and on every step down the tower this morning. She took a deep breath. It was the only thing she could do. "I knew about your custom regarding married women. It was part of the briefing Mr. Horton gave me before I accepted this assignment."

The duchess sat quietly, listening politely. "Go on."

Chewing on her bottom lip, Meredith stared at her shoes. This was going to be more difficult than she had thought. "Jim and I aren't married." There. She'd blurted it out. Not her most professional moment, but the truth was out. Almost immediately, she felt as though a great weight had been lifted from her conscience.

For a moment, the old woman sat silently, her head cocked to one side as if she were suddenly overcome with a mixture of sadness and pride. She smoothed her dress and cleared her throat.

"I was wondering if you'd have the courage to tell me the truth, my dear. I knew you hadn't married your young man when you first came to the castle."

"How? How did you know?"

The duchess tut-tutted, shaking her head. "When

you've been married as long as I have, Meredith, you just know. It isn't that you don't love him, and he you. You haven't decided to dedicate your lives to each other yet." She looked wistfully at the portrait of her husband hanging over the fireplace. "I had hoped that a night in my tower would make you see that the feelings you have for each other are strong and able to last a lifetime. Maybe more. You are made for each other."

Meredith sat back, stunned. She could hardly deny the duchess's words, because she felt the veracity in them. The strong and pulsating sensation at the core of her very being. The rush of heat that raced through her at the very thought of Jim. These feelings pointed out a truth she could no longer ignore: She was entirely and thoroughly in love with Jim.

She just couldn't do anything about it.

"I know there are impediments between you and your Jim," the duchess continued. "Edgar and I discussed it last night. But, dear girl, that's the wonder of true love. It really does conquer all."

"I'm not sure it can conquer this," Meredith said sadly. "Not even love can bridge the canyons between our two worlds." She gathered her presentation materials.

"Nonsense. Wait right here." She walked to the door and whispered to the servant. "You remember our conversation last night over dessert? How the magic of the tower really works?" She sat again, patting Meredith's knee.

The Grand Duke, Edgar, came into the room. Meredith jumped to her feet. "Don't stand on ceremony, my girl," the duke said. "This is more in the nature of a family meeting than a formal audience." Edgar, just millimeters taller than the duchess, was dressed this morning in a soft, cashmere sweater that

matched his gray hair. His smile reminded Meredith
of her grandfather.

"My bride and I"—he grinned at the duchess—
"understand why this promotion is so very important for you. We talked about it late into the night."
He sat beside the duchess and took her hand. "We
don't know exactly how, but this will all turn out well
for you and your Jim."

Meredith started, thinking that he'd said "djinn"
instead of "Jim." She shook her head. There was no
way this man could know Jim's true identity. She
cleared her throat. "I appreciate your kindness, Your
Graces." She held up her presentation. "I won't be
needing this. I can't ask you to sign a contract."

The grand Duchess stood, all five feet of her. And
the duke followed suit, all five feet and a smidgen.
"You're correct about that, Meredith," she said. "I
would love to do business with your company, but
tradition is tradition precisely because it has worked
for so long." She laid a soft hand on Meredith's arm.
"Stay as my guests for the remainder of your trip. I
enjoy having young people about. Besides, the magic
in the tower room is very strong. Perhaps you will
find a solution that both of you can live with."

Meredith shook the duke's hand. "You're right
about the promotion, you know. I've already decided
I can live better not worrying about it."

He smiled and, standing on tiptoe, kissed her
cheek. "I know this is going to work, my dear." He
winked.

The duchess signaled for two servants to collect
the remains of their very short meeting. "You come
back after the two of you figure out how to spend
your lives together, and then we can talk about contracts and signatures." With the tiniest of bows, the
Grand Duke and the Grand Duchess of Hertzenstein

left Meredith to pack up her presentation.

"Well, there you have it. No contract. No promotion." To her surprise, she didn't feel angry or disappointed. She felt light and free, as if a weight had fallen away. Securing the vice presidency didn't mean as much as it first had, not when stacked up against the fate Jim would suffer.

She smiled wistfully as she thought of the duke and duchess's optimism. If only she and Jim *could* figure out how to spend their lives together. The duke and duchess had no idea, Meredith thought, of the insurmountable barrier that she and Jim faced. As far as she knew, there hadn't been any successful marriages between humans and genies. It was a dumb idea, anyway. Marriage to a djinn was impossible, beyond the limits of a mere wish.

She returned to the tower to find Jim curled up, asleep. Poor creature. She couldn't fathom what he'd had to do to keep his djinni energy charged through all of yesterday and last night. Frankly, she was surprised he hadn't had some sort of run-in with the Chairman for all the activities they had engaged in—she was sure their actions were somehow forbidden by moldy, ancient Djinni rules.

*I've had about enough of stupid rules*, she thought as she changed into something more comfortable, jeans and a "Visit Hertzenstein" sweatshirt. What had rules ever done for her, anyway? She took her cell phone from its pocket in her briefcase and tiptoed down the stairs, leaving her exhausted genie to rest.

She smiled. He needed his sleep. She had plans for him.

Meredith wandered into the formal gardens surrounding the castle's courtyard. She admired the beautiful flowers and the amazing carvings on the castle walls. High above her she recognized gargoyles covering rain spouts. One especially ugly one attracted her attention.

"I'll bet the Chairman of the Board looks just like you, with drooly fangs and protruding eyes. The horns are probably accurate as well." She sat on a stone bench beside a fountain and addressed her chosen gargoyle.

"Ahem. It has come to my attention that you have selected my personal genie for downsizing. I'd like you to know I think that's a big mistake. He's got talent, and he actually cares about what he's doing. He's not in it just for the glory."

She stopped suddenly, looking right and left. She was certain she'd heard a voice tell her that he wasn't supposed to care and that was what was wrong.

"Don't be silly. Of course he cares. And what's wrong with that? If you're so all-fired interested in getting the general population excited about magic again, I should think you'd want genies who cared."

*Meredith, you've really have lost it this time. First, you take on a genie and now you're talking to stone heads. Ugly ones, at that.* She stood up, cell phone in hand, and waved good-bye to the gargoyle. She looked again, certain she'd seen the stone beast scowl at her.

Too much sun.

Or wishful thinking. She just had to convince that dratted Chairman to spare Jim's life. She wandered around the rose garden, alternately reviewing her performance with the duchess and wondering what kind of surprises Jim had in store for their second night with the Heartstone.

"Hey, why didn't you wake me?" Jim loped toward her, hurdling boxwood hedges as he came. "How did the meeting with Her Grace go?"

Meredith accepted a long, satisfying kiss from her favorite person. She linked her arm through his. "I told her the truth about us. That we're not married. And, while she didn't exactly throw me out, she didn't sign the contract." She leaned against his solid form. "I guess Griffin wins."

Quietly, they walked together, absorbing the reality of her meeting with the duchess. Stopping at a stone bench that overlooked a duck pond, Meredith gazed into Jim's eyes. "The duke was very sweet. He seems to think we can figure out how to make this relationship work."

Jim chuckled. "He's never met the Chairman," he said quietly. "I expect he wanted to take the sting out of your meeting."

"I kind of like him. He's like a comforting uncle, the one who had all the right answers when you were growing up."

"No uncles here. Just the Chairman."

"Speaking of whom . . ."

"No." Jim took her hands and kissed the backs of them, sending chills clear to the top of her head. "I thought we had a date to go horseback riding over the duchess's north forty."

Meredith jumped into his arms and he swung her around, kissing her. "You looked worn out."

"You've never seen me worn out."

Not entirely true. There was that time when he turned blue. And the time he was transparent. But she didn't want to think about those times now. She had promised herself to just enjoy the moment.

Turning her attention back to the sexiest man she'd ever met, she said, "And what will it take to wear you out?"

"Stick with me, kid, and you'll find out." He set her back on her feet, took her hand and walked with her out of the gardens, along a wooded path to the stables.

"I'm not much of a rider," Meredith confessed. "If I were being absolutely truthful, I'd have to tell you horses scare me silly."

"Not you. You're not afraid of anything." Jim put his arm around her. "Seriously?"

"Seriously. When I was a little girl, I asked my father for a horse. I loved horses. I wanted a brown and white one." She leaned into Jim.

"So, did you get one?"

She wrinkled her nose as they rounded the corner into the stable yard. "Not really. My folks didn't have a lot of money. Dad did the best he could. He bought me a pony, a Shetland. Nastiest little beast on the face of the planet."

Jim laughed. "What did it do? Buck you off?"

"It didn't have to do that. I was quite accomplished at falling all by myself." She grew quiet. "I'm still rather good at it." She looked sideways at him, watching the play of shadows on his handsome face. She was falling right now. Falling for her genie.

"Tell you what. Let's take a walk instead of a ride."

Snuggling closer to him, she said, "Works for me."

They'd wandered for about a hundred yards when Jim stooped to pick a daisy from one of the flower beds. He handed it to Meredith. "Are you okay with the duchess not signing the contract?"

Meredith took the flower and began to pluck off the petals. "She bought it. She didn't buy it. She bought it." She twirled the daisy and stuck it behind her ear. "Yes. I just couldn't continue to lie to her." She stopped and put her hands on Jim's shoulders. "I like her. A lot. She's trying to help her country and, while I know I could do that with the plan I've created, I couldn't continue to let her think we were married. You don't create lasting business relationships by fibbing."

Putting his hands on her waist, he leaned his forehead against hers. "Good for you. I'm proud of you." He kissed the tip of her nose. "And don't you feel good, being true to who you are?"

Come to think of it, yes, she did. She nodded. "She did say the proposal was very solid and that I should come back." She stroked Jim's cheek. "I'll get the contract, just not in time to also get the corner office." She took his hand, the electric warmth of it sizzling up her arm and into her heart. "I'm tired of walking. How about you?"

Jim grinned mischievously at her. "And how do you propose we pass the rest of this beautiful day?"

"I don't know, I am sure we can think of something." She met his grin and raised him one. "Maybe reading in bed. I noticed the duke and duchess have a wonderful collection in their library."

"Reading, huh, not exactly what I had in mind." Jim leaned down and gave Meredith a long, lingering kiss that left her wondering only one thing: How quickly could they get back to the tower room?

They spent the entire afternoon in bed, alternating between hot, impatient lovemaking and slow, languorous explorations of each other's bodies.

"Tell me about your life," she asked after a particularly vigorous session. Flopping back on the bed, she closed her eyes.

"You don't have enough time and I don't want to waste what we've got."

"You call what we've been doing wasting time?"

He turned on his side and traced her eyebrow, then her lips, swollen from his kisses. "Absolutely not."

"Really, tell me about you." She kissed the palm of his hand.

"There isn't much to tell. I'm a djinn. I do magic things, make trouble for people, you know, normal stuff."

"Have you ever been in this situation before?"

"You mean, have I ever goofed up on a wish? Not this big."

That wasn't what she meant, but she let it drop. He didn't want to talk, and she could understand why. She was watching the end of a genie's existence. She couldn't believe that he'd chosen to share his last days with her. It brought a lump to her throat and an ache to her chest.

Except, these weren't his last days, she reminded herself. She was confident she could change the course of events by talking to the Chairman. Heck, her first big assignment at Horton's had been to clean up a mess her predecessor had left. And that had meant talking to the chairman of a very important client. Not only had she talked him out of dropping Horton as his consultants, she'd gotten him to agree to an additional half million dollars of services. Yes, chairmen generally were M & Ms in her hands—hard on the outside, soft and melty on the inside.

She considered how she might be able to contact Jim's Chairman. "I can call you on my cell phone," she said.

"Right."

"How do you get in touch with the Chairman? Does he have a special sign, or a code or something?"

"Meredith, I've told you, you can't talk with the Chairman. He rarely takes time to talk to his djinni. He won't be amused if you stay on this course."

"But I can change his mind."

"No. Let it go." He rolled over and got out of bed.

He walked back and forth around the room, running his hands through his hair. "There's only one way that you could talk with him, and that's if I'm gone."

He stopped at the foot of the bed. "You understand what I mean by gone?"

Nodding, she said, "Yes."

"Listen, Meredith. What I said in that park, by the stream? It was a decision I made. *I* made. I knew what was at stake and I thought you did, too." He stooped to pick up his jeans, then pulled them on. "This was a strictly short-term thing, you and me." He slid into his loafers and stormed out of the room.

"Does this mean you don't want me to talk with the Chairman?" she called out. Little did he know. She wasn't sure how she was going to get around the fact that the Chairman would only speak with her when, and if, Jim was gone, but she'd work on it.

She pulled the sheet up to her chin and ran through the conversation she'd just had. Either she'd pushed Jim a little too far and, because he cared about her, he'd gotten irked. Or, behind door number two, Jim really was a mischief-making, trouble-causing, underhanded genie whose main purpose in life was to create chaos. Was it possible this whole "genie expiration date" thing had been a complete fabrication designed to get him into her bed?

She thought about that for a nanosecond. Not possible. He could have had her that first day, in her office on her antique red Turkistan carpet, if that was what he was after. No, there was something bigger bothering her Jim.

She hoped.

Jim ran down the curved stairs two at a time. He had to get away from Meredith and the stark knowledge that he was doomed. He'd never asked for much during all the centuries he'd been granting wishes, but he would sell his very essence if he could figure out a way to stay with Meredith forever.

He wandered down a long hall and found himself in the castle library. An old man sat in an ornate chair, smoking a pipe and leafing through a very large book. He looked up as Jim came in. The Grand Duke.

"Ah, taking a break from the tower, are we? Come in, come in, my boy." He waved Jim into the room. "You look like you swallowed a jarful of spiders. What's wrong?"

Jim edged into the room and leaned on the bookcase. "Nothing. I appreciate your hospitality, Your Grace. It's a lovely castle."

"Nonsense, my boy. It's a moldering old heap of stones, that's what it is. Drafty, cold." He set down his pipe. "Come in. Sit. Tell me what's wrong."

"I told you, nothing's wrong."

"You're not a very convincing liar, son."

Jim came around the end of the long sofa and sat on the arm. "It's Meredith. She thinks she can fix everything with her charts and diagrams and plans."

"She might be right."

"Not this time." He picked up a fringed pillow and played with the tassel on the corner.

"You don't see it now, my boy, but your woman is right. She can fix the problem, if you'll just trust her to follow her heart." He lit his pipe once more and drew a long, satisfying breath of fragrant smoke. "You'd be surprised how true love can overcome any obstacle in its way, if you just let it."

"I'm not in love with her." Maybe if he said the words out loud, he could make them true, he thought wistfully.

"Nonsense. How can you not love her, my boy?

She's your soul mate. You provide balance for her life, she provides focus for yours."

Jim shook his head. "It's true, I care for her. More than I have anyone else. But . . ."

"But, you're afraid it isn't in your character to devote yourself totally to one woman. Since you don't seem to fit in with your coworkers and especially your boss, you can't see yourself completing a different jigsaw puzzle." The duke cocked his head and examined Jim.

Jim felt like wriggling under the intense scrutiny. The duke seemed to understand their situation so well—it unnerved Jim.

"How do you know about the quarrel I have with my boss? No one knows about that. Not even Meredith."

The duke tapped the side of his nose. "Not everyone has the chance you do, son. Very few of us actually meet our true soul mates." He puffed on his pipe, watching the smoke curl in an intricate baroque pattern to the ceiling. "When you do, it's imperative you grab hold and never let her go."

Jim skipped past the never-let-go part. "Us?"

The old man winked at Jim. "Us men, son. Us men. Most of us hurry when picking a woman. We hook up with the first one who makes our blood sing." He cocked his head again. "I can see that you've waited a long, long time." The tobacco burned red in the bowl of the pipe as the duke drew in a breath. A smoky, cinnamon fragrance filled the room. "Trust is a powerful thing, my boy. Give your Meredith a chance."

Jim stood up and paced the room, studying the books lining the shelves. His mind didn't take in any of the titles, though. He thought only of Meredith. Trust. Wasn't that what he was always asking Meredith to do? And she'd done it, time after time. No matter how badly he'd botched things, she continued to trust him.

"Perhaps it's time to return the favor, son," the duke said with a yawn. "I've got a long day tomorrow. I'm dedicating a bridge, so I'll say good night now. You can stay here if you want, but I'd recommend going back to that young woman of yours. This room is drafty, but in the tower you have love to keep out the cold." He smiled and shuffled out of the room.

How had the duke known what he was thinking? It was almost as if he were a djinn himself. Jim shook his head. It couldn't be. It was not possible. And yet, the signature djinni fragrance came from his pipe. Was it possible the old legend might be based in fact? That, once every so often, a djinni was created with an abundance of human emotions so strong that he . . . Jim shook his head. Not possible.

He reconsidered what the duke had said and, for the second time since he'd come to Hertzenstein, he made a very important decision.

Whatever he was, the old man was right. He needed to trust Meredith and the love he had for her. He ran back down the hall and up the stairs.

He'd managed to avoid making the worst mistake of his life. If he was very lucky, she'd take him back and together they'd make their final days in Hertzenstein the best.

# *Chapter Fifteen*

## *"Djinn Trap"*

Jim guided Meredith through the crowds of people at the Horton Consulting Gala, pleased with himself and happy for the first time he could recall. He'd done what the duke suggested. The rest of their brief stay in Hertzenstein had constituted one of the happiest times he'd ever had. He'd even quit worrying about what the Chairman would do to him. It didn't matter anymore.

He was with Meredith, where he wanted to be. Whether they were in an enchanted tower room or in this expansive, beautifully decorated grand entry to the National Gallery. He stopped grinning long enough to pay attention to the people she introduced him to. Her colleagues.

"Jim, you remember Bill Horton, president of Horton Consulting." Meredith smiled. "Jim's the assistant with the specialty on the British market who helped with my presentation last week." The first thing she'd done when she and Jim had gotten back from Hertzenstein was to go to Horton and tell him about her failure to secure a signed contract. He'd been sad, rather than angry. Then he had seemed more interested in her relationship with Jim. Why had she broken her golden rule and dated someone from the office? He had not been accusing—after all, Jim had been more of a consultant than an assistant, and they were only working together temporarily, Horton had pointed out as he uncharacteristically babbled on about how happy he was that she had found someone with whom she really seemed happy.

Meredith had wondered briefly whether she had some secret message inscribed on her brow declaring, "This woman must be married to achieve supreme happiness." First her parents, then the duke and duchess and now Horton. Everyone seemed to be thrilled at the prospect of her marrying Jim. Maybe they knew what she had only recently realized: It took more than a successful career to make her happy—she needed her genie.

She gazed at the crowd gathered for Horton's annual Gala, wondering how much true love there was in the group sipping wine and nibbling canapés.

The National Gallery was the perfect place for a reception. The open, two-story space was big enough to hold a small athletic competition. Off to the right were the offices and the Gallery's extensive library. To the left the open area led to smaller, more intimate halls with exhibits. Above them, to one side of the wide staircase leading to the upper floor, turning slowly in the air currents caused by the heat rising from the crowd, was a huge, steel mobile suspended from the ceiling. Alexander Calder was a genius, she thought, as she watched one of his signature pieces. It looked sort of like an airplane wing.

She brought her attention back to the stunning man at her side. Although she hadn't told Jim, she had given up the silly idea that she could find another man who made bells ring the way Jim did. As a consequence, she was resigned to the fact that she'd have to rely on her business acumen to save Jim's life.

"Of course, of course. Couldn't forget our resident gentleman." Horton stuck out his hand. "Jim, glad to have you aboard." He unleashed his legendary charm. "Meredith is one of our stars, in spite of the outcome of the Hertzenstein assignment." He took Jim's elbow and leaned close. "Smart. Tough. You'd be a lucky man indeed if she decided to make your partnership permanent."

"Thanks, Bill, I appreciate your vote of confidence." Meredith slipped her arm through Jim's. "Let's mingle, shall we?" She smiled at her genie. The very last place she wanted to be was here, among all these people. Jim had nine days left. The second thing she'd done when they'd gotten back was to take that time off. She intended to spend the next nine days with Jim, and only Jim. But, she couldn't skip the Gala.

"Maybe we can chat later, Jim. Good to see you again." Horton turned to other guests.

"Delighted, I'm sure," Jim whispered into Meredith's ear, his warm breath sending shivers up her spine. "What was that all about? Permanent partnerships?"

"Variation number thirty-two on Mr. Horton's standard lecture." She maneuvered him across the expanse of marble floor toward the broad staircase. "He and his wife are happily married. Have been for going on thirty years. Deep in his heart, he wants each of his managers to have the same kind of joy in their lives. He's kind of like my folks in that regard. He's forever trying to play matchmaker." Could it be that Horton and his wife were another example of true love? Maybe there was more of this stuff around than she was aware of.

"He's right, you know," Jim said. "People in love glow." He smiled broadly and bowed as several sequined women wandered by, giving him looks of undisguised interest.

Meredith observed his movements with narrowing eyes. "Maybe bringing you wasn't such a hot idea." She felt an unaccustomed flush of protectiveness toward Jim. No, it was jealousy, plain and simple.

"Hi. I'm Jim. I'll be your genie for the evening." He leaned close and whispered into her ear, "I think it was a splendid idea. Look around. You can hear the buzz. Who is he? Where did he come from? Isn't Meredith the lucky one? If I can't actually grant your wish for true love, at least I can make them wonder."

She shivered. If they kept this up, and they really had no choice now that they were here, the crowd of this city's elite would have them engaged, married and pregnant before the night was through. Just like Her Grace, the duchess.

She placed her hand on Jim's chest and pushed gently. She could feel his human heart beating, pulsing beneath her touch. She took a deep breath. "We have a mission, oh, djinn of mine. For both of our sakes we'd better focus on that." She'd spent time helping Jim understand the finer points of the djinni marketing plan, so he'd be prepared to pitch it to the Chairman of the Board.

"Jealously and envy are strong motivators, Meredith. Let these fellows wonder for a while, then, when they least expect it, you swoop in and flatter away." Jim still thought she might find her true love

275

in this crowd, Meredith thought ruefully. How could he not know her true love was on her arm?

Jim stood back and began a slow ascent of the stairs. "Let's go look at the exhibit." As she joined him, he smiled broadly. "Promise me one thing, Meredith. Let me experience this evening as a man. I thoroughly enjoy being a man to your woman and we both know I will never have this opportunity again. I want to savor every movement, every sensation." His touch promised a night of savory sensations. She shivered again.

"As you wish, Cinderella. Just remember, you turn into a pumpkin at midnight a week from now. And, if you don't come to your senses and let me talk to your Chairman, you may just disappear altogether."

His smile was strained. "Not to worry."

Arm in arm, they walked up the grand staircase and into the exhibit hall on the second floor. This was the fourth year her company had taken over the National Gallery for their annual spring Gala. Guests had full access to the exhibits, while the main floor was festooned with tables of food, garlands of fresh flowers and athletic-looking waiters in white jackets. One offered Meredith and Jim tall flutes of champagne.

"None for me, thanks." Jim smiled at the waiter and handed Meredith a glass. "No alcohol, remember," he whispered.

Meredith snatched a second glass from the waiter's tray. "You want the full experience, have a glass of champagne." She offered the delicately golden liquid adorned with bubbles. "You may like it."

She could see him fighting the curiosity, and losing the battle handily. He took the glass. "Are you sure?"

"Manly men aren't afraid of the bubbly." She took a sip of hers. "And this is an especially good vintage."

He lifted the glass to his lips, sniffed and sneezed.

"Drink it, silly. Don't inhale it." Her laughter danced merrily around the marble hall, and she could see the heads turn toward her. He was right. Let them wonder.

"I think I'll pass on this particular experience, thanks. I've seen what these dangerous drinks do to people."

"Suit yourself."

Francis Griffin emerged from behind a large, black and red steel sculpture—another masterpiece by Calder, twice as tall as Griffin and a lot more attractive. "Gorgeous dress, Meredith. As I recall, you were modeling it in your office a week or so ago. Just after your 'date' conveniently disappeared." He glanced at Jim. "I guess the definition of office assistant has expanded considerably. Really, Meredith, I didn't think any woman who looks as good as you do would have to pay for it. By the way, I understand your trip to see the queen was less than satisfying." He smirked. "At least from a contractual standpoint."

"She's a duchess." Meredith stiffened, trying to ignore his underhanded reference to her relationship with Jim.

Jim took her elbow and said, "Why don't you go look at the display in the next room while Francis and I have a little chat." He pushed her gently toward the door.

She went into the next gallery, but quickly backtracked and followed Jim and Griffin at a discreet distance, concealing her presence beside a glass display case of smaller Calder works. She could just hear the conversation.

"I have really lost all patience with you," Jim said

as he led Griffin behind an especially large sculpture. "Cut her some slack, why don't you?"

"Really, of all the absurd things. Meredith's gigolo telling *me* how to act." Griffin poked Jim's chest with his index finger. "You're the one who should watch out, buster. I'm . . . a . . . very . . . important . . ."

"Yeah, you're important, all right, about as important as a bad file on a computer. Or a pig at a picnic." Jim shook his head.

"Don't get personal, pretty boy." Grifin poked harder. "You're a temporary employee, you know, and I'm going to be the next vice president. Whatever agency you came from, I'll see that you never get work in this town again."

Midpoke, Jim grabbed Griffin's hand and twisted it slightly. Griffin's face got red.

"Unhand me, you lout. Who do you think you are? Just because you're sleeping with little Miss I'm-Better-than-You doesn't mean . . ." His sputter slowed to a halt. Jim had begun to get taller, and nastier-looking. In seconds, he towered over Griffin with a menacing look on his face. He was still Jim, but Meredith was extremely glad she'd never made him angry.

"Who, wh-what are you?" Griffin's face was very pale, and he looked like the little boy who had just discovered that the bogeyman was real and living under his bed.

"I'm Meredith's assistant and her friend. Now, go away and don't bother her again." Instantly, Jim was back to being Jim. Handsome in a tux, sexy and strong. But, just Jim. The towering demon had gone back to its hiding place.

She walked quickly back to the gallery Jim had directed her to, thinking he should have turned Griffin into a toad. Oh, she forgot. He already was one.

She stopped just inside the door and watched a delicate red, yellow and black mobile twist in the air.

Darcie waved to her from across the gallery. "Hey, Boss Lady. You look great."

"You're not looking too shabby yourself." The iridescent fabric of Darcie's gown shifted in the light from rich purple to subtle gold, enhancing her perfect skin. "Where's Ben?" Tonight Darcie wore colorful beads in her hair to match her gown.

Darcie grinned. "Getting more champagne. He's so romantic."

"Lucky you. Romantics in this town are scarce as hen's dentures."

"I'd say we've both struck oil, then, because that yummy man who's been trailing after you all evening has romance written all over him, capital letters, forty-two-point font, bold."

Meredith smiled, picturing Jim with neon letters running up and down his tuxedo, alternately flashing "Romance" and "Get yours here." She shook her head. She was beginning to think like him.

"Where is he anyway? You shouldn't let any man who looks that tasty stray. There are too many trolling guests here this evening."

"Don't you worry, Darce. Any woman fishing for fun with Jim will surely flounder. They don't have his number. I do." She patted her black evening bag, reassured that her cell phone was safely tucked away with her lipstick and compact. "And I'm not sharing."

"Then, where is he?"

"He and Francis are discussing the finer points of Alexander Calder's choice of material in his stabiles versus his mobiles."

"That'll be the day. Francis couldn't spell 'art' if you gave him alphabet blocks and a diagram. Not to mention that he's absolutely unbearable since he got the contract and you didn't. I don't think you're going to be happy, working for him."

Darcie was right. "I've survived worse in my career."

"Perhaps. I've only worked with him for, let's see, less than a month, and I've gained a new respect for the words 'vengeful' and 'ambitious.' If this weren't a civilized land, I'd label him very dangerous."

"He's an overeager, frustrated, mildly talented man who can't deal with competition when it wears panty hose and heels." Meredith grinned at Darcie. "I sure miss you."

"Me, too, Boss Lady. But, I'll be back next week. As soon as I tie up all the loose ends from East Overshoe, Wyoming." Darcie's face lit up as Ben approached. "Oooh, baby. Thanks." She stretched to kiss his cheek, then took the flute of champagne. "You remember Meredith?"

Ben Johnson executed a perfect finishing-school bow and reached for her hand, which he kissed. "Who could forget such stunning eyes."

"Why, thank you, Mr. Johnson."

"A sentiment I wholeheartedly agree with." Jim took his place beside Meredith, putting his arm around her slender waist. "Of course, the rest of her is totally forgettable."

Meredith elbowed him in his side. "Impolite remarks will be noted on your report card, sir." She laughed. "Ben Johnson, meet Jim Goodman."

"Jim and Benny," Darcie quipped. "Maybe you should go into business together. Ice cream, perhaps."

The two couples wandered through the exhibit, talking and laughing. Meredith began to relax, observing how well Jim got along with Ben and Darcie.

Ben launched into his latest business plans, and Jim listened carefully, even offering suggestions. He chuckled at Darcie's outrageous jokes, and kept his arm protectively around Meredith's shoulders as they navigated the crowded rooms.

*What was wrong with this scene?* Nothing. Jim was perfect. He'd charmed her mother and father, handled her nieces with patience and humor, and dazzled Horton with his business acumen. He'd even held his own with the duchess. Most of all, he made her insides melt when he looked into her eyes. Even when his arm just briefly brushed hers, her heart sped up. There had to be a way to stop the inevitable chain of events piling up to take him away from her. There just had to. She took a deep breath as an idea from earlier began to unfold even further.

She did have that last wish.

Occasionally she looked over her shoulder, certain she saw, or more likely, felt, Francis Griffin following them. Being tracked by a rabid hyena would be preferable. She didn't trust Griffin as far as she could toss him. And, since she didn't have any intention of getting close enough to him to touch him, much less heave him across the room, she didn't trust him at all. He should have been happy with his promotion. Why was he still snooping?

"How about dessert? I detect the delicate scent of high-octane chocolate in the air." Jim, self-appointed, obsequious servant for the evening, nodded to the trio before him and went off in search of mousse and truffle.

"I'm sure he'll need help." Ben trundled off after Jim.

"Tell you what, Boss Lady. You need to option that one. He's even better than I remember him." Darcie

# Karen Lee

cocked an eyebrow and gave Meredith a knowing look. "Good men are hard to come by."

"I've been thinking the very same thing." She'd have to phrase the wish just right.

"Uh-oh. Skunk. Twelve o'clock high," Darcie whispered. "Hi, Francis. Where's your wife, Marianne?"

"Off powdering her nose or something. I know this is supposed to be an evening of fun and frivolity, but I need to talk briefly with you about some unfinished business. The mayor of Overshoe just paged me." He glowered. "It's imperative that we talk with him. Tonight."

Darcie rolled her eyes. "Of course it is. Let me finish my dessert. Meet me at the wine bar in fifteen minutes?"

"You know, Francis, Horton hasn't announced the promotion yet. I wouldn't get too cocky." Meredith smiled. "I could always have Jim talk to you again."

Griffin paled once more, and swallowed, grabbing for his handkerchief. "That won't be necessary, I'm sure." He looked at Darcie. "Wine bar in fifteen minutes. And, bring a cell phone. We may need to make a couple of calls. I want to be sure all the copies of the signed contract have been filed properly." He turned on his heel and stamped away.

"Sheesh. That man doesn't give up. In a spate of really bad planning, being under the impression that work was over for the week, I left my phone at home. Alone. Can I borrow yours?" She looked expectantly at Meredith.

He'd beaten her at a game she'd all but invented, but she didn't feel any regrets about Griffin and the corner office. "I detect a not-so-subtle implication that I can't leave work at work."

Darcie shrugged and grinned. "You said it, not me."

282

"As usual, you're right. I've got my trusty phone right here," she patted her bag. "But, you can't have it."

"Expecting an important call, are we?"

"You never know when Prince Charming or one of his brothers might need the odd marketing plan."

"Speaking of the Charmings, they've stormed the battlements and brought back treasure—mounds of delectable chocolate." She accepted a plate of assorted desserts from Ben. Jim set a similar selection in front of Meredith.

"I couldn't decide which you'd like more, so I got some of everything." Ben grinned at Darcie.

"The appropriate response when faced with chocolate choices." Darcie cut into a decadent devil's food cake and closed her eyes in ecstasy, inhaling the fragrance like fine wine. "The only real reason to live, besides you, baby."

Jim sat next to Meredith, missed the chair and landed on the floor at her feet.

"Are you all right?" She had never seen Jim execute a clumsy act before.

"Floors are our friends. I guess I misjudged where the chair was." He stood, shook his head and sat, this time where he wanted to. "I'm feeling just slightly dizzy."

"A normal reaction when in the presence of fair ladies and chocolate." Darcie waved her fork at him. "Low blood sugar. Have some chocolate cheesecake. It'll fix you right up."

Meredith doubted Jim's action had anything at all to do with blood, sugared or not. She wasn't certain genies had blood. "Maybe some fresh air would help. It is stuffy in here." She stood and took his elbow. "Let's wander the gardens, shall we?"

He rose, stumbled a bit and, apologizing to Ben

and Darcie, went with Meredith out into the garden.

"Are you okay? Are you going to be all right? I've never seen you like this. What's wrong?"

"One question at a time, please." He moved slowly to a stone bench under a blooming dogwood and sat. He rested his head in his hands. "I'm fine. As for being all right, I'm usually more left than right, so it wouldn't be correct to say I was all right. I'm about half right at the moment. Half left." He looked up at her and patted the bench. "Sit. It's easier to see you if you're closer."

She sat and put her hand on his knee. Something was definitely out of order.

"Third question again. I didn't quite catch it."

"What's wrong with you?"

"The Chairman of the Board is reminding me that I'm running out of time." He glanced at her plaintively. "You should have asked Tiburon to come to this gig with you."

"Absolutely not. I wouldn't have come with anyone else. We're a team, remember? We have a deal. Part of it was for you to come to the Gala. I don't welsh on a deal. Besides, he's in Australia."

"Tell you what. I could use a glass of water. Go get me one while I catch my breath? I'll be fine. Trust me."

"Whatever you say. You're the genie-in-charge." She moved reluctantly back toward the gallery, peering worriedly over her shoulder to reassure herself that Jim hadn't disappeared altogether.

Jim leaned back against the cold trunk of the dogwood tree. He didn't feel well at all. The Chairman of the Board must really be angry about his solution to Meredith's wish. He'd need to face it sometime.

Now was as good as any. "What? What do you want?" He addressed the air.

A deep voice boomed in his head, "Take care, Khalil. You've grown too fond of this woman. You forget your purpose."

"My purpose is to fulfill her desire for true love. I figured I could do a better job with this impossible wish if I got to know her better. You've never understood my creative approach to wish-granting." He could feel the anger of the Chairman of the Board build behind his human eyes, creating a splitting headache. All of Meredith's pain relievers couldn't touch this one.

"You have little time, Khalil Abu ben Kajii. I have been patient. I can be patient no longer."

"Hold it. I've got until midnight a week from today to unravel the answer. If you keep sapping my strength and making me fade in and out, how am I ever going to prove my worth?"

"I pose special challenges to you because of who you are. You are the First of my Djinni, created to have particular characteristics. I don't know where I went wrong, but you know I must not favor you over the others."

Particular characteristics? The legend flitted through Jim's head. Not possible. "Couldn't you just favor me as much? Do you have to pile troubles in my way?" As he suspected, there was no answer from the Mighty One. In fact, he appeared to have left the building altogether.

Jim slumped against the tree. Genies with human emotions. It was merely a bedtime story. And yet, with Meredith he'd been a better man than a genie. He shook his head wearily. He had to recharge. He straightened, shimmered, glinted and sparkled and changed his form back to standard-issue genie shape. He wriggled and expanded, comfortable in his own skin when he noticed a figure in the shadows at the edge of the garden.

Jim froze. It couldn't be Meredith, and if it were anyone else he was in deep trouble. No human had ever seen him in his true genie form. To be seen now, in this weakened state, would be to compromise himself utterly. As the figure moved out of the shadow, Jim pinged back into his human self, feeling somewhat refreshed, but apprehensive nonetheless.

"Who are you?" Francis Griffin strode toward him.

Jim stood, completely affronted. "I told you, I'm Meredith's friend. Remember?" Meredith. Whose wish he couldn't satisfy and who was breaking his nonexistent djinn heart.

"I remember. I haven't had that much to drink." Griffin narrowed his eyes. "I mean who are you, really?"

This guy must be stupid and dense. Apparently the earlier display of enraged demon hadn't penetrated. Or hadn't stuck. He had to do something. Soon. "Oh, you probably mean all the lights." Jim reached behind him and smacked the decorative pole holding up festive paper lanterns. "Must be a short in the cord or something. These things keep flashing on and off." He hit the pole once more and several of the lanterns flickered. "See?"

Griffin scowled. "I was sure I saw something, something very strange."

"Nope. Just blinking lights. If you want something strange, check out Meredith's phone." He paused to see if his comment registered at all in the man's meager mind, then slapped Francis on the shoulder. "I'm getting cold. Let's go back in."

\*   \*   \*

"Have you got a mirror in your purse? I need to see if I've gotten all the brownie out of my teeth before I meet Francis." Darcie ran her tongue around her mouth.

Meredith put down the glass of water for Jim and dug around in her bag, setting her keys, compact, lipstick, and cell phone on the table. She found the mirror and handed it to her friend. "You once said that chocolate made the perfect after-dinner attire and now you want to remove it?"

"Not cool in crowds. Especially those where your temporary new boss shows up. Hi, Francis. Have you met my presumed fiancé, Ben?"

Francis Griffin reached across the table to shake hands. "Pleased to meet you. And, congratulations. I didn't realize you'd made it official."

Jim sat next to Meredith and drank the water.

"We haven't," Ben said. "Darcie takes every opportunity to remind me I haven't said those four little words she's dying to hear." He grinned mischievously.

Darcie punched him playfully in the arm. "You shouldn't tease me, when you know the answer is yes."

Jim leaned close to Meredith, whispering, "What four words is she talking about?"

"The ones that come after the three words all women want to hear."

"Okay, we're up to seven words. Are you going to tell me which words or shall I guess? How about 'You've got chocolate sauce on your skirt.' That's seven."

"What Meredith is talking about, Jim," Darcie said, "is two simple sentences that get stuck in most men's mouths: 'I love you,' and 'Will you marry me?' Ben's gotten really good at the first one, but I can't seem to make him speak the second." Darcie looked hopefully at her man. "No time like the present."

"I believe you're right." Ben stood, walked around the table and knelt in front of Darcie. He took her hand and kissed it. "Will you marry me?"

The silence was ear-splitting. Meredith nudged Darcie. "I think your correct response is 'Yes.' "

"Yes." Darcie said obediently. Her face broke into a huge smile. She stood up and shouted, "Yes, yes. Of course I'll marry you." Ben folded her into his embrace.

Once more, Meredith felt a deep sadness. In Darcie and Ben she recognized the joy she and Jim had felt in the duchess's tower. Only for these two, it would last.

"Well, congratulations officially." Francis Griffin, reached for the cell phone beside Darcie's half-eaten chocolate cake.

Meredith's cell phone.

"I have seven words you need to hear." Jim touched Meredith's arm. "Griffin has your cell phone right now."

"Huh?" Meredith, excited for Darcie, didn't quite catch Jim's meaning.

"I said, Griffin has your cell phone right now!"

"Oh!" She stood and grabbed for the phone. "You can't use that, Francis."

"Really? Why not?"

"Because I've got it coded in a special way. For my fingers only." She snatched it back.

"I need to make a very important call." He took it from her and turned it on.

"It won't work for you. Trust me." She reached for it.

"And why won't it? What's so special about this

particular cell phone?" He held it just out of her reach.

As Griffin turned the phone on, Jim tried to snatch it from his grasp. But Griffin pulled it away from the genie. Meredith lunged forward. In the ensuing confusion, the phone, now activated, flew into the air over the table. Chairs tipped over. Ben pulled Darcie out of the way of chocolate shrapnel. Meredith, Jim and Francis all grabbed for the phone when a booming voice filled the room, "STOP!"

Jim grabbed the phone as everyone froze. Literally. The scene was a tableau of beautiful women in formal dress, men in tuxedoes, chairs suspended in midcrash. Bits of chocolate hung everywhere. Jim turned the phone off and carefully set it back on the table. "Okay, they've stopped." He addressed his superior, knowing he was in deep weeds.

He'd heard of only one other occasion when the Chairman of the Board had intervened. Djinni didn't speak of it; houris fainted when the subject came up. Only the demons seemed to know what had happened. Jim had made outrageous promises to get them to tell him.

He should have left that well undrilled.

He straightened and sauntered around the scene, ducking under outstretched arms frozen in midreach, tasting a fingerful of chocolate frosting. The panic on Meredith's face, the triumph on Francis's were captured in a three-dimensional snapshot of the genie's ultimate failure. He knew what was coming and it wouldn't be pretty.

"You've pushed my patience too far this time. You understood before you took this assignment that there could be only one client, as you put it. And, yet you let the cell phone fall into another's hands. And worse, you allowed him to *activate* it."

The Chairman of the Board's voice echoed around the room, anger hung from the chandelier while fury built to a reverberating pitch. At least he wasn't raging on about the genie's relationship with Meredith. Rules were rules, after all, and not letting more than one master have access to the lamp at a time was one of many.

"Let me guess. You're not here to hand out a Good Djinni Award." Jim could feel the Great Djinn's head shake.

"Why do you aggravate me so?"

"Because I'm good at it?"

"Khalil, my son, you have always been my favorite. I've spoiled you, I admit. And I take partial responsibility for your dismal state, but YOU KNEW THE RISKS!"

"Of course I knew them. You taught me to handle risks. You gave me the skills and beat the lessons into me. How could I not know the risks? I wanted the challenge."

"Explain to me then why you permitted this situation to deteriorate so far."

Jim sighed. His future as a djinn was clear. Short, but clear. This was his exit interview. He had no future.

He'd heard that humans' lives flashed before their eyes as they died. He cocked an eyebrow and gazed at the ceiling. Nothing even vaguely cinematic appeared. He tried to conjure up memories of other times, other masters, wishes that went spectacularly well.

The only image he saw was Meredith. Her smile, her determination to create the perfect marketing plan for him, her eager lips, her amazing body. Her caring, her concern.

He'd spent the better part of the month analyzing the various ways his last assignment could end. They all came to this: his absolute failure to grant Meredith's wish. He'd known as soon as the words were out of her mouth that he would fail. And he hadn't stopped it. He could have gone back to the Djinn Reorganization Board right then and there and let them know the problem he faced, turned in his djinn identification card, his keys to the locker room, and signed his outplacement forms.

But he hadn't.

And he knew precisely why. She was an intriguing puzzle and he couldn't resist a puzzle. Jigsaw, crossword, acrostic. This time it happened to be Meredith.

"The situation, as you call it, got out of hand because I've stumbled upon something that made it impossible for me to act otherwise." He stopped in front of Meredith and straightened her hair. "In fact, I suspect you knew before you gave me this assignment that I'd find out eventually."

"Yes. But I had hoped you might be spared the knowledge that magic isn't all-powerful. In the final analysis, Khalil, you are really too clever to be a genie. I should never have created you with human emotions. It was a dangerous experiment that has gone terribly wrong. At least I've learned that human emotions and djinni mischief don't mix." The great djinn paused. "For the record, then, what did you learn?"

"I discovered something more powerful than djinni magic." He took a deep breath. "I found love. I found Meredith. She's different from anyone I've served over the centuries. She didn't wish for riches or power. Her concern was always for me, never for herself." He slumped against the table. "I love her. The agony of knowing I couldn't be with her would have ended the assignment anyway, so I decided to accelerate the process, let Griffin possess the phone if only for seconds." He looked up at the source of the voice. "I figured you'd send in the troops, make a citizen's arrest. I had to stop before she fell in love with me."

"You may have acted too late."

He shook his head, felt a tear form. "No, please, no. It isn't fair. She should be able to find happiness with one of her own, not be saddled with a memory of a defective genie barred from returning her feelings. Please, do something. I know you can do something. Make it right."

The Chairman of the Board cleared his throat. "There is nothing I can do, Khalil."

"Nothing you will do," he snorted. "So. It's over."

"Except for some minor paperwork." As the Chairman of the Board spoke, dozens of pages fell through the air, collecting at Jim's feet. "The standard release forms, in triplicate. Read them, initial in the boxes, sign at the X and we can wrap this up."

"I really think you're taking this bureaucracy thing too far." He gathered the pages, whipped a pen into existence and read, initialed, perused. "Before I sign away my very being, I have one last request."

"Highly irregular."

"Call it an old human custom, granting the prisoner one last wish before the firing squad uses him for target practice. It won't cause any problems and it's really a very simple request. I want to say goodbye."

"To the woman?"

"She stood by me through all this. If I don't, she'll think it's her fault I'm gone. I can't let that happen."

He stood firm, waiting for the Great Djinn to decide.

"Done."

Meredith, reanimated, made her grab for the phone exactly where she'd left off. Only the phone wasn't there anymore. "What is going on here?" She collapsed into Jim's waiting arms. "Are you doing something magic? Why isn't anyone moving? How can chocolate hang in the air?"

"Which question would you like me to answer first?" He smiled at her confusion and pulled out a chair. "Sit. I'll explain.

"Yes, it's magic. No one's moving because they've been frozen in place for the time being. It's my fault. When Francis grabbed your phone and turned it on, he technically became the master of the djinn inside. Me. And that violated my assignment. You and only you were to have possession of the phone."

Meredith stood and started to walk around the room. "What are you saying?"

"I'm trying to explain. If you'd just stop pacing and sit down." He made a plush chair appear and led Meredith to it. "Sit. The Chairman of the Board has allowed me a brief minute to say good-bye."

"He's here?" She shook her head as if to clear away some invisible fog clogging her vision.

"Yes, in full voice if not in form."

"Hello, Mr. Chairman. Nice to almost meet you. I want to tell you that Jim has done a wonderful job under trying circumstances." Silence. "I want you to know I'm very satisfied with his work." Silence. She frowned at Jim. "I don't think he's listening."

"Oh, he's listening." He sat on the arm of the chair and took Meredith's chin in his hand. "It boils down to this. I'm leaving. My assignment is over. I need to tell you some things before I go."

"You can't leave. You're not finished."

"Rest assured, I'm finished."

"But, we haven't delivered the marketing plan."

"You're on your own with the plan. I gave the Chairman the folder, but he's not having any of it." He looked toward the ceiling, then back at her. "Listen, Meredith. Being with you has been worth everything it cost. I learned that not all humans are greedy. That some have a great capacity to care." He stopped, watched a tear form at the edge of Meredith's eye and wiped it away with his fingertip. "I want you to know this isn't your fault. I failed on my own. So you can't feel guilty about it. Promise?"

Meredith nodded.

"I'm running out of time. I have three words to say to you." He swallowed. "I love you." He leaned over and kissed her. "Good-bye," he whispered.

And vanished in a fine red mist.

Meredith couldn't let this happen. Not this way. Not now. Not when she'd found what she'd been looking for. Anger swiftly emerged at the top of the emotion heap.

"Wait just a minute!" Meredith stood. "Mr. Chairman of the Board? You can't downsize Jim yet. You haven't seen the whole marketing plan. And, I have one wish left. The whole genie/master contract is void if I don't get to make it. And if the contract is void, he hasn't failed."

The chandelier rumbled. "Is this what you marketing types call a pitch?"

She gulped in a deep breath of air. This was *the* Chairman she was talking with. This was her last chance to save Jim. She had to do the best sales job she'd ever done. "The plan? I guess you could call it that." She rapidly organized the most important facts in her head. She just had to convince the Chairman of the Board that the plan would work. And that Jim was the only one qualified to implement it. That it was her fault he'd failed with her ridiculous wish. "Give me a minute of your time and you'll see just how well my plan will help you and the djinni." She waited.

"Very well. Proceed."

She cleared her throat. "It would be more effective if I had my materials, but here's the essence of the plan. You need to use magic in carefully targeted ways to increase overall awareness of djinni and magic to the general population. I suggest a market-segmentation plan aimed at capturing the natural imagination of the eight-to-fifteen-year-old and cap-italizing on the nostalgia of the over-forty group. These two segments tend to have the broadest set of characteristics to which magic will appeal." She stopped and looked around. "How am I doing so far?"

"Interesting approach. Then what?"

She took a deep breath. Jim's life was on the line. "For the younger set, I suggest developing a series of video games, action figures and a cartoon show on Saturday mornings staring Jim the All-Powerful Djinn. I have some core ideas for scripts, but we'll work on those later. There will be fast food tie-ins, of course, and a line of clothing with the Djinni logo. Oh, and a Web site.

"For the over-forty segment, the approach needs to be more substantive. First, buy a sports franchise and use the djinn as the mascot. Basketball would work, or hockey. That will bring in the men. Then, bring out a line of calorie-free desserts, emphasis on chocolate and loads of flavor, and you'll clinch the female group without trouble. Support it with a dynamite ad campaign, including radio, TV and print ads."

She strolled around the room. "Well, when should we start? We can have ad copy ready by Monday afternoon. With your approval we can be in the top hundred markets by next Friday."

The chandelier jangled. "Don't be pushy. I hate pushy humans. You have some good ideas and I'll take them under consideration. However, Jim, as you call him, cannot participate in any way. He has failed in his assignment, and in my organization we don't promote failures."

She'd lost around one. Time to move to round two. "My first wish was defective. You can't hold him responsible for my mistake."

"I knew you'd try to argue this point. He knew it was defective and he chose to act on it, without any success, I might add, in spite of the consequences. He's responsible."

Her heart sank. "Wait. Jim told me there was a way to bind a djinn."

"There is."

"All I have to do is name him, right?"

"Right."

"I named him Jim. Jim Goodman, Ph.D."

The Chairman's chuckle rumbled around the room. "You have to name him with his real name. His djinni name."

"Jim is his real name."

"Sorry."

Round three. It had been worth a try. "What about my third wish? If you read the part of my plan on warranties, you should understand how important it is to the general population to be able to believe in magic." She walked to the center of the room. "I want my last wish."

The floor shuddered. "Very well. A valid technicality. Make your last wish."

"If I refuse to make it, will Jim survive?"

"No. He's gone. Make your wish."

"He didn't fail, you know. My first wish was for true love. I found it."

"Really?"

"Yes. With Jim. I love him. He makes me laugh, he brings me sunshine in take-out containers. He is the balance I've needed. Without him, I'm just a sketch, not a full painting."

"I can see why he admires you. Your thought processes are frighteningly similar. However"—Meredith heard the shuffling of papers—"you distinctly wished for a man. It says so in his first report." Papers crinkled. "And, since he's a djinn and not a man, loving him doesn't fulfill the wish. Nice try, though." She thought she heard a chuckle. "Last chance. Wish your final wish and be done with it."

"Fine." She felt hot tears sliding down her cheeks. "I wish that Jim's life be spared."

"AAARRRGGGGHHHHH!"

With a shudder, everyone in the room came back to life, impervious to the life-and-death events that had unfolded around them. Jim's chair crashed to the floor, a glass of wine spilled and chocolate splattered everywhere.

"What in the world happened here? It looks like a herd of sugar-starved executives raided the place." Darcie brushed chocolate cake crumbs off her lap. "Where's Jim?"

"He was sitting right here." Ben righted a chair. "Then everybody stood up, fighting over the phone."

"Where's that phone?"

"I've got it. Here, Francis. Would you like to borrow it?" Meredith handed him the now-lifeless object.

"Yes, thank you." He took the phone and turned it on. "Isn't this supposed to do something more interesting than just beep? I thought it was enchanted."

"Not anymore. Just simple electronics. Magic to the uninformed, but not to us." Meredith's eyes filled with tears.

"Nothing here to fight over." Francis handed the phone back to Meredith. "Your pal Jim lied to me."

Meredith held her breath. He had done it on purpose.

Darcie took hold of Meredith's hand. "Is Jim gone?" Her large, dark eyes searched Meredith's watery ones for an answer.

"Yes. Gone." Her voice caught on the Everest-sized lump in her throat. Gone for good.

Horton walked up to the group. "Enjoying yourselves?"

"Yes, sir, just had a little accident with the dessert plates." Darcie motioned to the mess. "I bumped the table reaching for my glass of champagne and everything went everywhere," she said. "I know it looks like the aftermath of a food fight, but it isn't."

"Don't worry about it. I'll get some of the staff to clean this up. You go get some more food and relax. This is supposed to be fun." He turned to Meredith. "Where's that fine young man of yours? I wanted to talk to him about joining the company on a permanent basis."

"He had to leave suddenly. Another obligation." There was that mountain once more, blocking her words. *I can't cry. I can't cry.*

"That's okay. Have him call me on Monday." He motioned to Darcie and Ben. "Would you excuse us, please? Meredith, Francis and I have some things to discuss."

"Not a problem." Darcie took Ben's arm and they headed back toward the dessert table.

Pity the Chairman of the Board hadn't understood the relevance of calorie-free chocolate. It was a killer idea.

"What did you want to talk about, Bill?" Francis inquired.

"I wanted you to know I won't be announcing the appointment of vice president this evening."

"But, why not?" Griffin whined. "I brought in the contract, I should get the job. That was the challenge."

"True." Horton nodded. "Look, Griffin, I'd rather not discuss this here, among our clients and guests."

"Again, why not?" His tone was a little stuffier this time. "I don't mind. In fact, I insist." Just a shade too confident, Meredith thought.

Horton scratched his head. "Well, if you insist." He motioned Meredith and Griffin to a quiet corner. "I'm giving the job to Meredith."

"But, but . . . you can't do that! It's my job. Mine, I tell you! *I* brought in the contract. *She* brought back chocolates for your secretary." Francis sputtered angrily.

"It would be difficult indeed to give you a promotion at Horton Consulting, Francis, because, after the investigator's report clears our legal department, you will no longer be employed by my firm."

"What are you talking about?" Francis sat solidly in a chocolate-covered chair.

"I took your presentation, and Meredith's, and gave them to an associate of mine. Someone who investigates corporations. He confirmed what I've suspected for some time now, Francis. You've been

# Karen Lee

slipping vital information to Gordon-Strunk, a clear violation of company policy, not to mention highly illegal. Don't be surprised if the authorities have some questions for you." He paused. "Damn, why wait. You're fired. Don't bother to come in on Monday. I'll have your personal items boxed and couriered to your house." He took Meredith's elbow and began to walk away. "Leave your ID, keys and company credit card with Darcie."

Shocked, Meredith allowed Horton to lead her away. "Meredith, I just want you to know how happy I am to give this promotion to you. In my gut I wanted to give you the vice presidency, but I felt it was only fair to let you both have an equal chance at it. I initiated the competition to see how you would both react under pressure. You stuck to your principles, even sacrificing getting a contract to be honest, while Griffin cheated to try to achieve his goal. Both of you showed your true colors. I only want honest people I can trust working for me. Meredith, you earned this promotion and I am glad we are going to be able to continue to work together."

"Thank you very much, Bill. I hope I can live up to your high expectations for me." The formal thanks was all Meredith could manage. She simply couldn't process any more information.

Horton led her back into the throngs of people and began to introduce her around, announcing her new position. She smiled and shook hands as if in a trance. The congratulations rang hollow in her ears. She had no one at home with whom to share her success. Jim wouldn't be popping out of her microwave. Nor would he be lounging in her Jacuzzi sipping wine with a "come-in-the-water's-fine" grin on his face.

He was gone.

She excused herself from the group toasting the new VP and went to the ladies room. She caught sight of herself in the mirror. The exquisite dress Jim had created for her set her figure off perfectly. He had done so many little things for her. Meredith couldn't help herself; she sat down and cried.

She'd known from the beginning that she had him for only a month. But she hadn't come to grips with how much she'd miss him. How much she'd gotten used to his clever phrases, his raised eyebrow, his touch. Him. And now she'd have to go on without him. She'd hoped it would be different with a genie, that he wouldn't disappear like all the men in her life. She'd held on to the hope that the duchess had been right about love's ability to overcome anything. She sniffed. She'd been hoping her love for Jim would satisfy the Chairman of the Board and that the marketing plan would excite him. Then, she had reasoned, Jim could visit from time to time.

That wouldn't happen now. The Chairman of the Board had made it clear. Not ever. She'd have to go to Plan B.

Except she didn't have a Plan B.

# Chapter Sixteen

## "Vir-Djinn"

Meredith woke Monday morning, rolled over and squinted at the clock. She closed her eyes. Her cheeks were still hot, her skin tight with dried tears. Somehow she'd managed to drive home from the Gala on Saturday. Somehow she'd managed to sleep. She'd spent the better part of Sunday in bed, trying to cope with the knowledge of what she'd lost.

She sniffed.

The sun filtered through the Roman shades on her windows. Birds sang in the trees outside. She could hear the children next door grousing about having to go to school. Everything in her life had tipped upside down, but the rest of the world just kept going on like nothing had happened.

She sat up, swung her legs over the side of the bed and slowly stood up. Her head hurt horribly. She hugged herself, shivering. Taking a deep breath, she put on her robe. Somehow she'd manage. Somehow she'd survive. She walked slowly downstairs, wanting Jim to be in the kitchen whipping up bacon and eggs with a silly smile on his face.

Today, she'd eat the bacon gladly and never worry about its fat content.

Stanley followed her down the stairs, aware, as cats often are, that something was amiss with his human. He rubbed against her legs and hopped into her lap when she sat at the table.

"Thanks, pal. I know you're trying to cheer me up." She buried her face in his soft fur. The tears would start again, she knew, if she spoke. Instead, she held the big black and white cat, stroking his head, taking some small comfort in his rumbling purr.

She heard Jim inside her head telling her to trust him. Okay, she could do that. Trust. But not believe. Never again believe. Not in magic, not in love. Regardless of what the duchess thought.

She felt tears slip past her eyelashes and knew she didn't have to talk to make them fall. *What the heck, Montgomery, let it go. Have a good cry and then pick up the pieces and move on.* She held Stanley close and sobbed, rocking back and forth.

"What am I going to do without him?"

There was his voice again, in her head. "You're a survivor, Meredith. You'll do just fine without me. You've got your promotion to look forward to, don't you? A new office and the possibility of a new man. Tiburon would be a good catch."

She didn't want a new man. She wanted an old genie.

She wiped her face and stood up. "How about some food, Stan? Starve a cold, feed a fever. Isn't that how it goes? I wonder what you do for a broken heart."

She snagged a tissue and blew her nose. "Okay. I'll

concede that I won't die. I just wish I could."

Without spirit she moved around her kitchen, relying on the comfort of routine to buffer her from her despair. Stanley got tuna as a treat for being so understanding. She fixed herself strong coffee and instead of her usual healthy yogurt, she had a large bowl of frosted cornflakes she kept for visits from her nieces.

She could be healthy tomorrow. Today she was in mourning and wanted to wallow in her misery.

Halfway through breakfast, Meredith decided she couldn't face work. She called Darcie.

"I'm feeling like ten cents' worth of day-old garbage. I'm staying home. I'm here if you need me, but please, don't need me."

"I'm sorry about Jim. I was so sure he'd stay where all the others hadn't. Guess I was wrong."

"Guess so." Meredith hung up the phone, wishing with all her being that things had turned out differently.

He loved her. It was his parting gift. How did couples cope with the death of their partner?

It was a pity there were no support groups for women without genies.

Around noon, her mother called.

"Meredith, honey, I called the office. Darcie said you were working from home. Meredith, you don't sound well. If you're coming down with a cold, you take yourself back to bed. Remember to drink lots of fluids. Can I bring you anything?"

*Yes, bring me my cell phone and my genie.* "Thanks, Mom. I'm fine. Allergies, I guess. I don't need anything."

"Good. How is your friend Jim? He was such a nice man. Friendly, polite. I'm so glad you're seeing him instead of one of those boring corporate types you usually bring home. I hope I'm not being too forward, but I have a feeling about him. I think he's the one. You two were so cute together. I would be glad to call him my son-in-law if it comes to that."

*Great. Just getting myself together and she brings up the genie whose "use by" date has expired.*

"I'm glad you approve." She turned a sob into a cough. "I need to go, Mom."

"I'm going to bring you some chicken soup. You've got a cold whether you know it or not." Her mother hung up.

"I don't exactly feel like having visitors," Meredith addressed the row of African violets, neat in their pots. She filled the watering can and gave each one a drink. "What would you do? How would you go on? I didn't even really get to say good-bye." No gifts, no mementos, no pictures, except the single painting she'd yet to finish. She stopped in midpour.

"My camera!" She dropped the watering can into the sink with a resounding clang and raced to her car. In the backseat, half hidden under files from work, was her camera. The one she'd so recently used to take pictures of Jim for the ad people. She'd used up the entire roll of twenty-four pictures on the genie.

Eagerly, she raced upstairs, pulled on an old pair of jeans, a slightly used T-shirt and some sandals. She ran a hand through her hair, but didn't succeed in making the ends stick any way but straight up. She shoved an old baseball cap on, grabbed her car keys and headed off to Quik Pics, the one-hour film developer near her house. For the first time since Jim disappeared Meredith felt her mood lighten.

Pictures weren't much, but they were better than nothing. She pulled into the little cluster of stores and ran into the shop.

"May I help you?" The clerk put down her magazine agonizingly slowly, Meredith thought as she practically paced in front of the counter.

"I need this developed. I'll be back in an hour."

"Okay, fine, whatever." The clerk took the roll of film, had Meredith fill out information on an envelope and dropped the film into it. "See you at two." She turned back to the magazine.

At precisely two o'clock Meredith got back out of her car, where she'd spent an anxious hour watching people come and go in the parking lot. She burst into the little photography shop. "I'm back."

"So I see. I'll get your pictures, although I don't know what the big rush was all about."

How could she not know? She must not have looked at them, Meredith reasoned. Who could be impervious to a gorgeous guy in a genie suit?

"Here you go. That'll be eight ninety-five."

Meredith pulled out a ten-dollar bill. "Keep the change." She grabbed the envelope with the pictures in it and fled to the sanctuary of her Mercedes.

Her hands shook as she opened the envelope. Suddenly she stopped, clutching the pictures to her chest. Could she deal with photographs of Jim? Or would they merely make her grief greater? There was only one way to find out.

She slowly pulled the photos from the envelope and turned them over. *Open your eyes, Montgomery. It's easier to see that way.* She opened her eyes and looked eagerly at the first picture of Jim.

It was blank. Sort of.

Oh, the office was there, with the wall of awards and the view of the Potomac. Jim was missing. There was just a dim blue blur where he should have been.

Quickly she flipped through the stack of twenty-four photos. There were lots of great shots of her office interior, but only big empty spaces where Jim should have been.

Like the big empty space in her heart.

Defeated, she drove slowly home, ignoring the angry motorists blazing past her at the speed limit and shaking their fists. They'd get over it.

She would never get over Jim.

As she turned into her neighborhood, a big black motorcycle rumbled past her, the driver resplendent in black leather jacket, worn jeans and boots. His black helmet gleamed in the afternoon sun.

Just what the neighborhood needed, its own version of Hell's Angels. *Go away, please. I've already lost my mad biker*.

Letting herself in the front door, Meredith closed it quietly behind herself, tossing the useless photos on the living room coffee table. She grabbed Stanley and slumped on the sofa. Her last fragment of hope had evaporated. She closed her eyes and imagined Jim as he had appeared that first time in her thoughts. A prince out of the desert, proud, strong, hers.

Sounds of the motorcycle got louder, then stopped. It must be in her driveway, beside her Mercedes.

Under normal circumstances she would have been out of the door in a shot, letting the hapless biker know exactly what she thought of his machine and his noise. Today she didn't have the energy. If he wanted to park his hog beside her car, so be it.

She heard footsteps on her front porch, then a knock at the door. "This better be good. I'm in no mood to buy a subscription to *Biker's Weekly*." She yanked open the front door without looking through the peephole. "What?"

He stood before her, broad shoulders clad in black

leather, tight jeans that left no room for speculation about his gender. Carefully he undid the strap on his helmet and pulled it off, shaking the hair out of his eyes—his magnificent dark, exotic eyes.

"Jim? Oh, God! You're all right. You came back." She stammered, knowing she sounded vaguely moronic. She jumped into his arms.

"Of course I came back," he said after she'd stopped her furious barrage of kisses. "I didn't have a choice, you know." He set her down. "When you named me, you coupled our fates and bound me to you forever."

"But, I thought . . . the Chairman of the Board said . . ."

"Forget what that old magician said. He was wrong." Jim smiled. "You could invite me in, you know."

"Oh, sorry. I'm just so surprised."

"Speechless? Overwhelmed? Astounded?"

"All that and more."

She led him to the sofa, afraid to take her eyes off him for fear she was hallucinating again. She reached out and touched his leather-clad arm. It felt solid, reassuringly human. "You're really back."

"Yep."

"The motorcycle is an interesting addition."

"It isn't as quiet as the carpet, but it's a whole lot of fun. Besides, you seemed to like it."

For a moment Meredith drank in the sight of him. "But how? How did you manage to come back?"

"It was all your doing, really. The marketing plan was a big hit. Look for calorie-free chocolate in your future. But that wasn't what really did it. Your last wish. The Chairman of the Board had to honor it. Djinni rules."

"So." She relaxed back into the cushions. He was

safe and had stopped by to say thanks. "This is just a quick stop before you go off to find a new subject and start granting wishes all over again."

"Not really. I stopped by Horton's office on the way here. The ad agency wants me to model for them. More or less permanently."

Good for him. "So you've taken a leave of absence from wish-granting, then?"

Jim set his helmet on the floor and took off his leather gloves. "No." He unzipped the jacket.

Meredith frowned. "What do you mean?"

"No more wishes. No more magic. No more genie." He took her hands. "You wished that my life be spared. The Chairman of the Board did the only thing he could. I was a bad boy djinn, now I'm just a bad boy. He made me human."

She knew her heart was breaking, this time from too much joy. She saw bright lights before her eyes and her throat squeezed up all tight. There were tears in her eyes.

He slid close to her and put his arm around her. "You remember those three words every woman wants to hear?" She nodded, unable to say anything. "I meant them when I said good-bye. I love you. I've loved you almost from the beginning, Meredith. I think that is why I didn't immediately give up on your wish. You pulled on my heartstrings—never had I experienced such a feeling. You were an enigma I needed to figure out. But the more I tried to help you the more I fell for you, and the more confused I became. I didn't think I could love, and yet my feelings toward you were so strong. It was not until Hertzenstein that I finally gave up trying to fight my feelings and gave into my desires. I decided to believe in my love for you even though it couldn't really exist." He grinned ruefully and squeezed her shoulder. "Boy, am I glad that I did.

"As it turns out, the Chairman created a few genies with the capacity to have human emotions. It was an experiment that backfired. I was one of the last of these genies—that is why the Chairman was so hard on me; I was one of his last chances to prove the experiment wasn't a total loss. It failed. My love for you clearly showed that a djinn with human emotions can't succeed at just granting three wishes and disappearing. Complications always arise."

"What happened to the others like you?" Meredith asked, gazing up at him in astonishment.

"It is classified how many others have existed. But I think the duke might have been one."

Meredith grinned up at Jim. "Really?" She laughed. "Well, that would explain his twinkling eyes, and all that talk about true love." She snuggled closer to Jim.

Jim kissed the top of her head lightly. "I love you."

Tears of overwhelming happiness glistened on her cheeks. "And I love you."

Jim cleared his throat. "There were four other words I learned that evening that are very important between a man and a woman. Do you remember them?"

"Something about chocolate?"

"No. Something like will you marry me?"

Meredith blinked and sat up straight. "Could you repeat that, please? My ears are ringing so loud I wasn't sure I heard you correctly."

Jim got down on one knee and, holding her hands in his, said, "Will you marry me? It'll be challenging to civilize an ex-genie, but I promise it'll be fun. Will you? Marry me?"

"Absolutely." She felt him pull her to her feet as he

stood. He kissed her, thoroughly, tenderly. She broke the kiss and gazed up at him.

"What's wrong?"

"I wasn't sure it would be the same without the genie magic—kissing you as a human, I mean." Meredith grinned up at her Jim. Her genie. Her love. "I shouldn't have worried. With you there'll always be magic."

Determined to locate his friend who disappeared during a
spell gone awry, Warrick petitions a dying stargazer to help
find him. But the astronomer will only assist Warrick if he
promises to escort his daughter Sophia and a priceless
crystal ball safely to Byzantium. Sharp-tongued and
argumentative, Sophia meets her match in the powerful and
intelligent Warrick. Try as she will to deny it, he holds her
spellbound, longing to be the magician's lover.

\_\_\_52263-2                               $5.99 US/$6.99 CAN

**Dorchester Publishing Co., Inc.**
**P.O. Box 6640**
**Wayne, PA 19087-8640**

Please add $1.75 for shipping and handling for the first book and
$.50 for each book thereafter. NY, NYC, and PA residents,
please add appropriate sales tax. No cash, stamps, or C.O.D.s. All
orders shipped within 6 weeks via postal service book rate.
Canadian orders require $2.00 extra postage and must be paid in
U.S. dollars through a U.S. banking facility.

Name_____
Address_____
City_____State_____Zip_____
I have enclosed $_____ in payment for the checked book(s).
Payment <u>must</u> accompany all orders. ❑ Please send a free catalog.
        CHECK OUT OUR WEBSITE! www.dorchesterpub.com

# More Than Magic
## Kathleen Nance

Darius is as beautiful, as mesmerizing, as dangerous as a man can be. His dark, star-kissed eyes promise exquisite joys, yet it is common knowledge he has no intention of taking a wife. Ever. Sex and sensuality will never ensnare Darius, for he is their master. But magic can. Knowledge of his true name will give a mortal woman power over the arrogant djinni, and an age-old enemy has carefully baited the trap. Alluring yet innocent, Isis Montgomery will snare his attention, and the spell she's been given will bind him to her. But who can control a force that is even more than magic?

# A Gentle Magic
## EMMA CRAIG

When cattleman Cody O'Fannin hears a high-pitched scream ring out across the harsh New Mexico Territory, he rides straight into the heart of danger, expecting to find a cougar or a Comanche. Instead, he finds a scene far more frightening— a woman in the final stages of childbirth. Alone, the beautiful Melissa Wilmeth clearly needs his assistance, and although he'd rather face a band of thieving outlaws, Cody ignores his quaking insides and helps deliver her baby. When the infant's first wail fills the air, Cody gazes into Melissa's bewitching blue eyes and is spellbound. How else can he explain the sparkles he sees shimmering in the air above her honey-colored hair? Then thoughts of marriage creep into his head, and he doesn't need a crystal ball to realize he hasn't lost his mind or his nerve, but his heart.

\_\_\_52321-3                                              $5.50 US/$6.50 CAN

**Dorchester Publishing Co., Inc.**
**P.O. Box 6640**
**Wayne, PA 19087-8640**

# Something Wild

# Kimberly Raye

Dependent only upon twentieth-century conveniences, Tara Martin seeks to make a name for herself as a top-notch photojournalist. But when a plea from her best friend sends her off into the Smoky Mountains to snap a sasquatch, a twisted ankle leaves her in a precarious position—and when she looks up, she sees the biggest foot she's ever seen. Tara learns that the big foot belongs to an even bigger man—with a colossal heart and a body to die for. And that man, who was raised alone in the wilds of Appalachia, will teach Tara that what she needs is something wild.

____52272-1                                     $5.50 US/$6.50 CAN

**Dorchester Publishing Co., Inc.**
**P.O. Box 6640**
**Wayne, PA 19087-8640**

# HIGH ENERGY DARA JOY

Zanita Masterson knows nothing about physics, until a reporting job leads her to Tyberius Evans. The rogue scientist is six feet of piercing blue eyes, rock-hard muscles and maverick ideas—with his own masterful equation for sizzling ecstasy and high energy.

___4438-2                                    $4.99 US/$5.99 CAN

**Dorchester Publishing Co., Inc.**
**P.O. Box 6640**
**Wayne, PA 19087-8640**

Please add $1.75 for shipping and handling for the first book and $.50 for each book thereafter. NY, NYC, and PA residents, please add appropriate sales tax. No cash, stamps, or C.O.D.s. All orders shipped within 6 weeks via postal service book rate. Canadian orders require $2.00 extra postage and must be paid in U.S. dollars through a U.S. banking facility.

Name_____
Address_____
City_____State_____Zip_____
I have enclosed $_____ in payment for the checked book(s).
Payment <u>must</u> accompany all orders. ❏ Please send a free catalog.
CHECK OUT OUR WEBSITE! www.dorchesterpub.com

# LOVE ME TENDER

# SANDRA HILL

Once upon a time, in the magic kingdom of Manhattan, there lived a handsome designer-shoe magnate named Prince Charming, and a beautiful stockbroker named Cinderella. And as the story goes, these two are destined to live happily ever after, at least according to a rhinestone-studded fairy godfather named Elmer Presley.

__4457-9                                    $5.99 US/$6.99 CAN

**Dorchester Publishing Co., Inc.**
**P.O. Box 6640**
**Wayne, PA 19087-8640**

Please add $1.75 for shipping and handling for the first book and $.50 for each book thereafter. NY, NYC, and PA residents, please add appropriate sales tax. No cash, stamps, or C.O.D.s. All orders shipped within 6 weeks via postal service book rate. Canadian orders require $2.00 extra postage and must be paid in U.S. dollars through a U.S. banking facility.

Name_____
Address_____
City_____ State_____ Zip_____
I have enclosed $_____ in payment for the checked book(s).
Payment <u>must</u> accompany all orders. ☐ Please send a free catalog.

# Golden Man
## Evelyn Rogers

Steven Marshall is the kind of guy who makes a woman think of satin sheets and steamy nights, of wild fantasies involving hot tubs and whipped cream—and then brass bands, waving flags, and Fourth of July parades. All-American terrific, that's what he is; tall and bronzed, with hair the color of the sun, thick-lashed blue eyes, and a killer grin slanted against a square jaw—a true Golden Man. He is even single. Unfortunately, he is also the President of the United States. So when average citizen Ginny Baxter finds herself his date for a diplomatic reception, she doesn't know if she is the luckiest woman in the country, or the victim of a practical joke. Either way, she is in for the ride of her life . . . and the man of her dreams.

___52295-0                                     $5.99 US/$6.99 CAN

# KIMBERLY RAYE
# FAITHLESS ANGEL

Faith Jansen has closed the door on life and love. After the death of her young ward, she is determined not to let anyone into her little house again. So when she finds Jesse Savage standing on her stoop, a strange light in his eyes, she turns the lock against him. But Jesse returns to her home each morning, gardening tools in hand. Despite her resolution never to reach out again, she finds herself drawing closer to him. So when she finds herself deep in the desert night with him, the doors of desire are flung open, and the light of something deeper is let loose to flood her heart and lead her to a heaven only two can share.

___52296-9 $5.50 US/$6.50 CAN

**Dorchester Publishing Co., Inc.**
**P.O. Box 6640**
**Wayne, PA 19087-8640**